**Praise for *What Doesn't Kill You*, the debut novel
in the Willa Pennington, PI Mystery Series:**

"Tight plotting, edge-of-your-seat suspense, and a protagonist in
PI Willa Pennington you'll want to read about again and again. I
couldn't put this book down."

—Maggie Barbieri, author of *Once Upon a Lie*

"A debut that saddles tough-girl noir with the heart of a cozy."

—*Kirkus Reviews*

"This is a solid beginning to a character and setting that could go
on to very good things." —*RT Book Reviews*

"Aimee Hix is an up-and-coming author everyone should watch."

—*Crimespree Magazine*

"The book has plenty of twists and surprises, but what stands out
is the tight writing and fast narrative of the author's debut novel."

—*Ellery Queen Mystery Magazine*

D1052154

DARK STREETS
COLD
SUBURBS

DARK STREETS
COLD
SUBURBS

AIMEE HIX

MIDNIGHT INK
WOODBURY, MINNESOTA

FIRST EDITION
First Printing, 2019

Book format by Bob Gaul
Cover design by Shira Atakpu
Editing by Nicole Nugent

Midnight Ink, an imprint of Llewellyn Worldwide Ltd.

This is a work of fiction. Names, characters, places, and incidents are either the product of the author's imagination or are used fictitiously, and any resemblance to actual persons, living or dead, business establishments, events, or locales is entirely coincidental.

Library of Congress Cataloging-in-Publication Data
Names: Hix, Aimee, author.
Title: Dark streets, cold suburbs / by Aimee Hix.
Description: Woodbury, Minnesota : Midnight Ink, [2019] | Series: A Willa Pennington, PI mystery.
Identifiers: LCCN 2018044221 (print) | LCCN 2018046050 (ebook) | ISBN 9780738756004 () | ISBN 9780738754703 (alk. paper)
Subjects: | GSAFD: Mystery fiction.
Classification: LCC PS3608.I95 (ebook) | LCC PS3608.I95 D37 2019 (print) | DDC 813/.6—dc23
LC record available at https://lccn.loc.gov/2018044221

Midnight Ink
Llewellyn Worldwide Ltd.
2143 Wooddale Drive
Woodbury, MN 55125-2989
www.midnightinkbooks.com

Printed in the United States of America

For Eric. With you, everything is possible.

CHAPTER

1

THE WINDOWS WERE ALREADY fogged from the humidity inside the building clashing with the icy February night. I hesitated for only a second; out of the corner of my eye, an image, a reflection in the glass—two men coming at me too fast. I had just enough time to drop my bag and turn to block the blow. I wrapped my fingers around the first man's wrist and twisted while pressing my thumb into his median nerve. He dropped a blade. Taking the offensive, still holding the first man immobile at the wrist, I stepped forward to kick the knee of the second man.

Block.

Hold.

Target.

Strike.

"Go, now," I barked. "Call 911."

I set my mind to the situation and felt the immediate shift. My adrenaline amped down. Not flight, fight. Letting go of the man's wrist, I danced back two steps and put my hands up to block. Prize-fighter stance.

Neither noticed my back leg planted and when I pivoted and slammed the taller of the two with a roundhouse kick to the ribs, he toppled. One attacker on the ground, I took a wider back turn to set my foot down and kept turning, throwing my elbow high into the shorter man's face. Spinning the rest of the way, I grabbed the back of his neck, bringing his face down to my knee. I pushed him off me and turned my attention to the instigator.

The taller man scrambled to his feet and glanced briefly at his partner then eyed me angrily.

He was furious at being put down by a woman. I could see it in his eyes and knew it would cause him to make a mistake. He did. Instead of taking a moment to assess what to do, he just rushed me. He got within a foot of me and I sidestepped, punching him in the kidney as he passed. He fell forward. I took two steps over to him and kicked him in the sternum as he scrambled to his feet, knocking the air out of him.

I felt another attack coming and threw my arm up to protect my head.

"Stop."

I looked at the instructor. He was smiling. "Great job, Willa."

"I missed the third attacker."

"You immobilized two armed men efficiently while urging your partner to flee and call for help," Adam said. "I couldn't expect you to do any better."

"Clearly you could have or you wouldn't have sent in the third attacker. I want to do it again."

"I think we're done for tonight." He smiled, but it was firm. Adam turned to the men—boys, really—playing the attackers. "I appreciate you guys coming in tonight for this drill. It was extremely effective."

"Your girl is a bruiser, Adam. I thought she was going to break my knee but she pulled it at the last second. You sending her to the ring?" the second attacker asked.

"I'm not his or anyone else's girl, jackass," I said.

"Sorry. Woman, female, lady, whatever," he said. His tone made apparent that he didn't understand, or care, why I was annoyed.

I grabbed my water and took a long drink. Putting it back, I turned to eye the teenage MMA students who'd been drafted as attackers. The other students sitting on the floor, most of them young women, watched us wide-eyed. I was the oldest woman in the class. A woman, not a girl.

"Listen, meathead, when you're done playing at being a brawler with pads and headgear, ask me about the neo-Nazi I had to fight last year. Until then, keep your sexist, macho crap to yourself."

"Bullshit," said the guy with the fake knife. Adam frowned, possibly at the curse, but didn't say anything or make a move to step in.

I nodded, biting my lip to keep the harsher expletive I wanted to say inside my mouth and dug my phone out of my bag. Pulling up the photo album, I tossed it to him.

"Talk to me about bullshit now, junior."

They clustered around, looking at pictures that Seth had taken at my insistence. I was still in the hospital and the harsh, florescent lighting exacerbated the purple and blue. Butterfly tape on my eyebrow, stitches in my lip, blood in the white of my left eye, elastic bandages on my right arm and ribs, the machines all in full view. I looked at them when I was tired of training and felt like quitting. Nothing was more motivational than your own battered features staring back at you, reminding you what you were training for in the first place and it wasn't a fucking trophy or belt.

Adam reached over and plucked my phone from the boys. "Well, with that lead-in, I guess it's time for you to share your story, Willa."

My gaze found the others in the room like me. The ones with watchful eyes, suspicious and appraising. The ones who had secrets they weren't ready to share. Stories that were probably worse than the others even dreamed of. Stories like mine, of being attacked in their homes and brutalized. One looked me dead in the eye, her fragile smile encouraging.

Acid poured into my stomach. I wasn't ready to go tonight. I wanted to sit in the back like every other time and listen. I wasn't ready for these people to know the details of what I had been through, but I'd mouthed off and gotten everyone curious. I slipped on my workout jacket as slowly as I could, debating a swift retreat. I didn't care if it looked like I was stalling.

While the room was settling down after the drill and verbal altercation, I had a moment to get this fear under control or let it take me down.

"Hi. Welcome. I see we have a few new people tonight. I'm glad you're here. The more, the merrier. I do want to reassure you that you won't be expected to do a drill like you just saw. Willa isn't one of the beginner students, as you may have realized, but I'll let her tell you her story."

I slowly walked to the front of the room, pulling the lightweight fleece fabric of the jacket tightly around me as if it could shield me from the looks I knew I'd be getting. Me and my stupid mouth. I needed training to get that under control.

"Like Adam said I'm Willa."

"Hi, Willa." Their expectant faces looked back at me.

"Wow, I never realized how much this looks like those AA meetings in the movies."

That earned a mass chuckle.

"I'm a former LEO. Uh, that's Law Enforcement Officer. And, I, um, well, I'm former because I quit about a year ago. My best friend was killed in Afghanistan and I decided that I didn't have it in me to be the person on the porch telling someone their loved one wasn't ever coming home again."

It was so much harder than I'd feared. I was struggling to push down a quiver that was threatening to turn into shaking. Hand-to-hand with a bigot had been terrifying, but physical pain was a lot easier to deal with than letting people see what I had on the inside of me. It was hard enough with loved ones; strangers, some who had mocked me a moment before, was a mountain I wasn't used to trudging. All the stuff I didn't ever want to share with anyone was the top of the peak.

"So that was about nine months ago, Michael's death. I kind of went into a tailspin after and bailed on my life for a while."

I had gotten through talking about Michael without feeling like I'd swallowed a rock. My therapist would have been proud.

"My dad, former military intelligence, former cop, is now a private investigator. I decided to come back and work with him. While he was out of town I kind of ended up caught in a case and it got out of hand. Like crazy out of hand. I can't really talk about the specifics because it's an ongoing prosecution but … I mentioned a neo-Nazi a minute ago. He wasn't a fan of mine, for obvious reasons." I gestured vaguely to my mixed-race skin and female form.

I could hear muttering. Sweat poured down my back like I'd been exercising hard for hours. My heart raced and struggled to keep my breath even. I unzipped my jacket and stripped it off.

I had been babbling a little. I was definitely going to lose some eloquence points from the European judges. Oh well, I'd try to stick the landing.

"Sorry, public speaking's not really my thing."

Adam nodded encouragingly. I wasn't done yet?

"Anyway, I ended up learning a lot of important lessons on that case. The most important is that as a woman, I couldn't ever rely on brute strength like a man can. I don't have the muscles for that. I needed to learn how to use what I did have. My brain. My training, definitely. But the training we received in the justice academy wasn't enough. I mean, they gave us guns and tasers and batons. A uniform alone is a self-defense tool. Very few people walk up to a cop in uniform and start shit. That's suicide. But I didn't have the uniform anymore. I needed some new tools. So the second I got clearance from the doctors, I started training with Adam. Hard. I don't let up. I can't. Because the most important thing I learned is that sometimes it's fight or die."

I was done. I weaved my way through the stunned women wearing pink sweats and sorority t-shirts. In my gray ATF t-shirt and black leggings, from day one I had looked like a rock in a carton of Easter eggs.

I'd started in private lessons because, honestly, even weeks after I left the hospital I hadn't been ready for a public class. Or a public anything.

Seth knew Adam Carson from the Army and wouldn't stop bugging me until I agreed to meet him. He had an unexpectedly gentle and non-threatening nature for such a big guy. He's like the human version of a Muppet.

We worked one-on-one for weeks; mornings before he opened the dojo, evenings after he closed, Sundays when there weren't any classes. I needed the privacy. I was bruised and battered and scared shitless. Our first few sessions we just sat and talked about movies, dogs, anything but the incident that landed me in the hospital. The fourth day I walked in to find my brother, Ben, waiting for me.

Adam positioned Ben behind me and said, "Defend your brother." He gave me no other warning before he lunged and I had less than a full breath to decide what to do. I fought back. My wrist, badly sprained still, screamed at me with every grapple or blow blocked, but picturing Ben bruised and beaten like I saw in the pictures of my own face spurred me on. Adam stopped the drill after a minute. I'd been gasping for breath within ten seconds.

As he iced my wrist, Adam asked me why fighting to protect Ben got me past my fear. I didn't have an answer other than I loved him and I'd been protecting him for seventeen years. But I had gotten over the hill. I was in for another mountain, so I strapped in and started climbing hard. I left most of those sessions frustrated. I was impatient. It took too long to learn skills, I lagged in energy, my decision-making stalled if I was overstimulated. I berated myself for tiny mistakes. Adam patiently explained that my body needed time to catch up to my will.

Adam clapped his hands to get everyone's attention. The MMA dudes were doing pushups in the corner. That made me smile. I looked around and my gaze landed on one woman standing by herself, wearing a Rolling Stones hoodie. She had an *I don't give a damn* expression and a nervous habit of rolling her ankle out. I hadn't seen her before. I nodded my head over in her direction, silently asking Adam. He shrugged.

I walked over, intrigued. She reminded me of myself. Especially the *go away* vibe she radiated. Another rock, like me. "First class?"

Up close, she was much younger than I had thought. She'd dyed her hair darker. Like she wanted to look tough. Late teens, at most. I could see her fighting the urge to say something snarky so I decided to let her off the hook.

"I can tell because you don't look like a frosted cookie yet."

It probably wouldn't make Adam happy to hear me make fun of the other students, but I sensed that she needed an ally more than the rules needed to be unbroken. And I've got my own smartass issues. She giggled, confirming my assessment of her age. I wondered if she went to Ben's school.

"You're wondering if this is the right place for you. You don't see yourself in these other women."

She nodded, biting her lip, her eyes following the duck line of women walking behind Adam.

"If you're here to learn, you're in the right place. And it looks like you're stuck with me as your partner, so you're going to learn a lot. Not to brag or anything, but I'm Adam's favorite."

I moved to the front of the room, feeling the girl trail behind me, and took my place near Adam. The girl stood in front of me, uncertainty on her face.

Adam ran us through some basic drills to help us work on our muscle memory, stuff I'd mastered months ago. My new friend did a good job. She kept her focus and when she made a mistake she didn't act silly like some of the pastels. She worked hard too. We were both sweaty before the halfway mark and I had stripped off my t-shirt to my sports bra. The Rolling Stones hoodie stayed put.

We stopped for a water break. Our guests were still doing pushups in the back. Adam had been very annoyed. I watched the other women pull out their color-coordinated water bottles. The fountain was closer than my gear bag and good enough for me. I knew Adam kept the place spotless.

"I'm Aja, by the way."

The girl had followed me to the water fountain even though she had a water bottle too.

"Like the continent?" a voice asked from behind us. It was one of the college girls. Her shirt had the school mascot on it. One of the other non-pastels.

Aja blushed. "Uh, the album title."

"Cool. I haven't heard of it, but that's still awesome." College Mascot girl took her place at the water fountain I'd just abandoned.

"I agree. It is awesome. I love Steely Dan," I said.

"Oh my god, you've heard of them?" Aja asked, blushing a pretty shade of rose that was at odds with her attempt at toughness.

"My dad is a big fan."

Her smile was suddenly shy, like a little girl. My chest squeezed a little bit.

Adam didn't work us as hard physically during the second half of the class. We ran through some scenarios—how to be aware, what to look for, giving yourself options. I could see some of the candy-colored women weren't really engaged. These were harder exercises. They required you to imagine yourself in danger, needing to think several moves ahead like the scariest game of chess you'd ever played. That some students were disconnecting from this part of the class wasn't a surprise.

"I know it's hard to think in abstracts. Try imagining it's a television show you're watching. It's late and dark. The lead actress is playing with her phone and absentmindedly starts walking to her parking space after her shift at the bar. What are you yelling at the TV?" Adam asked.

"Put your phone away."

"Have your keys out."

"Check your car first."

"Walk with friends."

The whole class was getting into it, yelling answers. Adam was an astute teacher to take them back a step, noticing they were resisting playing the victim. I knew what it was really like to be in danger. You yell those things at yourself too. After. Pay attention to your surroundings. Even at the grocery store, shopping with your boyfriend and your brother. Full-on daytime, store packed with yuppies looking for quinoa and arugula. You found yourself checking the locks at stoplights. You felt them look at you, knowing what you were doing, not saying anything, not having to. Because you saw it in their eyes. And then those close to you start doing it too. Before you can. Wanting to make you feel safe. Wanting to take some of it off you. Wanting to make it better. And knowing that they can't.

Adam ended the class with a reading from one of the dozens of inspirational books he had in the dojo. He firmly believed that it was his job to help people learn how to master their bodies *and* their minds.

I watched as Aja packed up her messenger bag. I took a chance and got out one of my new business cards. I wrote my cell number on the back and handed it to her.

"Pennington Investigations? Your initials spell out PI and you're a PI?"

I nodded. Dad found it amusing. I found it slightly less amusing. It was a conversation starter if you needed one beyond a father-daughter private investigation business. Or girl PI. That one was annoying. Those two were novel enough for most people. Aja went up again in my estimation.

"Look, I don't normally do this, but if you need help, you can call me. Any time, day or night."

"Why?" Her face had that wannabe-tough look again.

"I can tell you've got something going on and that you don't want to talk about it. That's fine. But I've got a brother who's about your age. If he needed help, I'd want someone to make sure he got it."

She looked down at my card and shoved it into the pocket of her hoodie. "Thanks."

She skirted around me and was out the door so fast I hadn't even bent to pick up my own bag. I took my time getting cleaned up, letting the other women file out the door.

"Looks like you made a friend. Good for you."

Adam knew I didn't have many women friends. Or any women friends. I'd never been the kind of girl who had girl friends. I'd had Michael. And I hadn't needed anyone else. Then I didn't have Michael anymore. At least now I had Seth, though in a very different way.

"I'm not sure we're friends just yet but she interests me."

Adam gave me a knowing look. "You've found a project then. Something else to think about and worry about instead of dealing with all the stuff you need to deal with."

"I already have a therapist, you know."

"I know. The practice is mental and physical. When you're in a bad place mentally, you're not a good martial artist."

"So I'm not a good martial artist?" It was a pointless question. We both knew that wasn't my goal.

"You have the skills and the right intention. The rest we can work on. It's the intention that matters most."

"So tell me about Aja's intention."

Adam smiled and shook his head. "You're not fooling me."

CHAPTER

2

I STARED AT SETH sleeping. He looked so unguarded. And hot. Sweat matted his short hair to his scalp, darkening it from blond to brown. The air in the room was stuck on eighty and I didn't dare go to the motel's front desk to get it fixed. Mostly because I didn't want to risk missing anything on the surveillance job we were on. Okay, the surveillance job that I was on and he came along on to keep me company. *Keeping me company* being a euphemism for trying to get into my pants. His plan had some merit, as he was the only thing in the place I would have felt comfortable letting my naked skin touch. Except I wasn't about to have sex in a place where I'd have to keep one eye open to make sure the cockroaches didn't steal our wallets.

I didn't think anyone working this hellhole would do anything about the temperature even if they could do something. You stayed in a by-the-hour motel, you got what you paid for. Which wasn't much. Four walls, a ceiling, a door with a flimsy lock, and the filthiest space I had ever seen in my life. I didn't need a black light to know the place was crawling with enough bacteria that it had formed its own civilization and was holding elections. I was afraid if I squinted too hard I'd actually see the "dirt" move.

I wanted the money shot so I could get home and get a hazmat shower. Wash the whole damn day off me—class, baring my soul, and a cheating stakeout that was just gross on principle. On the bright side, it was likely we'd both developed immunity to pretty much every disease known to man and probably a few percolating on the edges of the human gene pool.

Using a tissue, I pulled back the curtain the barest inch. The black Cadillac my mark drove still sat in the parking space in front of the room I'd been surveilling.

"Dammit."

Seth snuffled awake and sat up rubbing his face.

"What's wrong?" he asked. It was little more than a slurred mumble. The man slept like he had an off switch. If I'd yelled out in panic, he'd have been full-on awake and doing a detailed threat assessment but my quiet curse hadn't alarmed him. He could fall asleep at a stoplight if it ran too long. After struggling with insomnia for the better part of a year I wouldn't say it was his most annoying personality trait, but it was up there.

"My subject is just hunkered down in that room. Something needs to happen before I lose my mind."

He snickered. I glared at him, the man who'd been sleeping for the past four hours, daring him to laugh again. He'd never touch my bare flesh again.

"Sunshine, just chill. It'll happen when it happens and you'll catch it. Especially since you won't be in the bathroom anymore bitching about getting hepatitis from the toilet."

"Says the man who doesn't actually have to touch anything in order to pee."

"Look, this is surveillance. If you can't handle this simple job, tell your dad and—"

If glaring could kill, he'd be dead five times over.

"Why are you here again? You can annoy me and act like a superior ass when I'm not trying to work."

"Are you working? I thought you were bitching about working."

I gathered up his clothes, also just lying on the floor, and barely avoided gagging. I pressed them into his body where he was standing too close to me for the tone of our encounter.

"So we getting out of here? You giving up the game?"

"No. I'm throwing you out. While you were sleeping you were annoying me and now you've pissed me off so much my options are kick your ass out or kill you."

His motions were stiff as he dressed and while I knew the mattress was old and full of dead coils, I was pretty sure it was because he was mad at me. Fine. So be it.

If I hadn't had a job to do, I would have stepped toe-to-toe and started something. I had gotten better at not taking the bait on slights with him lately, but I wasn't immune. I checked the parking lot again. Nothing happening.

"You're seriously telling me to go?"

I stared at him, wearing a look that indicated I was baffled by his behavior. Possibly the look was more *what crawled up your ass and died?* but it was open to interpretation.

Seth, standing barefoot on the grime-crusted carpet, looked angry out of proportion to my "offense."

He'd bitched and moaned when I'd ended up in one of his cases and I'd never said one word about his attitude or professional capabilities. Not unprovoked anyway.

It was four in the morning and I'd been in this grimy motel for hours waiting on a cheater and had he not been in the place, he'd never have heard my complaints. Yet, he'd invited himself to my job and critiqued how I did it and how I felt about it.

He'd interfered when I was setting up the camera and tripod. He'd even bitched that I got the room in the first place, insisting real surveillance was done from the car. He'd put in his two, three, and four cents on every decision I'd made then lain down and fallen asleep, clearly exhausted from criticizing me. And I'd taken it all with aplomb because I loved him and he had been "just trying to help."

That was done. I was full-on done.

"Seth, are you under the impression you are the aggrieved party? Do you feel like your behavior or treatment of me has been appropriate?"

I was busting out everything I'd learned in therapy. And I had some big damn guns to use too.

I kept my eye on the screen of the DSLR camera. I had a feeling something, besides the fight that was brewing, was getting ready to break open. He must have, as well, because he kept his mouth shut.

The door across the way opened a crack. I held the shutter button down and let the action mode do the work for me. A man and a woman perfectly silhouetted in the doorway kissed. Money shot.

I pivoted the camera slightly and trailed the man from the door to his car. Closeup on the license plate.

A little frisson of excitement worked its way up my spine.

"Hey, you were right. It happened when it happened. Thanks for the bumper sticker platitude. Super helpful."

I dissembled the tripod and stowed it and the camera in the bag.

He came up behind me and wrapped his arms around me. His skin was still hot with sleep sweat.

"I'm sorry, Sunshine. I'm tired and cranky."

I didn't move to get free, but I also didn't make any motions to hug him back. The heat on his skin had intensified the spicy smell of his guy shampoo. I wanted to close my eyes and lean back into him. I didn't though because that was his MO—the hit-and-run fight. He laid traps for me and waited while I set them off and then bailed on the fight, making me look like the bad guy.

"Next, you'll try to blame it on PMS. Don't you think it's kind of shitty to take out your fears and frustrations about my safety on me? Your 'suggestions' about how to do my job are about you, not me. So you can quit trying to manage me. I'm a grown-ass person and if I want to bitch about my job or where I have to do it, then that's none of your business."

"You know, Will, there are places in the world worse than this crappy motel."

"And I don't want to work in any of them either, but I did my damn job."

He dropped his arms and stepped back. "I don't want to get into anything this morning," he said.

And yet he clearly did if his body language was any indicator.

"Me either so I'm out of here, but we're all paid up until noon if you'd like to stick around and prove what a trooper you are."

He threw his hands up in the air. I was momentarily distracted by his hip cuts hovering just above the waistband of his unfastened jeans. I regained my faculties after a brief struggle with a naughty fantasy that involved his handcuffs. Fatigue was wearing down my defenses against the crazy amount of physical chemistry we had. But it wasn't good enough to make me entirely forget that Seth Anderson was the one being a giant ass, not me.

"What? What are you so annoyed about? I'm the one who should be mad. You've been bitching since the moment you got here except when you were asleep. And you were probably bitching at me in your dreams."

"It's called constructive criticism, princess."

Constructive criticism? Princess? And I'd never been more offended by a name. Not *mongrel bitch*. Not even being called the C word.

I wasn't pulling a punch on this one. He drops in on my case, offers unsolicited "constructive criticism," then calls *me* a princess?

Loud banging on the wall broke into our bickering. Clearly, our fight had disturbed some of the other patrons. I felt bad for them being woken in the wee hours of the morning to the sounds of fighting from the next room. It shouldn't have surprised them considering the venue, but I still felt a little guilty.

"You could at least be grateful for the company and help." His voice had dropped to a harsh whisper.

I started to wonder if he'd had a stroke or suddenly developed some previously unknown fast-acting mental illness that resulted in his bizarre behavior. Maybe he had recently had a blow to the head.

"Grateful? For your help? You've belittled me and questioned my professional skills and commitment. That's not help. That's sabotage."

"I—"

"And now, for the record, I'm super motivated to move in with you, she said sarcastically."

"You already live there!"

The pounding began in earnest again. I walked over and slammed my hand against the wall three times.

"I am a cop on a stakeout and my boyfriend is with the ATF. You bang on the damn wall one more time and the next thing we'll fight about is who gets to arrest you."

The banging abruptly stopped. A moment later we heard the door slam as our neighbor fled.

"Nice," Seth said. Another criticism.

"They're no longer annoying me, unlike you, and odds are, based on their hasty exit, were here doing something illegal. You wanna go catch them to apologize? Feel free."

I snatched up my bags and jacket and wrestled the door open. I managed to remotely unlock and open the passenger door, slinging everything into the back seat. I was so mad I didn't even spend a moment admiring the new-to-me truck. I wanted to get the photos to my dad and close this case.

As I backed out of the parking lot I saw the door to the room was still sitting open. I contemplated going back but decided that Seth was a big boy and he could take care of himself. Sunrise was three hours away. Nothing was open yet. I had to go home. Not back to the apartment, since that was the first place Seth would go and I was really afraid I might get physical with him if I saw him again so soon. Not the good kind of physical either.

When I pulled up in front of the house, I could see Dad sitting in the kitchen. Like he knew I was coming. I made sure I was quiet opening the door so I didn't wake up the rest of the family.

Ben had at least another hour before he had to get up, despite the ridiculously early start time for his high school. Of course, he probably would just bounce out of bed and make breakfast. He was a morning person. So was our mother. And Dad and I were the ones up at an hour even the Army considered the middle of the night. I'd like to cash in on their *we do more before nine a.m.* bet—I guarantee that documenting infidelity, thwarting a possible crime, and contracting a new strain of diphtheria was a winning hand.

I dropped down in the chair next to him and dug the camera out of the bag. Sliding it in front of him, I raised an eyebrow at him. He didn't normally accept cheating spouse stakeouts (what can't you get via a cell phone and computer anymore?) so I was curious about this aberration. He took the camera and popped out the memory card. I raised my eyebrow a bit higher. He put the memory card into the pocket of his robe. My eyebrow reached my hairline and I feared I'd sprain it if I pushed it any farther.

"Dad. Give already. What's up with this case?"

"You needed to do a stakeout." He looked guilty.

I couldn't believe it. I had just been scammed. No, I'd been hazed. By my own flesh and blood. I got up and poured myself a cup of coffee.

"Seriously, you're the worst boss ever." I was only half kidding. That motel had me contemplating any other career where I would be exposed to fewer germs. Like sanitation engineer. Or Peace Corps nurse. Or Band-Aid handed out by a Peace Corps nurse *to* a sanitation engineer.

"I'm not your boss. I'm your partner. And why are you here?"

I was just hoping I made it through my apprentice hours and got my license and didn't get his revoked in the process. I hadn't even been thinking about partnership.

"I came to do my write-up on the case and ... weren't you expecting me? Why are you up?"

"Oh, I was expecting you but not for five more hours. I figured once my friend left the motel, you'd head home."

"I am home." I avoided his eyes as I blew across the top of my coffee.

CHAPTER

3

"HE'S BEEN ANTSY AND distant. Cranky, picky, stubborn. Pretty much the textbook signs of a cheating spouse. Not that I studied for my stakeout or anything." Choke on the guilt, old man.

"You two have a lot of history. It's not always going to be easy. And he's not cheating on you. He wouldn't dare."

I wasn't sure if Dad was intimating that I would do something to Seth or that he would.

"I'm not expecting it to be all easy. Or even any easy. I am expecting to be an equal partner. But he doesn't ... he won't treat me like one. He doesn't want to let me out of his sight, but when we're together he's picking fights."

He chuckled. And I saw the humor in it too. Or rather irony that I was the one complaining about people picking fights, since I was the master at it.

"I'm saying that he's picking fights and even I'm looking back at them and being baffled. It's about everything now. Popcorn and the dishwasher. It's like we jumped from the conflict mediation to the honeymoon phase and then we jumped twenty years into the future to old married couple who can't get along once the kids have gone off to college. Again, classic cheater behavior even if we both think we know better."

"I very much hope that when we get your brother off to college, your father and I have something in common still. If only that it's planning a big party when you get your PI license. And Seth's not cheating on you. He adores you. He's adjusting."

I hadn't even heard her sneak into the room. I'd consider it an indictment of my sleuthing skills, but my mother—stepmother, technically—was the queen of stealth. It was in the handbook, I was sure.

"Shit, Mom, I'm ... and now I've said *shit*. I know you hate that. Crap. I've woken you up and—"

"Sweetie, it's fine. You guys were being quiet. I just had a hard time sleeping with you out on that stakeout."

I got up and started to make her a cup of tea. In my peripheral vision, I saw her run her hand over Dad's head and lean into him. For some reason, that little gesture said home to me regardless of where I lived and it made me feel safe. I knew they were solid and trusted each other.

And then she was at my elbow with her hand on my back. How do moms know?

"What's going on, sweetie?"

Therapy had made my emotions too easy to access, in my opinion. I was sure normal people thought that was a wonderful breakthrough and something to be pleased about, but the fact was I didn't feel like myself.

"I don't know what's wrong with him or me or maybe both of us. I'm not acting like me anymore and I think that's a problem for him."

"Anyone who really loves you wants this for you, Willa. You've always been reserved, but when Michael died you closed off almost completely. You changed when Seth came back into your life. You got your spark back. Hold on to that."

I rubbed my hand over her arm. It was possible that my mother was a better therapist than the one who had her shingle out. Then again, she knew me a lot better.

"How's the sex? That's still fine, right?"

I could feel Dad cringe from across the room. And since he'd sent me on a fake stakeout at Motel Disgusting, I was going to torment him more than a little. I turned around to face her.

"No, that's still amazing. Like, uh-mazing. Even when we're fighting we're one step away from tearing each other's clothes off."

I heard a clank as Dad banged the mug down on the table before fleeing. She laughed, smoothing my hair down and then caressing my cheek for a moment. Then she reached around me to grab the tea I'd started for her.

"We're terrible for torturing him like that," I said.

"That's what he gets for sending my baby on a made-up case."

She winked at me. Never mess with Mom. He hadn't learned that lesson in the almost twenty years they'd been married.

I slid down the stairs to my room. It had been mostly denuded since I'd started spending more time at the apartment with Seth.

And it was true. It was a mere technicality that I was holding onto saying I didn't really live over there with him. And it wasn't just the fear that once I made it official, we'd pack up the last of Michael. I didn't want to lose my space. A place that was just mine.

I checked my phone. Nothing from Seth. I couldn't deny something was going on with him. The only thing I was sure of, bone deep sure, was that he wasn't cheating on me. I'd mentioned it to Dad mostly to make him feel guilty for my fake stakeout. In high school, Michael and I spent a lot of time bantering about Seth being a player, but he'd never been a cheater. And if he was going to start, it wouldn't be with the woman who knew his whole playbook. Would he?

Dammit, he was making me doubt all the things I thought I knew about him. He wouldn't be pushing me so hard to move in if he was trying to get something over on me or trying to end it. I had to hold onto that faith in him. I had to believe that whatever was bothering him wasn't about us. If it was his work, I couldn't do much of anything. Maybe I could check in with Gordon, Seth's de facto partner. After last fall, I trusted him and I knew he'd be honest with me, as honest as he could. If it was a case, he'd tell me.

Maybe it was his family. Seth's relationship with his parents had gotten extremely rocky since Michael's death. Seth and I hadn't spent much time with them since we'd gotten together. Barely an hour at Christmas. He'd been in a bigger hurry to get out of there than I had. They had both been excited to see us and even happy that we'd reconnected after the years apart. Neither of us had enlightened them to our "reconnection" being a drunken hookup the night of Michael's memorial service. They didn't need to know and, honestly, it wasn't something either of us were particularly proud of.

He'd even forgone Thanksgiving with them. I was still a mass of injuries and physical damage. It had made sense he'd want to be with me and that I'd want to be with my family. I hadn't even thought about the Andersons and what they were doing with no children home for Thanksgiving.

I took a quick shower, just to wash off the feeling of cheap motel and stupid fight. I had time to have breakfast with Ben before he left for school.

What greeted me in the kitchen was pancakes. Real pancakes. Nothing wheat germ or flax. Pancakes and syrup and, god bless the woman, bacon. I gulped down half my cup of coffee from earlier. It was slightly warmer than room temperature but that left room for a top off. Ben played it cool but he was happy to see me. He must have been because he didn't say a word as I slathered butter all over my stack of pillowy, carb-laden heaven on a plate and dumped a cup of syrup over it. I chewed a piece of bacon and watched him spread all-natural almond butter on his. No butter or syrup. Mom had a single pancake on her plate. A cup of herbal tea seemed to be the only thing she touched. Dad used the rest of the bottle of syrup on his plate, drowning the bacon too. Talk about a house divided.

I had just cut into my stack when I heard the front door open. The pancakes had been a trap. I gave my mother a look filled with betrayal but she just shrugged. Either I was losing my touch and my expression of pain and outrage had come across as merely vexed or she'd had nothing to do with Seth's presence. I looked at my father and he had conveniently found a newspaper to read.

"Dad?"

"Hmm, yeah, sweetie?"

"Why is Seth here?"

"What makes you think Seth is here, pumpkin?"

"The awesome skills of deduction you've been training me in literally my whole life."

25

I slammed my fork back down on the table and got up. I got another plate and filled it with the now understandable overabundance of pancakes. I set the plate in front of Seth as he sat down and returned to my seat across from him.

Dad offered him a faint smile. It was like blood meant nothing to him. Ben passed him the butter dish. Traitors in my own family.

"Good morning, Nancy," Seth said.

I stuffed a large forkful of pancakes in my mouth and chewed viciously. I had just wanted a few hours to process the whole scene at the motel. Why in the hell did he have to show up and ruin breakfast too?

"Willa."

I swallowed and shoveled in another forkful. If I kept my mouth full it would be impossible for us to fight. If we couldn't fight then I wouldn't cuss. If I didn't cuss, Mom would be happier. I was doing it for her. I was literally eating my feelings. Of course, once I was full or the plate was empty then I'd be out of excuses to avoid talking to him.

"She's really pissed, dude."

And there was my baby brother wading into the emotional sewage for me. I really loved that kid.

"Yeah, I know she is, man. She's right to be. I was a jerk."

I took a deep breath forgetting I had five square inches of gummy pancake paste in my mouth. I coughed hard and then ran for the sink so I could spit the food out before I choked. I spit a few more times to make sure I had it all out. And to buy myself some more time.

I turned back to the table to find all four sets of eyes watching me. I noticed no one got up ready to give me the Heimlich, just in case. Nice.

"Seth admits he's wrong? The apocalypse is imminent. Do we have a Bible?"

"Be nice," my mother said.

26

I thought I was being nice. I hadn't thrown anything at him. I hadn't walked out. I hadn't even cursed. I got any nicer and I'd have to offer him a mint and hot towel.

"No, she's right to be skeptical, Nancy. I've been pushing her buttons and then apologizing when she reacts. This morning I crossed the line big time intruding on the fake stakeout and trying to boss her around."

He'd known it was fake too? And he must have realized his mistake because he started to stand.

"You move from that chair and I will make sure it's the last thing you do. You knew. You not only knew but you kept me there while you took a goddamn nap. You are so dead it's not even funny."

CHAPTER

4

I NEED 20 MINUTES.

FOR? my reply read.

20 MINUTES OF YOU NOT ASKING STUPID QUESTIONS.

I had missed Detective Jan Boyd. We had kept in touch after the Joe Reagan case but it had been a few weeks since she'd let me buy her coffee and pick her brain on the cases I was studying for the PI licensing exam. She was the only person who'd been treating me remotely normally since the end of that case. Which mostly meant that she treated me like she was mildly annoyed with me and slightly proud at the same time. But she didn't hover or worry over me so it was a nice change.

SURE. BOB'S? I wasn't a fan of anything at Bob's. All their food went down like paint stripper but Jan liked the coffee.

CAN YOU MEET ME AT THE STATION?

I stared at the words for a moment. "At the station" was not something I figured Jan would ever say to me. I wasn't persona non grata at the PD, but I also wasn't one of them anymore. I knew she wouldn't want to meet there if it wasn't important so I texted back my agreement and grabbed a jacket.

It wasn't my workplace anymore, but the sight of all the black-and-whites in the parking lot calmed me almost as much as the front door of home. The little asshole voice in my head reminded me that I was much safer at the cop shop than at home. I stuffed her in the box as I disarmed and stowed my weapon—concealed carry took you most places but into a police station without a badge was not one of them.

I tried for *casual* as I walked up to the front desk and landed mostly on *not actively displaying signs of instability*. They were used to it though. Cops just made people nervous.

"Hi, I'm here to see Detective Boyd. She's expecting me."

"She's expecting you?" he asked, distracted with something on his monitor.

I wanted to swallow my smartass reply but he'd barely glanced at me. This was a public building with dozens of targets some crazy would love to put down. That annoyed the hell out of me because I knew how quickly a lapse in vigilance could go ugly. "I said she was."

He looked up. Ah, Cop Face, I know you well. His expression softened. "Pennington, right?"

My right eye started to twitch, my fifth least favorite reminder of the reason for my fame.

"Yeah." I jammed my hands in my pockets and looked away.

"Here's your access." I turned back to see him flop a lanyard on the counter. "And you're supposed to wear it, not just carry it in your hand."

I smiled at him and slipped it over my head. I'd never met him before but he'd obviously met my type before. The door behind him buzzed and popped open slightly. "She's waiting for you on the other side of the man trap."

I paused in the four-by-four space until the second door buzzed and Jan yanked it open. She didn't even say hello before she turned and walked back through the main aisle of the glass and MDF cubicle farm. Her hair was longer than the last time I'd seen her. It was almost pretty.

She took a right and I was worried I'd lose her. Then I remembered the building wasn't that big so I trailed back, taking it all in. The detective's cubes weren't something I'd experienced much of when I was a uniform, plus I'd been assigned to another station. This one was more modern, newer even if the computers were something out of a museum. The keyboards clacked at varying speeds. I was grateful that Ben made sure we always had the best bargain equipment because if I'd had to listen to Dad hunt and peck like I was hearing some of the old timers doing, I'd go mad.

"You done strolling down the runway, Beauty Queen?" Jan asked. Most women wouldn't complain about that kind of nickname, but since she'd deposited it on me when I was bruised from temple to chin, it chafed. I'd learned in the past few months that Jan did not value meekness.

"Sorry. I forgot you speed walk with the other old folks at the mall in the mornings."

There was a table arrayed with pastries and, blessedly, those giant coffee pots. I made a beeline for it and she watched with a quirk to her lips as I looked through the cups for one that seemed even slightly larger. They were all tiny. Why did they even make cups that small? They were tea party tiny.

"Dude, do you have a real cup I can use?" I turned to Jan. "These are cups for kids. I need a grownup cup."

Jan chuckled and opened her magical cubicle cabinet, producing a mug bigger than a baby's face. It had a smiley face with a bullet hole in its forehead. Giant and pithy. Yes. I could definitely work with that.

I overheard someone whispering, "Did she just call Boyd 'dude'?"

Jan handed me the mug. I took my time attempting to empty the vat of regular coffee and stirring in a single packet of sugar with a meager splash of half and half. I was practically drinking it black. Jan made an annoyed noise and grabbed the coffee from me, tossing in another sugar and a waterfall of the creamer.

"You can't think without cowboy coffee and we both know it."

She handed me back the mug and I took a long swallow, which I could do because it wasn't scalding hot anymore thanks to the extra half and half Jan had generously dumped in. She was right. It was much better with the usual condiments added.

Another voice whispered, "Did Boyd just fix her coffee?"

Geez, Jan's co-workers had no idea how whispering was supposed to work.

"Yes, I called her 'dude.' I do it a lot. Yes, she fixed my coffee because she knows I'm too incompetent to handle the task. If you have any other questions, you should ask them out loud. Some detectives they are. They're all under the impression that you're some kind of hard-ass ball breaker." I winked at her.

She tried not to smile but we both knew that it wouldn't last. "Kid, you're ruining my reputation."

I shrugged and had another over-large mouthful of coffee.

I scanned the desk surface and saw the usual cop paraphernalia—dirty cups half full of coffee, stacks of folders in no discernible order, and a stuffed pig in uniform. Hell, even I had that stupid pig packed in a box I'd jammed in a closet. All she was missing was the cartoons about donuts. And then my eye lit on the enclosed shelf space. I reached over and slid the door down. There it was. Cops, coffee, donuts, and pigs.

"Sit," Jan barked.

I dropped into her chair instead of the guest chair and spun around to annoy her. "I need a lawyer, Detective?"

"Up, smartass. You sit in the perp chair." We both knew no perp had ever, would never sit in that chair but that's what it was named and that's what we called it. Cops like routine.

I took an extra ten seconds hauling my frame up and over into the chair that didn't have wheels and slumped down, giving her my best sullen criminal stare.

"You having fun?" Jan dropped into her own chair and it kept going to the bottom of its adjustment level, stopping with a jolt. All those months of punishing martial arts training had been worth it. She'd never noticed I'd depressed the height button on the chair.

I smiled at her in earnest. "You done giving me shit, Jan? I am here out of the goodness of my own heart, you know."

She laughed and cranked her chair back up to the right height.

I had done an admirable job of ignoring the food but I had skipped out before finishing breakfast and, as I had pointed out, I was working for free. She caught me eyeing the table and gave me the nod.

I stole three donuts and a bear claw too big to dunk in the mug. These weren't pastries from a grocery store or chain donut place. These were the real deal. And enormous. *The sugar rush would take me through the rest of the week* enormous. I took as small of bites as my ravenous appetite allowed.

She grabbed a folder off the top of the pile. The spine was worn and soft and it was neat but overstuffed. She handed it to me.

"I need your help."

I must have taken the folder but I was too busy gaping at her to register doing it. I might have gotten over my hero worship and started calling her by first name—at her insistence—but Detective Jan Boyd asking for my help was still a shock. I recovered enough to start running my mouth, the only part of me that never seems to shut down.

"What? You need my help? With…?"

She nodded at the folder. "Give that a look and tell me if anything jumps out at you."

I began to flip the folder open and she put her hand on top. "Not here. Take it home. Give it a good going over. Call me in a couple of days and let me know if you've got anything."

She turned back to her desk. I had been dismissed. You bet your ass I'd be looking over the file if only to figure out what the best detective in the county needed my help for. Neither of us was under any illusions that I'd done anything more than stumble into a solution to one of her cases last fall, and that was with her and the ATF doing most of the heavy lifting.

I resisted looking in the folder until I had returned my lanyard and got back in my truck. I'd seen a few of these when I'd been in uniform. I'd even handled a few when I had to give the officer's notes for a case that was moving on from my hands to a detective's.

The first page in the file was a summary report detailing the contents of the folder: witness statements, crime scene photos, detective notes, and the evidence list. I flipped through realizing there was too much to get into in the front seat of the truck. I fanned out a few crime scene photos looking for the detective notes and not finding them. I paged through the file piece by piece in case they'd been put back in the wrong section. Nothing.

I slipped out my phone to text Jan.

Detective notes seem to be missing.

I want your opinion without mine leading you.

Huh. That made it easier and harder. I'd built enough of a relationship with Jan that I wasn't too giddy to speak to her coherently, but I'd never before been in the position she was asking me to assume—reviewing her work. It was an odd feeling.

I shuffled everything back in and laid the file on the passenger seat. I'd spread it all out when I got home with pen and paper and build my own detective notes. Then if she didn't give those over, I was going to need to take my own witness statements. On a case that was sixteen... no, seventeen years old.

I was ten. I had been destroying fractions in fourth grade. The legal wrangling to allow me to move in with Dad and my new stepmother had finished with minimal peeps from my biological mother, Leila. We were moving into our new house. My parents were a few months away from telling me I was getting a new brother or sister. The Andersons would be moving to the neighborhood in two years. And Jan had been trying to solve her first murder case.

CHAPTER

5

I PUT THE TRUCK in drive and headed back to the house. I hoped that Seth was gone. I needed to talk to my dad. Alone. Mom would already be out the door for her day at the local elementary school. Once I had hit high school, she had resigned at the hospital and taken a job as a school nurse. She said it would be better if she was home in the afternoons with us. Despite Dad being there. She'd never said anything, but I had always thought that because Ben was so much like her and I was so much like Dad that if she was home, she could ensure we all got balanced time. Or maybe she was just worried Dad and I would eat junk food all the time and die of a sugar overdose. I couldn't honestly say it wasn't a possibility.

"Dad?"

He was already in the office. The light was on. He was sitting behind his desk, still in his robe. A cup of coffee sat on a stack of files, unsteady as hell.

"You're going to spill that."

"You sound like your mother."

"Duh. Where do you think I got it from? You got a minute?"

He put down the file he hadn't been reading. His reading glasses sat folded on another stack of files. I may not have known the stakeout case was an elaborate play, but I could pick up a detail like that.

"Is this about last night?"

Dare I repeat *duh*? Better not. He was always going to be my dad even if he wasn't going to be my boss forever. I nodded.

"You're mad and not just at Seth. You're upset that I would send you off on a wild goose chase. You feel like it wasn't respectful. You're thinking that if I pull something like that again, you'll quit."

Wow, nailed it. Dad wasn't clueless, by any means. He was a damn good detective. But that was so on point I was more than a little stunned. It must have shown on my face.

"Nancy might have mentioned that it could blow up in my face."

Now that made sense. Dad ignoring her and doing what he wanted made even more sense. It blowing up in his face, that was pretty much guaranteed. You ignored Mom at your own peril. She was always right.

"If I promise not to do anything like that again, will you stick it out with me?"

I nodded again. That had gone much easier than I thought it would. So well, in fact, I hadn't had to say anything.

"You should know by now that not listening to her is a bad idea."

"You know, every time she doesn't say 'I told you so,' I think that. At least you kids are smarter than your old man."

"Us kids? Clearly you mean Ben because I am a huge dumbass for falling for that fake stakeout."

"Nah, you're doing great. I was treating you like a dad and not a supervising investigator."

I sat down at the chair that went with my pint-sized desk. It was like he found it at the Take Your Daughter to Work Day office furniture store. There really hadn't been room for a second desk so I didn't complain about it. It was a sweet gesture.

"Dad, I'm fine. I promise. You don't have to baby me."

I had even managed to make eye contact with him for most of that confession. I wasn't lying about any of it. Therapy had gone well. Martial arts training was too. And I'd always been a crack shot. He didn't need to baby me.

The fact that I still woke up choking down screams at least once a week, well, I hadn't mentioned that and he hadn't asked. It wasn't the first secret I had kept from him, it wouldn't be the last. I was great at keeping secrets. I could have won a gold medal in secret keeping at the Olympics and no one would even know.

Work through the pain, suck it up, keep going, never give in, never say die. Pick your hard-ass, tough-guy, stoic cliché. I had learned them and learned them well. And I only rarely complained. It took a lot too. I hurt less than I should and more than I wanted. The bruises and broken bones had healed.

"You're fine?"

"I'm mostly fine. It's not a light switch you can flip, Dad. No matter how much you guys want to watch me all the time, you can't. I have to be fine in the time it takes."

"Bah."

Who says *bah*?

"And that means what exactly?

37

"It means that's psychobabble."

Yeah, it was psychobabble. And as much as I hated to admit it, it was working. "I know you don't believe in therapy. I'm not sure I do completely either, but Mom insisted and you know I don't ignore her when she tells me something. Unlike some people."

"I just don't see how lying down and talking about feelings for an hour helps anything."

Typical Dad. He didn't understand it so it couldn't work. He didn't understand exactly how cell phones worked either but he used one. And I was annoyed he was putting me in the position of having to defend something I was only doing begrudgingly, no matter how effective it seemed to be.

"She didn't make me lie down."

"I'd just nod off."

"I get it, Dad. You think it's stupid. You think the problem can be solved by making me do fake stakeouts and lying to me." I pushed my chair back and started to leave but then turned back. "And if you ever pull that kind of shit on me again, I will quit so damn fast your coffee won't even have a chance to go cold. The ATF still has a spot for me."

That should do it. The ATF offer bugged him. It bugged him because he thought I should have taken it and he was worried I would still take it. It kept us at a nice state of imbalance; me knowing I had it in my hip pocket to whip out when I needed an ace in the hole and him thinking that he was being selfish to not encourage me to take it. The fact that Nancy was dead set against it kept us at stalemate.

He didn't need to know that I had only briefly considered the pitch. I liked my own rules. I liked knowing it was a family business. And we were a good team despite our differences but mostly despite our similarities.

I'd planned a quick nap and then I'd head to the apartment. At the door to my bedroom I checked my phone, the time showing it was just before nine. Seth would already be in his temporary office at the undisclosed location while he worked the unspecified task force.

He'd wanted to keep that low key considering the last time his job and mine had overlapped, there had been considerable mayhem. Which I now liked to refer to as The Incidents. I think the legal terms the district attorney had threatened me with were "obstruction of official duties" and "criminal mischief" before the ATF had shut him down. The poor guy had practically been swallowing his tongue when he'd had to apologize.

I laid down on the bed fully clothed and shut my eyes. I hadn't needed to use the trick the therapist gave me in a few days but I pulled it out since I was in a "troubled emotional state that might negatively affect sleep." I started to visualize drops of water falling steadily onto the side of a bowl and letting them run down into the basin full of water, no splash or sound just the slow drip and slip. That just reminded me I needed to take a shower and wash off the … everything from the Pay by the Hour but It's Not Really a Front for Prostitution motel.

As I finally rinsed off the perceived grime from the cheap motel (trying and failing not to catalog the odds of getting an STI from the air), washed and deep-conditioned my hair (a necessity in the dry winter air), and shaved (something I had to do regularly now that I was sharing a bed with another person I wanted to touch said legs), fatigue tried to take over but sleepiness was out on an errand. If I couldn't get in any rest, I'd survive. I'd gone without sleep longer than a night many times.

I combed my hair out and added leave-in conditioner. The way January had been, super cold and extremely snowy, I wanted to protect my mop as much as possible. I had become obsessive about it since someone had grabbed a handful of it to keep me from running away from him and yanked out a patch the size of a silver dollar. That was the part that had pissed me off the most. I mean, he'd done it to get a few more punches in and not out of any desire to wound me emotionally (wounding me physically was enough for him), but women are funny about their hair.

I knew it was stupid and vain but it was one thing I could control, so I was overly determined to care for it. The bruises faded in the time it took bruises to fade. The broken ribs healed slowly and still ached when it was cold—so pretty much all the time. And four months later the scars were fading too slowly for my liking as I caught Seth staring at them more and more. His jaw would clench and he'd get that look in his eyes and then he'd want to spend hours at the gym running through drills or at the range shooting silhouette after silhouette.

Too much on my mind and not enough space to shove it all down past the ignore line. My conscious could do it, but it just burbled back up when my subconscious took over. Then the fight began between the two parts of my brain trying to protect me and not being able to agree on how best to do that. But once my body shut down, letting my subconscious take over, the dreams began.

Nightmares. Of fires, which I knew too well. And explosions, which I had no idea about but I'd imagined was like if someone threw you into a brick wall. That was on fire. And terrifyingly silent after the initial blast took your hearing. And of a house that I didn't know and a room by room search for someone who I wasn't even sure was there. And the choking and raw throat of breathing and pushing through smoke. My eyes burned. The temperature rose as I climbed the stairs, knowing that going up was dangerous, that I could end up trapped trying to rescue someone. These weren't merely bad dreams but memories of being trapped in a fire. Of feeling the weight of responsibility on my shoulders for saving someone else. And then the chase was on as I felt rather than heard someone running up the stairs behind me.

Someone hunting me. Wanting to hurt me, not being content to let the fire take me. Wanting to do the damage with his fists. Wanting to watch. I didn't run. I knew running would be giving in. I stepped deliberately up into the hall that was finally in front of me and the door that lay at the end. I turned the knob and saw Michael. Not as I remembered him, but as I tried not to imagine him. Torn open, broken, bloodied, screaming in pain. And still I didn't wake up. His eyes were full of pain. And I still didn't wake up. His face morphed into Seth's and I felt the obscene heat of the fire reach me, finally overtaking me.

CHAPTER

6

I WASN'T GETTING BACK to sleep after that last bout with the man who wanted to kill me. Fire was scary. I had forgotten how scary. The sound of it, how alive it was, how the smoke curled and eddied. I had purposely forgotten how scary it had been. I stared determinedly at random objects in my room, grounding myself in reality as I waited for my heart to slow.

There were times in the days after the fire that my eyes would begin to water, my lungs would feel as if they were tearing open, the smoke slicing through them, my throat would burn just from the memory. I walked away from that fire with minor smoke inhalation and a healthy respect for the awesome power of flame. And the fire and all the scariness had then been eclipsed by later events. And then it was all over, as quickly as it had begun, and I was bruised and battered and broken. And none of it had felt much like a victory.

Getting the crap beaten out of you rarely felt like a win. Unless you were a masochist. Which I had been accused of a time or two. But getting punched in the face was not how I liked to spend an evening. Having someone try to knife me was not a good time in my book. Dropping out an open window the size of a boot box and falling fifteen feet to the ground so I could bruise my tailbone and have my boyfriend narrowly escape being burned alive was definitely not fun and games.

Masochist I was not. But I didn't shy away from the hard stuff. I couldn't. There were people I loved who needed to be protected. And I'd never back down from that. Not from knives or fists or fire. I didn't consider myself a badass although a few former coworkers, cops no less, had used that word when visiting me in the hospital. I hadn't set out to be a hero. But if putting one foot in front of the other and doing good ended up in some bad-assery, well, those were the risks you took.

I picked up my phone and pulled up the contact log.

"Agent Gordon."

He knew who was calling and answered like that to annoy me.

"Gordo."

"I hate it when you call me that," he said, weariness making him sound as close to whiny as he could get.

"I know. It's why I do it," I said, brightly.

I heard him sigh. It sounded exasperated. I had plenty of experience with that one.

"I just need to know one thing and it's not even for me. What's going on with Seth lately?"

"How is that not for you?" he asked. I heard a door shut. He'd probably gotten himself off to one of those privacy cubes they sequestered themselves in when non-work calls intruded on workspace. That way no one heard anything they weren't supposed to. I always envisioned them like those isolation booths on old game shows. I had to use my imagination because despite a job offer from the ATF, I had never been given a tour of even the lobby of one of their facilities.

"Because it's for Seth. You know, emotional support and whatnot," I said.

"Emotional support and whatnot." He chuckled.

"Jeez, someone sees your soft underbelly once and they lose all ability to remember you're a badass capable of action movie–level heroics."

He cleared his throat. "Sorry. Emotional support. Whatnot. Heroics. I'm taking this deeply seriously now." The only thing deep was his voice.

"Gordo, is this task force stressing Seth out or what? I just need to know."

He sighed again. "I don't know. We're not working together right now, Willa."

I bit my lip. We didn't exactly have a warm and fuzzy relationship, not like I had those with ... well, anyone, really, but he was someone I trusted.

"He's ... off."

"Yeah."

Silence racked up.

"Listen, I'll give him a call. Suggest a beer," he said.

"Okay. Thanks."

"It's the least I can do for the only superhero I know," he said, laughing again before he disconnected the call.

I knew Seth wouldn't be home until late afternoon so I headed to the apartment to pick up my laptop. I'd left it there two nights ago

44

and wanted to get it before I had to develop a plan to deal with his crabby ass.

Being in his space with his things made me angry at him again. I'd fought getting involved with him, and his behavior at the stakeout was exactly why. But I didn't have time to think about his weirdness so I distracted myself by opening the file Jan had given me and actually doing my job. I spread the papers on the couch and, as usual, got sucked into the puzzle of the case.

My sympathetic nervous system clicked on before I consciously recognized the sound of keys in the lock. I checked the time but saw that it was way too early for Seth to be home from work. The door opened and Seth's dad, the man we referred to as the Colonel, was standing on the other side. He seemed startled to see me too.

"Hi."

"Hi, Willa. I'm sorry. I thought you were at the office with Arch otherwise I would have knocked."

How many freaking people had keys to this apartment?

"Seth told me you were going to be out. He didn't want you here when I came to pick up Michael's things."

Of course he didn't. He hadn't talked to me about any of it, so why would he have mentioned that his father was coming to clear out Michael's room? Or that he was going to do it today? No, he'd much rather wait until he thought I wasn't home. I *was* surprised that he'd decided to have the Colonel come take the boxes.

"He's been packing up while I'm out. He doesn't seem to want me to be involved."

"I'm sure he's trying to … how are you doing with all of this, Willa?" the Colonel asked.

I looked for an uncomplicated answer to a complicated question. I didn't find one.

"I'm okay with letting go of Michael's things. That doesn't mean I'm letting go of him. He was my best friend. He made me a better person and he'll always be in my heart. I don't know that Seth is as okay as I am. He keeps saying all the right things, but I'm not convinced."

He looked surprised. Maybe my honesty was more than he expected. He started fiddling with the keys he held. It was uncharacteristic. The Colonel had always been self-possessed with a still, military air about him. I watched as his thin fingers wound a key off the ring. He handed it to me.

"You should have this now. Your dad tells me you're moving in."

My dad told him? Not Seth? Not his son who had asked him to come over and take away Michael's things?

"Um, thanks, but I already have one. You should keep it. For emergencies."

I couldn't meet his eyes so I focused on his hands as I pressed the key back into his palm. His hands were little compared to Seth's. And Michael's, too, if I thought about it. The Colonel's sons looked nothing like him. Or their mother. Both the Colonel and Barbara were small, fine-boned people while their boys were taller, sturdier, more substantial. Seth looked like he could muscle through walls. Michael has been taller and leaner, but he had towered over his parents.

"Thank you, Willa. For being Michael's friend. For taking care of Seth. My sons have been lucky to have you in their lives."

"I... I have no response to that."

He didn't laugh but only barely, I could tell, as he pressed his lips together tightly.

"Sorry, I just honestly thought you two hated me."

He looked baffled. At least it wasn't just me that was confused then.

46

"Why would you think that? We've always loved you."

I thought about it for a minute. Why had I thought they'd hated me? They'd never said anything overt.

"I really don't know why. I just always thought that you didn't approve of Michael spending so much time with me, that his best friend was a girl. And that if you didn't like me being Michael's best friend and knew that he didn't want me and Seth together, that this wouldn't be something you'd want either."

He shook his head. "We have always thought of you as a part of our family, just like your parents have thought of Seth and Michael as a part of their family. We'd always hoped you would rub off on Michael, get him to stop feeling like he needed to prove himself to everyone, especially me."

It was my turn to shake my head. I had to fight back tears and turned away knowing I was going to be unsuccessful. The Colonel didn't follow me as I moved through the living room and sat on the couch with my back to him. He may not have been good with his own emotions but he was pretty good at recognizing other people's.

"Sorry, it's been a really weird year," I said.

The Colonel came and sat on the other side of the couch, careful not to crumple any of the papers I'd strewn about. Out of the corner of my eye I could see him looking straight ahead, like he was trying to be close but still give me some privacy. It was sweet, and that was a sentiment I had never entertained about the man before. Stupid, really, considering he'd raised two of my favorite people.

"I know we haven't talked much since ... well, ever, but I don't know much about girls and sometimes that made me nervous around you. I suppose that's why you felt we never liked you. Barbara and I aren't the most effusive people, but we do care. I know it's been really hard on you since even before Michael died. I knew you were unhappy about him joining the Army. Honestly, so was I."

The man wouldn't stop surprising me, it seemed. Him telling me he hadn't wanted Michael to join up was the last thing I would have ever expected to come out of his mouth. I sniffed, embarrassingly, and grabbed a tissue from the box situated on the side table. Seth was a great housekeeper.

"You didn't? I thought that you wanted them both to join up."

"I wanted them to do what they wanted. Seth wanted it. Michael didn't. He thought it was what we expected of him. He was always doing what he thought other people wanted."

We sat in silence for a few moments before I got up.

"Can I make you some coffee or tea or ... um, a sandwich?"

The Colonel smirked at that. "Ben despairs that you're going to die of scurvy."

"Ben isn't that smart if he doesn't know scurvy has practically been eradicated. At least in the first world."

He followed me to the kitchen and sat down at our little table, miraculously clean of any crumbs or stickiness. Then again, we had eaten breakfast at my parent's house so we looked like responsible grownups who could clean up after themselves. Generally, we could but the breakfast table was a bit of a hot zone for fights, so one or both of us usually stomped off before we cleaned up.

Many a night we'd come home after making up via text or a lunchtime detente, only to find bowls of warm milk and cereal bits so mushy you couldn't tell if they'd started their lives out as Os or umlauts; plates littered with toast crumbs and crusted with egg yolks; sad butter pools on congealed syrup lakes. The breakfast leavings were the reminders of our inability to talk our problems out. The little nitpicky fights were too. Neither of us truly cared about popcorn as much as we'd made out, but it was easier than me telling Seth I knew there was something wrong that he wasn't admitting to me and, obviously, Ruby Reds were easier than him just telling me what it was.

"He's different lately. Seth. There's something bothering him."

"I know. He is with us too."

I am sure he meant that to be a comfort to me.

"What does he do when he brings Ben over?" I asked.

"Watches TV, sometimes. Mostly sequesters himself away on his phone claiming work."

I busied myself with the coffeemaker. During my discharge session at the hospital I had been ordered to cut back on the caffeine. Coffee had been off limits during my stay because something, something about the pain medications being contraindicated. Honestly, I wasn't paying too much attention due to the fun floaty sensation I got from the pain meds and Seth rubbing circles on the back of my hand. Yes, I remember that distinctly because, frankly, he was a lot better looking than the dour, mean doctor.

It was either the happy, no-pain drugs or coffee. And I wasn't about to give up the drugs with the broken ribs and bruised everything. Then they were kind enough to let me keep some of the great drugs to take home when I was discharged, bill paid in full by the ATF, but I still wasn't allowed coffee so my mother plied me with the herbal tea she and Ben loved so much and I was almost willing to give up the medication. Almost. Then Dad got everyone to agree to decaf and I don't care what anyone says, it's not as good as the real thing.

I had realized I was rambling, out loud, when the Colonel chuckled.

"You still do that, I see."

Well, that was mortifying. I'd hazard a guess that mortification was not one of those emotions easily masked. Proven out by his next remark.

"Don't be embarrassed. It's one of my favorite things about you. You always say what you mean."

This day was beyond full of surprises. I surreptitiously pinched my own hand to make sure I wasn't asleep and dreaming. All I found was that I needed to drink some more water as I was slightly dehydrated, indicated by the skin shrinking back down more slowly than it should have. My mom's a nurse, remember? We got tons of lectures on hydration. And antibiotic-resistant infections. She's more fun than she sounds.

"Maybe you and Seth could come over for dinner together. If you came we could all sit together and talk."

I was a little uncomfortable feeling like I was being used to get his son to come hang out with him. But I considered that it might get me some intel on what the hell had crawled up Seth's ass, so I nodded.

"Did you want me to help you load those boxes up?"

I'd hoped he'd say no. It seemed pretty crappy of me to not at least offer, but I really didn't want to haul those boxes down to his car knowing that they contained the last of Michael's possessions. And I didn't want to think of those pieces of my life, his life, jammed together, ready to be forgotten. To the Colonel and Barbara, I was sure it was infinitely harder, having lost a child. But I wasn't them. I was me. And this was the pain I knew.

"No, I think this has been hard enough on you. Both of you."

And suddenly I wanted nothing more than to have Seth walk in the door. I thought back to the night I'd almost lost him too. The fire of my dream had been nothing like the real fire we'd barely survived. He'd risked his life to save me, to give both of us a chance, no matter how small his chance was. Letting go of his hand as he'd dropped me out of that window had taken every bit of emotional strength I had left in me after Michael's death. That night I'd gotten as close as possible to a nervous breakdown, losing myself on a knife's edge of fear and grief, until the firefighters had dragged Seth free of the smoke-filled garage. Until I'd heard his voice again, I wasn't that far away from giving up entirely. I hadn't thought about my family, Michael, even myself. My only thought was that if I lost Seth, too, that would be it. I wouldn't be able to go on. I had thought I hated him. I had spent so much time pretending and that moment when I thought I wouldn't be able to pretend anymore, I knew I'd always loved him.

"Tell me what is wrong with him, please. Because I think you know."

The Colonel stared at me, his mouth slightly dropped open. The apartment was so silent I could hear him breathing across the room from me. He knew. His poker face was decent, but it wasn't as good as my ability to see through it. This had all started after Michael's death. Seth referring to them by their first names. And as formal as their home had been, this was a father who knew his child well enough to know what was really going on inside Seth's head.

"Please don't bullshit me. I need to know."

His expression had grown mulish. Fine. I knew how to break down walls.

"How much do you know about the night of the fire?"

He shook his head. He didn't want to hear about the night his son almost died. Losing one was more than he could handle. I had to agree with him.

"Your son put me out a window and held me twenty feet off the ground. With a metal window frame digging into his arms and his lungs full of smoke, he held my dead weight trying to give me as

51

much of his arms so the drop wouldn't be so bad. I weighed a hundred and forty pounds. Hanging me like that had to have been almost unbearable. He didn't have enough oxygen and he still held on. I had to pull free from him so I could save both of us."

He covered his face with his hands.

"He told me it was the only chance for both of us, but he was lying to me. He didn't think he was getting out alive. His only goal was to save me."

He opened his mouth and closed it again. I could see him wavering.

"I won't let go this time. I will do whatever it takes. You need to tell me."

And I wouldn't. Whatever shit Seth had put me through, we'd saved each other's lives. I wasn't letting go because he acted like an asshole sometimes.

The Colonel stared at me, his eyes shining, and opened his mouth. My phone chirped from the other room. The chirp sounded again. A text. It could wait.

"Seth and Michael aren't ours." His voice was quiet and raspy.

Seth and Michael aren't theirs. I had no idea what that meant. Then it hit me. The eyes, the hands, their builds. Seth and Michael weren't their biological children.

I drew in a shaky breath. "And Seth knows?"

It was a stupid question. Of course, Seth knew.

"And Seth is mad at you. He's been avoiding you, avoiding talking about it when he is with you, putting people in between you at every turn."

My phone beeped again. I went to the other room to quiet it.

Text alert from Seth. I saw a previous one from him. The one I'd ignored. This one was a terse time estimate of his arrival home. He was in a mood. I knew why now. I walked back to the kitchen.

"Let me see what I can do. I'm not making any promises. You know how stubborn he is."

———

A half hour later I watched the Colonel put the last box in his car and locked the door behind us.

I decide to go to the dojo. It would be a good way to deal with the nightmare; to literally sweat it out, punch it out of my system, work my lungs until they burned in a good way.

I was four stoplights away—a long one—when my phone chirped in my pocket. I needed a new tone for text alerts. I hadn't found one that didn't make me jump. The therapist said it was reaction to external stimuli that reminded my subconscious of being in danger. Whatever the reason, the most recent tone set my teeth on edge.

YOU SAID YOU WOULD HELP. DID YOU MEAN IT?

Aja. My stomach dropped. She hadn't indicated she was in danger, but my instincts screamed at me.

CHAPTER

7

THE LIGHT TURNED GREEN and I eyed the shopping center turn-in two lanes over. I checked my side mirror and saw I barely had enough room to jet over. A horn blared. Maybe *barely* hadn't been enough. Whatever. This was a possible emergency. I turned in and slammed the truck into park while calling the number back.

"Willa?" Her voice was shaky but didn't sound tearful.

"Aja? Are you safe?"

"Um, I don't know. I think so." I didn't hear panic. She probably was safe even if she didn't feel certain of it.

"Where are you, sweetie?" The term of endearment had been spontaneous and even if I didn't use them normally, it felt right. She needed reassurance and I was the person she'd turned to.

Aja took a shuddering breath and blew it out. Her breathing sounded steadier. "At home. My parents are out of town."

What kind of shitty parents left their teen daughter home alone when she was clearly having an issue so obvious a total stranger picked up on it? I shoved down the anger. It wasn't my job to fix her parents.

"Give me the address and I'll be right over."

She rattled off an address I knew wasn't too far from Ben's school and after assuring her I would be no more than twenty minutes, I recited it into the map app and floored it back into traffic. Once I got close enough to the address, and the school, buses began to cause the cars to crawl. I knew where I was going and navigated away from the stream of vehicles leaving the school's parking lot.

I pulled onto the street and my reflexes went on high alert. Aja had told me she was safe, but that was based on what she saw and heard. Danger sometimes lurked just on the edges. I knew that well. If I could, I'd try to make sure she didn't have to learn that fact today.

The houses in the neighborhood were a good deal bigger than the one I grew up in. Seth and I referred to the ostentatious displays as yuppie trailer parks—all the same houses, all the same people. Was it stereotypical and unfair? Yes. Did we care? No.

I rang the doorbell and the filmy curtain covering the side window pulled back barely an inch. Heavy black eyeliner ringed the eye that only partially showed. I heard at least three locks click before the massive door cracked open. I stood patiently. The teen was well and truly spooked by something. Or someone.

"You came."

I nodded. "That was the deal, wasn't it?"

Aja pulled the door open wider, stepping behind it to let me in or hide behind it. It could have gone either way considering the rest of her behavior.

"Did you see him?"

I pushed the door shut, manipulated the locks, and leaned against it. Three barriers between whoever "he" was and the terrified girl who obviously felt she had no one to count on. I stood staring at her, assessing her physical well-being. She didn't have any apparent injuries. No black eyes or other bruises. There was no blood that I could see. She was folded in on herself but didn't seem to be babying any limbs. She looked whole and unblemished. She didn't even have any tracks through her makeup, although that could have been reapplied.

"How long have you been alone here, Aja?"

She shrugged, popping one already-chewed-to-the-quick thumbnail in her mouth. I was sure she knew down to the second how long it had been since her parents had left. She kept her mouth shut. I couldn't fault her loyalty. I had certainly extended it to enough people who didn't deserve it, and most hadn't even been family.

"Sweetie, I'm not going to get your parents in trouble for leaving you alone. All I care about is your safety. You said 'him.' There's a man bothering you?"

Aja nodded. "I mean, he's just a guy. Not a man, really."

That was a relief. A teenager was going to be easier to deal with than an adult.

"Wait, weren't you supposed to be in school when you texted me? Did you leave school because this guy is bothering you?"

Her eyes shifted away from mine. For someone who called me for help, Aja was being a bit too reticent.

"I'm just trying to figure out what's going on. Why don't you tell me what you think I need to know and then we'll go back and fill in any blanks."

She shifted from one foot to the other and then led me down a winding staircase to the lower level of the house. There was a door at the bottom of the stairs sitting ajar. She slipped through it without opening it any farther.

I followed her through the door and my eyes widened. The walls and the ceiling were painted black. Even the concrete floor had been painted black. It was impossible to tell how large the room was thanks to the illusion the all black space created. We could have been in a decent-sized room or the entire footprint of the massive house.

"Your parent's decorator must have pitched a fit when she saw what you wanted to do down here."

Aja giggled and flopped down on the vast couch. She somehow managed to sprawl gracefully on the modern hybrid between a sofa and an aircraft carrier deck. It had no arms or backs just a flat plane of cushion and enough pillows that no princess would ever feel a pea. Or a boulder.

"There's a stupid suit of armor in the formal living room," she said. "Believe it or not, my parents were chill about the basement being mine. My granddad made a shit ton of money in the seventies and eighties, so they can pretty much do whatever they want."

The smile dropped from her face again. She'd reminded herself that her parents weren't the people she wanted them to be. I could relate.

"You know, Aja, my mom—my biological mother—is an actress. She never wanted to marry my dad. I was about two when she decided she wanted to take off and she didn't want to go alone. I spent the next eight years of my life bouncing around bedsits in New York and run-down summer camps taken over by theater people. There were even a few months in Los Angeles when she was cast in a pilot for a TV show."

When she perked up, I shook my head.

"When I was nine, I was negotiating with landlords to try to keep us from getting evicted. I finally told her I wanted to live with my dad. So I get it."

She was shocked. You always think you're the only one.

"There are more of us than you'd ever think possible, Aja. And you know, they're not all bad people. Leila is a good person, but she's not exactly built for motherhood. Some people are just … not ready to be parents and don't learn it until after they have a kid."

She turned away swiping her sleeve over the flood of black eye makeup coursing down her face. "Why are you making excuses for them?"

I sat gingerly on the couch and put my hand on the arm not covering her face. "I'm not. There's no excuse. My attitude is you have a kid, you get your shit together. But that's not reality sometimes. Even with my dad and my stepmom it took me a long … Jesus, such a long damn time to get on with my life. I don't trust people like I should. Still. But, Aja, even if they came through that door and everything was the complete opposite from this moment on, the past happened. You don't have to like it or even understand it. But you have to accept that it is."

"At least you got to have your dad."

She sniffled, still feeling sorry for herself. I didn't blame her. Something scary was happening to her and her parents were not helping her. Hell, they weren't even around.

"I did. And he taught me how to do what I do."

Aja looked over her arm, one eyebrow raised.

"Okay, is teaching me," I conceded.

She sat up and rubbed her hands, ineffectively, over her cheeks. The makeup smeared more and cleared at the same time.

"Why don't you go wash your face and think about what you want to tell me about this person you're afraid of?"

She started to protest and then looked at her hands covered in black smudges. While she wandered off to what was likely an all-black bathroom, I looked around the room. The dark expanse of wall was broken up with movie and rock concert posters. The kid had amazing taste even if there were no Coen Brothers movies represented. Which made me think.

"Yo, Benj. I found you a new friend. One your own age. Call me back." My brother hated it when I called and even more when I left voicemail messages. I just couldn't text as fast as he did. And I so enjoyed hearing him sputter and whine about it. It gave me older-sister warm fuzzies.

I was trying to calculate the dimensions of the humongous television when Aja returned. Her face absent any makeup, she looked much younger than her chronological age. I doubted she would appreciate the observation so I kept it to myself.

"I didn't realize they made TVs this big. It looks like something you'd see in an action movie when all the spy guys have to have covert discussion with their counterparts in the enemy state."

"I spend a lot of time down here lately. My parents don't even pay attention to the credit card bills so I figured . . . ." She shrugged again.

I squashed down the uncharitable poor-little-rich-girl thought that popped into my head. I knew my life wouldn't have been better with Leila even if we'd had this kind of money. Plus, it's not as if Aja had chosen her life.

"So you spend a lot of time by yourself or is anyone joining you?"

The thumb popped back into her mouth as her eyes sidled away. It made me wonder if she was even as old as I assumed she was. Seventeen was okay to leave alone for a bit. Fourteen? Not so much.

59

"Alone. Mostly since I broke up with Damian. He's the one ... he's kind of not letting go."

"Damian is who you thought I might have seen when I arrived?"

She nodded.

Okay, I'd been here twenty minutes and we'd finally gotten somewhere. Aside from the shit ton of money her grandfather made and that she had flighty, irresponsible parents.

"You broke up with Damian because?"

She shrugged again.

"Aja, listen. I want to help you. I told you I would and I'm here when you called, but you need to do your part. Did he cheat on you? Did you get underwater with schoolwork? Did you just change your mind and decide 'nope, not the guy for me'? What happened?"

"He got weird. He started hanging out with some new people. We're both seniors, but he dropped all his old friends at school. Then he stopped coming to school. He ignored my texts."

I nodded. Okay, we were making progress. Teen boy acts like teen boy. Teen girl gets sick of his shit.

"Had you two, you know ... ?"

Her eyes got wide. "Why would you ask that?"

"Sometimes when guys get what they want, they take off. Which is stupid to me because if you've gotten it once, your odds of continuing to get it only increase," I rambled.

"Okay, no. And ew." She pulled her hands up inside the sleeves. "It's weird that you'd even ask."

"It seemed germane to the topic. I'm sorry if I offended you."

"I'm not offended. It's just weird talking to a stranger about sex."

A stranger? I'd come when she asked me to without asking why, but I was a stranger? I mean, yeah, I was, but still, I was here.

"You've heard the two worst things that have happened to me. I shared that with a room full of strangers. We may not know each other well, but I think I've earned some trust by sharing my own personal and embarrassing stories."

She smiled for the first time since I'd arrived. "Yeah, you were kind of a dork giving your testimony or whatever it's called."

Ouch. This girl had no idea how to relate to people. Or Ben was just really well-versed in social niceties.

"Okay, so he started acting weird and you broke up with him."

She flopped back down on the football field of dark fabric and jammed a faux fur pillow under her head. Good thing she'd scrubbed all the makeup off or I would have lost sight of her in the black void.

"And then weird stuff started happening. The doorbell would ring in the middle of the night. The phone would ring an hour later."

Immature but nothing too scary.

"Someone wrote *bitch* on my locker."

Could be labeled a prank but vandalism nonetheless.

"Then I found the garage door open one morning when I know I had shut it."

That was a little more troubling.

"Then one day I came home from school and all the pillows on my bed had been cut open and there were feathers everywhere."

And we have a crazy-ass stalker move for the win.

"Did you call the cops?"

"What would I tell them?"

"That someone had broken into your house and gone into the room you sleep and destroyed the pillows you sleep on."

She made a face. "That's when I decided to go to the class."

I had the urge to shake her. "Aja, someone breaking in is serious enough, but cutting up pillows ... *your* pillows ... is a threat. You're alone here. In this giant house. I don't want to scare you ... except I really do. Anything could happen to you. There could be someone in this house right now."

I couldn't tell if she got paler but she looked freaked out. I mean, hell, I was freaked out and I was armed. That pillow thing was some obsessive horror movie shit.

"Here's what I am going to do. I'm going to search the whole house. You're going to come with me to direct me. If we don't see anything, we call a locksmith and get every lock in this place changed today. We'll light up your parents' credit card good. Okay?"

She nodded, eyes glassy and wider than I would have guessed they could have gotten.

"Are you freaked out?" I knew she was, but I needed her to take this seriously. "Do you think if we called your parents, they'd come home?"

I could see her calculating. Jesus, she didn't know. She wasn't sure if a PI called her parents and told them their daughter was being harassed if they'd come to her rescue. That truly sucked. Leila was a flake but she'd be stalking through the house with a baseball bat behind Dad and have to be pulled off anybody who hurt me.

"Okay, let's worry about that later."

I could tell by the look on her face she'd decided they would not and that meant if I wanted to call the cops in officially, Aja would fight me. Despite them not having her back, she'd have theirs. Dammit, being a kid was not like on TV.

"Let's go look around. We got this, kid." I'd switched from treating her (mostly) like Nancy would have and gone straight into Dad.

I needed that in case we did stumble across this ex who had some spectacularly bad decision-making skills.

I tried to walk up the stairs normally but with Aja pressed up against my back we were in Scooby Doo territory before we even left the basement.

"Why aren't we starting in the basement since we're already here?" she whispered.

"A top-down approach is best. We don't want to drive anyone to the top floor where there's no escape. People tend to get panicked when they're trapped. Panicky people do stupid, dangerous things."

"But what if he's already upstairs?"

And that was the rub, but you had to start somewhere and I was trained to start top down so that's what we were doing.

"Then he can run downstairs and leave and hopefully he's smart enough to stop the crap he's pulling."

We crept through the door to the foyer and circled up the stairs to the main hall. I reached back and pulled the snap free on the holster pocket. I wasn't about to search gun in hand. That was an unnecessary escalation. I was damn well going to have the weapon available though.

Aja gasped. "Are you going to shoot him?"

"Only if I have to. Worst-case scenario."

She pondered that for a minute. "How do you know if it's worst case?"

Oh, sweetie, I thought. *You know.*

"If someone's trying to kill you. Or me."

She didn't seem to have any more questions but she pressed up against me a little tighter. I didn't think the dumbass kid was here and maybe I should have done a better job of downplaying that situation, but I was gratified that she finally seemed to be taking it seriously.

A little guilt crept in that I was causing her more emotional trauma—she was already dealing with being neglected by her parents—but if it saved her life, I was willing to deal with a little guilt.

We took the final step up the main hall and I looked at it stretched toward a large picture window that provided a view of the sea of grass that comprised the front lawn. The hall turned and continued to the right of the expanse of glass. Another giant window behind us gave a view of the even larger backyard and the next house over. I'd need to interview the neighbors but knew no one saw anything. The people who lived in these kinds of houses paid the price for comfort, privacy, and the illusion of safety. And a good school for their neglected kids.

There were half a dozen doors spaced out evenly. There were probably an even number down the next hallway.

"Are these all bedrooms?" I asked Aja, quietly.

"No, those two are bathrooms and that one is a laundry closet." She pointed out the doors.

"Okay, you said this is the main hall. There's another floor above? Bathrooms, closets up there too?"

She nodded. "One of each. The closet's really more of a storage room."

There were dozens of places for someone to hide. Between ensuite bathrooms and walk-in closets, it was going to take me at least an hour to work my way down from the attic to the basement. And Aja spending the majority of her time in the basement meant a family of psychos could have set up in the attic and she'd never even have heard them. I wasn't about to walk her up there and trap us both.

I opened the door to the laundry closet and cleared the space. I shoved her inside, ignoring the shock on her face. I held my finger up to my lips. I took my phone out and waggled it. She pulled hers out of one voluminous hoodie pocket and showing it to me, nodded.

I leaned in, whispering. "If you hear anything that sounds like a commotion, you hustle your ass out of this house and call 911. Out first then call. From the middle of the street."

I dug into my pocket and pulled out my keys. "Better yet, get in my truck, lock the doors, start it, and then call."

She nodded again. I shut the door. I had slipped back into cop mode. I wondered, as I walked toward the window and around the corner to see the stairs up to the attic space, if I was ever going to lose that situational awareness that clicked on when I needed it most. I hoped not. It came in handy.

The door to the attic stairs was slightly ajar. Out of Aja's sightline, I took the Glock out and swung the door open. It was an awkward set up with the door open, it blocked the hallway. Good.

The staircase was longer than I'd expected. When I got to the top I saw why: the stairs ended directly under the peak of the roof. The ceiling sloped down at intervals giving the room what I was sure the salesperson called a "cozy esthetic," as if a house finishing at more than five thousand square feet was capable of being cozy, but really made it look as if a drunk had designed the floor plan. The room was sparsely and oddly furnished, given the style and quantity in other rooms. A daybed was pushed up against the wall in between two windows and there was a small, almost child-sized nightstand with a lamp on it. The bed was covered with a quilt and it wasn't rumpled.

There were cushions in the narrow dormer windows on either side of the daybed. They made the room feel even more designed for elves because there was no way a normal person was climbing up in one of those things to do anything. Except maybe clean them—they were in desperate need. That was also odd because the rest of the house that I'd seen was spotless, including the basement. In absence of any color variations down there though, the room could have been swathed in buckets of blood and even a forensic team would miss the signs.

The room seemed like half the size it should have been. Aja had told me there was a storage closet so I poked my head around the half wall guarding against a fall down the stairs and saw the door. I took a deep breath and blew it out slowly as I tried to slow my heartbeat. It had begun racing without me noticing it.

There was likely nothing out of the ordinary in the storage room. Boxes, maybe some of those plastic containers full of holiday decorations, a garment rack or two storing out-of-season clothing. I put my hand on the knob. Another few breaths, slow and deliberate. My heartbeat was a loud thump in my ears. At least it wasn't a frantic whoosh but I had to get it under control. If I didn't, I wasn't safe with a gun.

The knob turned easily and I gently pulled the door open. I stopped and stepped to the left. Flicking the light switch up and flattening myself against the wall, I anticipated a rush from the storage room. Nothing. I counted to five and pushed the door open with my foot. Nothing. I gave it another five count before I craned my neck to look in the room. Empty. No lunatic with bloodlust in his eyes. No nothing. The room was completely devoid of anything. I thought back. Had Aja said anything about there being anything stored in the closet or had I assumed? I was startled out of my thoughts by a thump. Aja's scream followed a second later and stopped as abruptly as it had begun.

CHAPTER

8

I POUNDED DOWN THE stairs and thumbed off the safety. I hit the hall with my right foot and planted to pivot and take the corner when I saw a flicker of motion out the picture window. Someone had just been in the driveway. Someone who had attacked the door and then heaved something through my windshield. Sonofabitch.

I didn't have time to worry about who was outside. "Aja?"

I wasn't relieved to see the door to the laundry room still shut. The thump I'd heard could have been the door slamming shut after someone grabbed her. My heart stuttered.

"Willa?" Aja's voice, shaking and weak, came through the door just as my hand closed on the knob. I pulled it off and transferred the Glock to my left hand, sliding the safety back into place.

"It's okay, Aja." I was reassuring myself as much as her. I opened the right-side door, keeping the gun concealed by the left. "Are you okay?"

She was seated on the floor with the dryer door open blocking much of her body. Clever. Her terrified eyes peered over the top. "What was that noise?"

"Okay, from now on we stick together. You stay behind me while we go check the front door." I had reasoned that the only thing capable of making a noise loud enough that it scared Aja into screaming two floors away and I could feel it three floors away was the front door. The thing was made of something impossibly heavy and thick, like redwood or unobtanium.

She shut the dryer and crawled out toward me. I kept an eye on the stair landing as I helped her up. She seemed smaller and shrank even further into herself when she saw the gun in my hand.

"We're okay, Aja. I just want to make sure we stay that way." Even if she didn't agree, I wasn't holstering it.

She pressed up against me even tighter than she had when we'd come up the stairs, and this time I was grateful for it. If I had to let her out of my sight being able to feel her, still alive, still breathing, making tiny whimpering sounds that flipped my stomach and reminded me how young and alone she was, eased my stress level.

We slipped down the stairs on proverbial little cat feet, our steps in sync. If we'd had music, we would have gotten tens from the celebrity judges.

The front door was shut but I could see the frame had bulged above the lock. The handle sticking out through my windshield had to be a mini sledge. A full one would have done more damage to the door and an axe would have gone right through the cheap wood of the decorative molding.

"Okay, I'm going to open the front door." I felt her nod.

"I'm not scared." I was sure that wasn't true, but she got points for trying. My earlier frustration with her had completely fled.

I cranked the locks open, probably the only thing that kept that sledge from caving in the frame was the reinforced bolt plate that had to be installed to manage the multiple locks. I opened the door and we pushed forward just enough to look out into the lawn and driveway. I saw an older man staring at us. He had a small, white fluff ball on a leash. It was so furry I couldn't tell if it was a dog or a cat or a baby harp seal.

I raised the hand not carrying a gun and pressed my gun hand slightly behind me.

"Hi. This is going to be an odd question but—"

"Are you girls okay? I saw the truck. And the door. It looks like you're both kind of scared."

Both of us? I may not have felt it but I sure as hell looked calm. It was the only thing I managed to pull off perfectly lately. Looking fine. Aja, of course, looked like she'd just left a horror movie. A 3-D one. With interactive popup villain planted in the audience.

"We're fine. But did you happen to see the guy who vandalized the door? And the truck."

He stared at me, a little smile on his face. Like he was enjoying that someone had tried to break in. In broad daylight. With a teenager at home. I hoped it was that frisson of excitement one got from watching a cop show or reading a particular thrilling book. Something to bust up the boredom of retirement.

"Nope. The missus heard it though and insisted on calling the police."

And you decided to snap the leash on Fido and check out the scene.

69

"Awesome. Thanks so much." *Brava, Mrs. Old Neighbor.* Calling the cops and getting some official eyes on the house was now out of my hands. I didn't have to convince Aja to let me do it and I didn't have to worry about her loyalty to her parents keeping her from doing it.

I turned back to the inside of the house, still concealing my gun and changed hands with it again. I did another one eighty to holster it. I wasn't about to have it in my hand in a ritzy neighborhood when the black-and-whites came screaming in to check on the well-being of the Richie Riches even if I was protecting one of them.

The man was still staring at us while the cotton ball tugged and ran in circles trying to get the show on the road.

"We're fine. I promise. We're going to wait out here for the police." He looked annoyed that I was rushing him along. Like I cared.

"He's the neighborhood snoop," Aja whispered. "He's hoping you'll ask him to come up and look at the damage."

Fat fucking chance. I kept smiling and waving. "Really. We don't want to keep you from your walk."

"I don't know you. You don't live here." He'd taken a few steps into the yard, the little dandelion puff barking now. So it was a dog.

"She's my friend, okay?" Aja said. Her voice was not the sad girl or the scared girl. This was black eye makeup goth girl and she was pissed.

"Down girl," I said, quietly, trying not to laugh. The tension from the adrenaline started to dissipate from my limbs. Watching Aja go snarly on the busybody was perking my mood back up.

My ears picked up the sirens the little dog had heard thirty seconds before.

He stomped down the grass, pulling the dog along just when it had started to relieve itself.

The cops came, ones I'd never met before, and took a report. They weren't as deferential as they'd have been if Aja wasn't a teen and I wasn't a PI, but they did reassure her that they'd talk to the neighbors. They seemed even less concerned about my truck. I believe the quote was, "That's what insurance is for, right?" Said the guy who didn't have to explain to her partner/boss/father why there was an insurance claim.

After a call to a locksmith where we got extremely deferential treatment for the extra money Aja threw at him, I made one to my dad to have him come pick Aja up.

His reaction was, as predicted, unthrilled. He didn't say a word about Aja, though. Just came, introduced himself, made sure she was okay, and said he was sure she was hungry so they'd better get her home. That was it. I got a look leveled at me then he smiled, perhaps reminding himself that he'd lied to and tricked me only a few hours earlier.

I had to make a call to a glass replacement company for the windshield, but after that I called Seth's cell and got his voicemail. I didn't want to leave any of this in a message so I called the number for the task force.

"This is Willa Pennington. I need to leave a message for Seth Anderson to call me as soon as he can, please."

"One second, Ms. Pennington. Let me look up your access."

Standard operating procedure. All the task force members had to compile a list of people who were authorized to leave or receive messages or, in case of an emergency, receive notification. Seth and I had fought over that list. He'd left his parents off. I'd told him that I would call them and he told me he couldn't control me and then I'd told him he was a stubborn ass and that if I was the one who had to call his parents and tell them he was dead I was going to find some kind of witchcraft to bring his selfish ass back and then I was going to kill him myself. He'd added them to the list.

"Ms. Pennington. Agent Anderson has left a message for you." There was a click and the recording began.

"Sunshine, I have to go out of town for an undetermined amount of time. I'll call you when I know more."

I stood in the front yard of Aja's house, staring at the ground as the recording clicked off. My chest was tight. He hadn't called me. He'd left a message for me in case I called the task force.

I called his cell phone again. Now I had a message I definitely wanted to leave.

"That is some coward bullshit right there, Seth. I mean, who does that? Who just takes off without a word? I ... I'm so pissed at you right now." I disconnected the call before I said something I'd regret.

I chewed on his message over and over until the locksmith arrived, the windshield repair truck following a few minutes later.

"You know I can't repair the damage to the decorative frame, right? There's a nasty gash in the wood. It'll need to be replaced or puttied."

I nodded. "We just want to make sure the locks are changed and whatever you need to do to make sure they're set properly in case there was any damage to the wood around the bolt and strike plates."

"Um, lady. There's a sledgehammer in the windshield."

I turned my attention to the truck. I resisted the urge to say something sarcastic. It wasn't his job to move the implement. I was pissed the cops didn't take it, but their attitude was if there were fingerprints they wouldn't be in the system and it was a waste of time and resources. Had I caught a call like this when I'd been a uniform you can bet your ass I'd have taken it as evidence, but I wasn't a cop anymore and I couldn't dictate their judgement. Or lack thereof.

I hauled out my tool case and got out a pair of latex gloves. I was preserving evidence either way. I laid it on the backseat and grabbed the file Jan gave me. I could go over it inside while I waited for the work to finish.

I wandered the first floor looking for the kitchen and found a vast room of white marble and stainless-steel appliances. It looked like a meal had never been cooked in the room. A table with eight chairs sat to one side and I knew that a syrup bottle had never touched its surface. The refrigerator was filled with bottled water and not much else. What did Aja eat? I grabbed a bottle of water and dropped it and the file onto the counter while I snooped through the cabinets. All I found were box after bag after package of processed, chemical-laden, artificially colored, mass-produced junk. It was enough to put me off my stubborn clinging to the diet I'd indulged in most of my life.

My phone beeped.

GOT AJA SETTLED AT THE DINING ROOM TABLE TO DO HER HOMEWORK.

You had to love Nancy. I threw an almost full-grown teenage stalking victim at her and her only response was "Did you do your homework?"

My phone blipped again: OMG! UR MOM IS IMPOSSIBLE.

I chuckled. Poor girl had no idea that she was about to fall deeply under the spell Nancy Pennington wove. First it was homework, then it was fresh fruit, and before you knew it you were turning in early to get a good night's sleep. There was no use fighting it. I never bothered. I side-stepped it on occasion, but we both pretended I didn't.

Beep: SHE REMINDS ME SO MUCH OF YOU WHEN YOU WERE HER AGE.

Translation: I'll break her like a breadstick.

Blip: She's making me eat a cut up apple with homemade peanut butter. She made peanut butter from scratch just now.

No fighting it. She'd already started falling.

Beeeeeep: Poor thing just needs some attention and love.

And Mom was gone too.

Bliiiiiiiiiiiip: I love ur mom!!!

Beeeeeeeeeeeeeeeeeeeeeeeeep: I'm keeping her.

I texted them both back Talk to each other and put my phone on silent.

I unscrewed the cap and took a long drink of the water.

Had the guy been lurking when I'd gotten here? Where would he have hidden himself? Where had he gotten the sledge from? Had he brought it with him? Where had he gone when he left?

And what the hell was hightailing it out of town without so much as a phone call supposed to mean? I shook my head. I couldn't think about that. Seth would call and I'd hear what he had to say. Or he wouldn't call and that was that too.

I had Aja to worry about and the case Jan had asked me to review for her. I grabbed the file off the counter and spread the photos out on the table. It wasn't like being at the crime scene, but it was the best I was going to get. I looked at the short list detailing the exhibits displayed in each. I flipped back to the case overview.

The decedent, Amanda Veitch, known to her family as Mandy, was found dead in her room at 14:17 on November 26th by her mother, Marilyn Veitch.

I flipped to the coroner's report.

Manner of death: Homicide

Cause of death: Blunt force trauma resulting in middle meningeal arterial rupture

A small amount of blood had been found on the dresser corner. I took out my phone and Googled *middle meningeal artery*. She'd hit her head. It was an easy way to die. The skull thinned out over the ear, the artery located outside the dura. An unlucky blow and you could be dead in minutes without ever realizing there was an issue. You could feel fine, suffering what seemed like a small bump to your head, you were walking and talking and then down for the count.

Had Amanda Veitch been conscious after the fall? Had she been alert? Had she seemed fine to her killer? Had it been an accident? Boyd didn't think so and neither did the coroner. Manner of death was listed as homicide. But why?

I went back to the summary.

Attempt made to cover the death with fire. Assumption is homicide pending autopsy. Initial suspects: brother, Kevin Veitch, and boyfriend, Kyle Warnicky.

Initial suspect was the brother? What kind of screwed-up family dynamic led to that assumption? Boyfriend, sure. I'd been on enough domestic calls to see what love could twist into—hell, if my own boyfriend had been in front of me, I'd cheerfully bash him on the head—but fratricide wasn't a radar hit for me. Maybe because I couldn't ever imagine being pissed off enough at my own brother to contemplate worse than ratting him out to our parents.

Mother's witness statement indicated the victim and brother fighting the night before, Thanksgiving. Jeez, the mom had been out shopping for Christmas presents when her daughter was killed. Brother and sister had been close in age and emotionally until the summer before. Mother didn't know what had started the estrangement.

Okay, they had a dispute, which having a brother I knew was a normal state of affairs. How does that lead to murder or even suspicion? Boyd wasn't the kind of cop to pull a flimsy assumption like that out of nothing. I read further.

Alibis:

Kevin Veitch, none

Kyle Warnicky, none

So the brother and the boyfriend had no alibis. That still wasn't enough to list either as an official suspect, not even counting a recent estrangement. Had Jan played fast and loose with the case because she'd been a rookie? There had to be something more. She was a fantastic detective and she didn't cut corners. And the case was cold, so whatever her reasons for suspecting the two men, they hadn't panned out into real evidence.

I got an alert on my phone that the windshield was done.

Too bad it hadn't been the locksmith since it had started to get really cold in the house with the door open.

I went out through what looked like a pantry or mudroom to what I was assuming was the garage based on where the kitchen was laid out in the house.

I opened the door to the garage and sent the automated door up. I didn't want to get in the locksmith's way going out the front door. Three cars sat in the bay. Two shiny sports cars and a black Mini, I assumed was Aja's. She really liked the color.

"Man, you guys have the worst luck with cars. Who did you piss off?" The windshield repair guy pointed at the back of Aja's car and I could see *bitch* had been gouged into the paint. Bare metal gleamed under the garage's overhead light. Damian had been angry and dedicated.

"Yeah, we're dealing with a bad breakup."

He handed me a business card. "We've got an association with an auto body repair place."

"Most windshield repair isn't due to sledgehammers wielded by jilted teens?"

He chuckled, probably relieved I wasn't all shriek-y and weepy. "That's a first for me."

I motioned to Aja's car. "Stick around. I have a feeling if I don't catch her ex soon enough, we'll be giving you more business."

"Catch him? I thought you were like her sister or something." He flushed. I narrowed my eyes at him. *That "something" damn well better not have been "her mother," buddy,* I thought. *Maybe something slightly older, like "cool aunt." Or "cousin."*

"Nope, friend who happens to be a PI."

He smirked. "You're a PI? Right. Let me see your badge."

Fun. Another man who thought that PIs came in only one variety—penis-laden. "How about a business card?"

"You don't have a badge?" He looked skeptical.

The locksmith came over with his toolbox. He was smiling. "She's the real deal, dude. She was all over the news a couple months ago—some joint county-feds operation."

Now it was my turn to smirk. I didn't usually like it when someone mentioned the events of the previous fall, but it was nice to see the stupid look on the guy's face. It had been bad enough being a female cop. The force hadn't officially been a misogynistic cesspool of boob jokes and fatheads offering to help me pick up heavy objects, like their dicks, but it happened. You had two choices: strident ball-buster who needed to get a sense of humor or one of the guys laughing it off. Either way, you still endured it.

Being a female PI brought out all kinds of raised eyebrows, jokes, and questions. It was long past time that we put all that sexist bullshit into some Viking ship and turned it into a funeral pyre.

I tipped my imaginary cowgirl hat at the locksmith. "Just doing my part, sir."

He laughed and handed me the receipt and a set of keys. I tried not to look as shocked as I felt, but there were more numbers on the left side of the decimal point than I'd been expecting. Higher numbers than I was expecting too. All that for the one door.

"That's for the whole job. I'll be back tomorrow morning to change out the locks on all the other exterior doors, put in window security pins, and assist the alarm technician."

That was more like it. He looked at Aja's car. "I'll make sure we install manual locks for the garage door too."

I watched both men drive off and returned to the kitchen to grab my water bottle and case file. I needed to take pictures of the damage to Aja's car before I returned home.

I rolled my neck trying to diffuse the tension in the muscles running from the base of my skull to the middle of my back. I needed to get to a heavy bag and beat back the escalating anger I was feeling.

On the drive home, the mess with Seth popped back into my head. I still couldn't do anything about it except maybe consider giving him the benefit of the doubt. Maybe. I could consider it and still discard it. I could choose to be the bigger person and get Ben to figure out how to delete the message I'd left. I could. I wouldn't. I hadn't had that much therapy. I didn't think that much therapy existed.

So he'd get the message and he could damn well call back to give me a decent explanation for how someone who'd been bugging me relentlessly to move in with him as recently as forty-eight hours before could take off for parts unknown without even a text. Damn him!

Aja and Ben were out front playing with Fargo when I pulled up. "Playing" was a euphemism for training her to rip off an enemy's arm, of course. I wasn't sure why Ben thought a washout from federal training would be a good guard dog, but I knew he needed to do something to feel productive after my attack. And if it took the form of a companion, especially since my human one had lit off for parts unknown, I wasn't going to interfere anymore.

Fargo caught sight of my truck and began to run frantically toward me.

"Phooey," Ben yelled. Fargo stopped her flight and looked back, her head tilted. She wasn't the only one who looked confused. Aja stared at Ben like he'd lost his mind.

I laughed. "*Hier*, Fargo."

The puppy resumed her gallop toward me and I got down on one knee to accept her exuberant, and damp, puppy greeting. It had felt like weeks since I'd seen her beautiful eyes. I hated the overnight weeklong training Ben had insisted on. In retrospect it seemed like a great idea since I needed someone that happy to see me when I got home. I wasn't about to tell my brother he'd been right though. I'd rather poke myself in the eyes with a sharp stick. Twice.

"Who's my pretty girl? Who's the prettiest girl in prettygirlville, huh? You are. Yes, you are."

As I rubbed her head, I looked up at Aja, questioning look still on her face. "She's being trained in Dutch. Genius there thought it was a good idea and I don't have the energy to argue with him about everything."

"Dutch?" Aja turned to Ben.

"If she responds to commands in Dutch, her focus can't be broken by someone who only knows standard English dog commands."

Aja looked thoughtful. She was probably considering whether getting hooked up with my weird family was in her best interests. "Smart. Have you thought of using multiple languages in case the person knows Dutch?"

Oh, shit.

Ben blinked. "That's an interesting approach. We'd need languages that were linguistically similar to ensure the trainee wasn't too confused by sentence structure since she's unlikely to make heuristic language developments."

"I'm sure the dog is smart enough—"

"He's talking about me, Aja," I said. "And for the record, he's not correct. I've already trained Fargo to understand my own sentence structure. Watch."

I pulled a treat out of my pocket and showed it to the dog. "Tell me a story, Fargo."

She instantly laid down on the grass and rolled on to her back. It wasn't what she was supposed to do, but I wasn't about to let Ben know that.

"Good girl!" She sat back up and I gave her the treat. I'd figure out way later to make sure she knew what she was really supposed to do.

"What was that?" Ben demanded.

"I asked her to tell me a story and she acted out the Venice Beach League Playoffs 1987 scene."

"You let the dog watch *The Big Lebowski*?" He sounded annoyed. "She's just a puppy."

I blinked at him and hauled my bag back up onto my shoulder. I turned to look at him as I walked past, heading toward the house. I'd given up hoping he was playing with me when he said stupid crap like that. He might have been a math and science genius, but sometimes he was a dumbass. I shook my head. He was worried about a dog being too young to see a movie.

I chuckled and went into the house.

"Mom? I'm home."

"In here, sweetie." I followed her voice into the kitchen. She sat at the table with a black hoodie in her hand re-threading the drawstring.

"If we keep this up, I'm going to have to get more of those name-tags." She smiled.

"I'm sorry. I didn't know what else to do," I said.

"Willa Elaine. Don't you dare apologize for helping someone. Besides, Aja is lovely."

Lovely? Okay. She must have turned on the charm because I hadn't seen anything approaching lovely. I'd gotten full of attitude, annoyed, rude, and scared. Of course, my mother engendered different feelings in people than I did. It's probably why she had lollipops and I had a gun. Or maybe it's because she had lollipops and I had a gun. It really was a chicken-and-egg dilemma. Or was that carrot and stick? Damned if I knew.

"I appreciate it either way. She needs to feel safe and I figured there's no safer place. Plus, the cabinets at her place are full of junk."

She raised an eyebrow but she kept her lips pressed tightly together, holding in a laugh. Yeah, I got the irony too.

I grabbed a bottle of water and considered how best to dump my annoyance at Seth. I didn't want to come across as whiny. Not that it would have made a difference. She was my mom, not his. I could whine about him being an inconsiderate, rude, inconsistent, cowardly asshole and she'd tsk my language choices but she'd still be firmly Team Willa.

"Seth took off for … who knows where." Discretion being the better part of valor, I unscrewed the cap and took a long swallow while avoiding her eyes.

"For work?"

I nodded. "I assume so. He left a recording with the message center. He didn't even try to call me or text me."

I wasn't sure if it was okay to tell my parents about Seth and Michael being adopted. But the Colonel had made it my secret too and I needed advice.

"Seth found out that he and Michael were adopted sometime after Michael died and...."

She just looked at me trying hard to keep her face neutral. Her attempt to act like she didn't know told me she'd known.

"How long?" I asked. I wasn't mad. I wanted to be, but it made sense that the Colonel and Barbara would have told their best friends.

"After Michael's memorial service." She looked chagrined. "They were so bereft and it seemed like keeping it a secret any longer was another burden."

"Did you think about telling me? So I'd understand why ... dammit, Mom, this morning I told you I knew something was up with him."

She thought for a minute. Had it been Dad in front of me, I'd never have known what he was thinking about—box scores, what was on TV, whether he needed to mow the lawn—but my mother was as opaque as the herb tea she liked. It was obvious she hadn't agreed with keeping it a secret. I decided to let her off the hook.

"It wasn't your secret to tell." Relief showed on her face. "Unlike those cookies on the top shelf of the pantry behind the giant box of bulgur wheat."

Her eyes widened and she looked away. I had to laugh. No poker face at all.

"And the embarrassing part is that Seth had to show me. I'm such a great detective my health nut mother who doesn't have an ounce of deceit in her body is hiding junk food from me and I missed it."

She grabbed me in a surprisingly rough hug. Hugging her was usually like hugging a marshmallow, soft and comfortably dry, sweet all around, reminding you of gentler times.

"Mom?"

She sniffled.

"Mom, it's okay. I'm just teasing you."

She pulled back and looked in my face. In another surprise, her voice was deep and brusque when she spoke. "I *am* your mother. I always will be. Never forget that. Promise me, Willa? You're my daughter just as if I'd known you since before you were born. You have to tell me you always know that."

Fear pooled in my stomach like a swirl of acid. She was dying. She had cancer or a heart condition and she was going to die and leave me. Tears prickled, a not unusual sensation over the past year, and I didn't fight them. Get used to discomfort, the therapist had said.

"Oh, sweetheart, don't cry. I didn't mean to make you cry." She seemed as stunned by my reaction as I'd been by her words.

"You're dying." The words crawled out of my mouth like molasses, thick and dark, chokingly cloying.

Her gentle smile was back. "Not any more than anyone else, Willa."

Feeling silly, I leaned away from her and swiped my hoodie cuff under my eyes, mopping up the tears.

"Then what the heck, Mom?" If that was what getting used to discomfort was like, then screw that.

She fluttered her hands at the kitchen windows overlooking the front yard where Ben and Aja played with Fargo. "That little girl out there. She's taking care of herself and … I just …."

"And Aja reminds you of me when I came to live with you here."

There it was. Mom hated to say anything bad about Leila. I'm sure she'd read in some step-parenting book that you didn't criticize the child's biological parent. But I wasn't a child anymore. And I knew Leila's faults.

She looked stricken. "Your mother did her best—"

"Neither of us believe that, Mom. Even Leila doesn't. I can't say it's okay. I can't even say I'm over it, but she knows. She even can admit that you've been a better mother than she ever could."

"I'd never say that, Willa."

And she wouldn't. Not even under threat of torture.

"You don't have to. I know the truth."

I gave her a kiss on the cheek and went to my room to change into clean clothes for dinner.

I texted Jan about the situation at Aja's and the sledge I'd maintained as evidence.

My mother called out from the kitchen as I finished up. "Can you let the kids know it's time to come in? And they need to wash their hands since they've been playing with the dog."

I just smiled. Aja would get more attention than she knew what to do with. She was going to have an overflowing well of meddling and hovering mothering. She'd just have to adjust like I had.

I opened the front door and stopped for a minute, observing the teenagers. Ben tried to school his face into a stern model of authority and kept failing. Aja and Fargo were having too much fun. That made me happy. She had too big of a burden and not enough happy. I knew being angry at her parents was pointless but, hell, they could have at least gotten her a pet to keep her company if they were determined to be off jet-setting.

CHAPTER

9

AJA HADN'T EVEN BEEN gone a day and the place looked even lonelier than it had when she was living, existing, inside it. It didn't help that it was barely dawn and another gray, overcast day had been predicted. I thought it would be a good idea to check Aja's house to make sure the ex hadn't come for one of his nighttime visits and left anymore presents.

The perimeter search yielded nothing out of order so I circled the house, eyeing the windows and doors, especially in the back. Nothing.

It began misting so I yanked the keys out and tried to unlock the front door. I met resistance, barely getting the key into the deadbolt. I pulled back and looked at the key ring. The locksmith had labeled them for me so I knew the key was right.

I pulled the key for the handset up and the same thing happened.

I pocketed the ring again and pulled up my flashlight app. Both locks had been jammed.

That sonuvabitch had been here and sabotaged the locks, probably hoping that Aja would be trapped outside. Checkmate, you little asshole. I flipped up the hood of my jacket and went back to check the slider. That was, at least, under a deck, which would keep off the worst of the moisture that seemed to hang in the air, not falling so much as just suspended like film on a window.

I slipped walking down the minor slope that was dug into the backyard property allowing the basement, fully underground in the front, to open onto backyard. Just like our house but worth at least a million dollars more.

I let out a yelp, louder than I would have liked since most of the neighbors were probably still snuggled up in their cozy beds, while I slid my dampening ass down the grass that was unnaturally green after a snowy winter and must have been super expensive fake grass. Rich people.

I was pushing off the ground when I saw a figure dressed much like I was—jeans, flat sneakers, dark hoodie. Unlike me, the figure attempting to slip around the far side of the house away from me was wearing a Guy Fawkes mask. Super inconspicuous in case anyone comes upon you sneaking around a house in the early morning hours. A mask. Sheesh. Someone watched too many movies.

"Hey!"

Stupidly warning him—and it was definitely a him, the lower body straining against the fabric, showing musculature definition even through denim—I watched as he took off at a sloppy run over the damp ground. I tried to push up off the grass harder and into a run, but I wasn't having any more luck with my slippery-soled shoes. I made a mental note to get something that had traction and put on speed. He wasn't even to the front of the house by the time I turned the corner and, like a good PI, calculated his height. Specifically, that he didn't have much of it and his shorter, heavier legs made him a good deal slower than I was.

He jagged right into the trees, cutting through to the paved path that wound through the development—another nice perk for the upper, upper middle class that lived in the subdivision. His shortcut hadn't saved him much time because I was still gaining on him and I wasn't even running full speed, conscious of taking a spill and losing him entirely. Oh, and hurting myself.

On the asphalt, though, I poured on the speed. "Stop!"

I didn't care about disturbing the inhabitants at that point. We were in a shallow wooded area, the nearest house five hundred yards or more in the distance. He was pumping his arms at a speed that would have been sufficient had his legs been able to keep up.

"Stop! Police!"

Cop instinct, not a year out of uniform, kicked in. I hoped he didn't ask to see a badge like the windshield repair guy.

I pushed off extra hard with my back foot and launched myself, grabbing him around the waist, and twisted us off the pavement into the mulch. I didn't want anyone breaking anything when I had falsely, if accidentally, identified myself as police.

Instead of deflating like expected, like any scared, stupid kid would, he kicked back hard and caught me on the jaw. He nailed me in just the right spot and I saw proverbial stars.

I heard him scrambling up and running off while I shook my head like a cartoon and tried to count all my teeth, especially the back ones. When I was finally back in the land of the fully cognizant with a wet ass, ripped jeans, and scuffed Chucks, I listened for the sound of a vehicle. The only thing I heard was a very optimistic mourning dove cooing and the chirp of a text alert. The figure was gone, so I pulled out my phone.

I NEED YOU AT A SCENE.

Either Jan's cold case has just gotten super-hot or she had a second case for me. That made three I was juggling, in case anyone was counting.

The rain began coming down in earnest as I limped back to my truck, my knee competing with my pride to see which smarted more.

———

The rain was an icy drip-drip-drip on my neck, sliding off the umbrella. Despite the chill, the air was warm enough to melt the snow. The soft mounds covering the bushes were disintegrating quickly and chilled air hung foggy low on the ground in between the trees that ringed a little pond. There were dozens of these neighborhood ponds scattered through the subdivisions all over the county. The crime scene turned out to be in the neighboring subdivision, so I'd arrived in under five minutes.

Anything built during or after the nineties had community spaces like this that the older neighborhoods like mine lacked. There was also less space between the houses in these newer ones too, so I didn't bemoan missing the fifty gallons of water that collected leaves and a bench pitched at such a steep angle as if it wanted to slip you into the water while you weren't paying attention. It was just a place for toddlers and dogs to get muddy while their moms chatted.

"I do not miss this," I said, remembering the last time I'd been at a crime scene in the rain. Just like the uniforms standing watch now, I'd only had my police uniform hat to protect me from the elements. At least that time it had been summer and the rain running down my back hadn't been cold. Man, that guy had bitched about his ticket from the nice dry car he'd maimed while talking on his cell phone. Another thing I did not miss—entitled middle-aged assholes in their midlife-crisis-mobiles.

I was still having a better day than the uniforms. Or Jan. Or the dead guy they'd found face down in the small pond. I'd been at the scene of another body in a pond no more than a year before. That time I'd been the uniform who'd arrived in response to the 911 call. This time the body had already been whisked from view and was in the unmarked coroner's van. That time the body hadn't shown any outward signs of what had happened other than the water. This time Jan had told me that it was obvious the guy had been in a fight, at least. *At least* was her out in case the cause of death wasn't beaten to death.

Unlike TV, where autopsies were instantaneous because the coroner had nothing better to do than wait for a well-timed murder, Jan would not be dropping in to get the autopsy results later today.

"Not that I'm not enjoying this frigid walk down Being A Cop Sucks memory lane, Jan, but why am I here?" I asked. The closest uniform, a guy I didn't know, smirked and then his face settled back down to the barely concealed misery I knew he felt.

Silently, she handed me her phone. A young man stared back at me from a DMV file. Damian Murphy. He was as nondescript as they came—an average teen you would have seen a hundred of wandering around the halls of the high school. Unless you knew him, loved him. Like Aja might have once. It couldn't be a coincidence that a kid named Damian about the right age was found dead near her house.

"Never seen him before. Not that I remember anyway." I wasn't lying. I hadn't seen him before.

I shrugged and tried to hand the phone back, but Jan shook her head. I flipped to the next photo.

The picture displaying on the screen was of my business card.

"My business card was at the scene? Okay, that's unusual but—"

"Flip to the next shot."

I scrolled to the next picture on her camera and saw my handwritten cell phone number and the words *any time, day or night.*

"Willa?"

Fine. I was here to answer questions so I'd answer questions. "I gave this card to a young woman I met at one of the self-defense classes I attend."

"I'm assuming you generally don't give out your cell number," she said. "The card was in the vic's back pocket. Do you have any idea how my victim had the specific business card you gave this young woman?"

I curled my toes inside my boots. I counted to ten.

"Her ex-boyfriend has been bothering her. There's been some vandalism. Someone's been getting into her house."

I'd let Jan draw her own conclusions, but even an idiot could add two plus two. Either way, Aja's stalker was likely in a body bag.

"The boyfriend's name?"

"Damian. I didn't get a last name from her."

"I'll need to talk with her."

I felt a flare of mistrust that I buried. "If you were any other cop, Jan..."

She nodded under her own umbrella. "You'd tell me to go pound sand. I know. And you know I'd have to talk to her anyway."

Last fall had left me with big trust issues for the police—an organization I'd once belonged to, an organization I'd once sworn an oath to. Having a civilian police employee looking through my records, giving my address to his neo-Nazi cousin, letting his aunt, the neo-Nazi's mother, have my hospital room number ... I understood people made choices, but that didn't mean I trusted the organization anymore if they chose those kinds of people.

Jan was different, but the information she got went straight into the same computer system that everyone accessed regardless of their intentions.

She nodded. "I'll do right by her, Willa."

I stared at the pond and then looked around at the trees surrounding the area. I'd turned off the main road a mile before the high school but as the crow flies, walking through the woods, the pond couldn't have been too far from Aja's house.

I pulled out my own phone and tried to juggle my umbrella, tiny and ineffective as it was, and the phone with my chilled hands. Jan sighed with impatience and yanked the flimsy travel umbrella from me, covering us both with her giant, police-issue one. Detectives rated a little better than unis that way.

I pulled up the GPS and inputted Aja's address, indicating I wanted walking directions from my current location. Siri started trying to route me. I punched voice commands off and scrolled back up to the map. Sure enough, it was less than a half mile to Aja's house through the wooded area. I held the screen up for Jan to see.

The height on the driver's license made Damian too tall to be the guy I'd encountered.

"I'd bet you money that your vic was on his way back from Aja's house when this happened. I might have even met the guy who killed him."

She peered at the small screen, her face grim. "Met? Please back up the narrative to when you might have met the killer."

"I was at Aja's house when you texted. I had just given chase to a guy wearing a Guy Fawkes mask and lurking."

"Your friend—"

"She's safe. I took her to my parents' house yesterday."

I jammed the phone back in my pocket and grabbed my gloves, dragging them slowly onto my hands, trying to make the point that we could be doing this in a nice warm car, or coffee shop, or anywhere but where we and other people were currently freezing our asses off.

"Okay, so you gave chase and lost him, I'm guessing based on your near-immediate arrival and ripped jeans. And we know it wasn't Damian because he was already dead when I texted you."

"Got it in one, boss."

"Description." She'd pulled out her notebook and was ready to take notes.

"Can we get a witness statement done someplace warmer and drier?"

"We'll do a full statement later but for now, a description, please? So uniforms can start a door-to-door."

I thought back. I knew he wasn't tall, but how short was he exactly? "About my height, maybe an inch shorter or taller. Jeans, dark hoodie—navy, green, black, one of them—Guy Fawkes mask. Heavily muscled, straining the fabric heavily, slow runner, hard kicker."

"Hmmm, that DMV photo of Murphy is a year old but he doesn't look like that anymore. He was a big guy. Muscled, I mean. Like your lurker. Do you think the guy you saw would be capable of beating someone to death?"

"Anyone's capable of anything, Jan. I could beat someone to death given the right weapon."

She nodded. Then dismissed the uniform. She stared at the pond for a minute, marking the scene in her memory to compare to the crime scene photos later.

"Let's go meet your friend. The vic *might* not be her boyfriend. Business cards travel."

But I had a better idea and I drove to Aja's house with Jan following in her unmarked. We were barely out of the vehicles when the nosy neighbor popped out of his house.

"Young lady, you are responsible for all the commotion around here and I simply will not have it."

My scalp tingled with anger. "You don't get much of a choice, buddy. And if you'd been a halfway decent busybody you'd have noticed the guy bothering your neighbor. Frankly, you're responsible for all the commotion around here since you didn't pay any attention to the little girl living alone next door and help keep her safe. Stick that in your pipe and smoke it."

I stared him down until he broke eye contact and went back inside his house.

I stomped up to the front door with Jan trailing behind me chuckling. "Stick that in your pipe and smoke it? Where do you get all these old-timey phrases?"

"My grandpa's big on them. I used to spend summers with them and my aunt while my mom was doing summer shows and I wasn't with my dad."

She put her hand on my arm stopping me. "School was out and there was no one else. My parents weren't always getting along... legally. And they weren't ever married so ...."

She nodded but the reality was she either got it or she didn't. The words could make sense to her, but unless she'd been torn between parents she wouldn't know what it felt like.

"It's kind of hard to trust or depend on people if you're not sure when you're going to see them again," she said.

Too close. And too sharp. Jan's job was to dig for information and I knew in her own clumsy way she was expressing support, but I wasn't in the mood for revisiting my own childhood dysfunction.

"Aja's been left alone by her parents for weeks now. I promised I wouldn't get the cops or Social Services involved if I didn't have to but...I don't know what I'm doing with her, Jan."

"Err on the side of keeping your promise. Then she knows she can trust you." She smiled and continued. "She'll be fine, Willa."

I showed Jan the jammed locks. "This is a pretty good example of some of the crap he pulled."

I walked to the garage door and flipped the cover up on the electronic keypad and we both saw the gum he'd smooshed into the keys. I had never hated a dead guy more. He really had been an immature prick.

"Wow, this kid was a royal douche."

For some reason hearing Jan say *royal douche* was hilarious. I bit my lip to keep from laughing but couldn't stop myself.

"And that neighbor? You're right that he's probably a font of information about all the vandalism that's happened over here. Too bad he's insufferable."

I stopped snickering and looked over at the house he'd squirreled himself away in—probably watching us out the window.

"Insufferable doesn't mean he won't give up the goods if you slap him in an interrogation room and sweat him."

That made her laugh. "You want me to throw him in the hole while I'm at it and threaten his family?"

"He's got one of those yappy dogs. Maybe you could call animal control."

"How about I just go ask him some questions, politely."

I shrugged. "You do what you think is best."

"Why don't you meet me at your place? I think you glaring at him will make him less cooperative."

I was a little bummed. I loved playing good cop, mean apprentice PI and I really wanted to piss off the old fart a little more. Vent a little of the anger brewing inside me. Instead, I did as Jan asked and headed home. I passed a black-and-white on my way out of the cul-de-sac. Jan must have called them to do a vandalism report.

When I pulled up to the house, I could see Aja and my mom through the picture window. They were sitting at the kitchen table. I had a momentary flash of that table knocked out of position and the room filled with EMTs and cops the night Mark Ingalls had broken in. I needed a moment before I went in and possibly devastated Aja.

I pulled up the photo album on my phone and looked at a few photos of Fargo when she'd been a puppy in the ATF program. Seeing her in the bulletproof vest she'd never get the chance to grow into made me happy. I knew the working dogs got loved plenty and truly enjoyed the work, but Fargo was mine now. I wasn't even able to picture her sniffing out accelerant at a crime scene. And just like that my memory dragged me back to the hulking shell of the burnt-out garage, the buckled and crumbled cinder block walls looking like jagged, black dragon's teeth, a beast that had tried to eat me and Seth.

I knew I was supposed to do something, anything other than the path I'd committed to take. Muscling through post-traumatic stress wasn't even possible. You didn't just grit your teeth and double down on stubborn. I knew that. I even mostly believed that. I just wasn't capable of it. Not yet.

I got out of the truck, grabbing my keys and phone, jamming them both in various pockets. Ben was opening the door to take Fargo for their afternoon walk. She strained at her halter and leash for only a second before she plopped down on the wet cement stoop.

I heard Ben praise her after he turned back from locking the door behind him. The doors were always locked now. People home, people away from home, the doors were locked. It was a habit we were all in now.

I waited on the front walk for them, trying not to show any emotion. Ben felt that training Fargo to not be the center of attention was safer for her. I hated it, of course, but he was right.

I waited until she sat down again in front of me and Ben gave her the release command before I bent down to scritch her ears.

"Who's a sweet girl? Who's my sweet girl?" I cooed.

Ben wisely suppressed his normal response to me gushing at the dog. Either that or he'd become inured to it. He'd certainly heard it enough.

"We need to get her a raincoat if this weather's going to continue through spring."

It had been a cold, snowy winter which meant lots of time indoors and lots of family time that had chafed. I spent more time with my family and Seth than I really was comfortably built for. The spring was turning out to be rainy and gray. It felt like I hadn't seen the sun since I'd been in New Mexico the previous summer. The bright sun there had felt like sharp little stabs to my grieving heart. Gray, cold rain would have been better suited.

"She's a dog, Will," Ben said.

"She's a dog that takes forever to dry, sport. And I'm tired of washing muddy blankets."

"How's a raincoat going to prevent her paws from getting muddy?" He looked at me in horror. "You want to get her boots too, don't you?"

I smiled at him, a mean little smile, knowing that it would torment him. "And one of those little hats with holes for her ears."

He shook his head and walked the dog around me, down the stairs to the sidewalk. He was muttering just loud enough for me to hear that he was grumbling but not loud enough that he couldn't deny it and call me crazy for hearing things. I knew he was going to get her extra muddy to pay me back. It was still worth it.

I stared up at the window again as I walked up the path and saw Aja waving at me, an actual smile on her face. Mom was healing the lonely little girl in her. Good. She needed it and my mother could spare the love. I couldn't put it off any longer though. I got my keys out and undid the locks and punched in my alarm code as the keypad started its frantic beeping. I hated the damn thing but it made Mom feel safer. Tolerating it silently was the least I could do.

"Your mom ... sorry, step-mom is super awesome," Aja said, giggling, slipping in her sock feet on the hardwood floor of the entry.

Giggling? Had the kid developed Stockholm Syndrome?

"One, she's totally my mom. Two, she's better than super awesome. Three, you're in a good mood."

Damn. She was in a good mood and I got to ruin it. Good times.

She nodded. "I'm in a great mood. Ben just totally cleared up this issue I was having with calculus and now I'm going to ace my test."

I had somehow managed to bring home another genius for my parents to fawn over. Speaking of parents ....

"Have you seen my dad?"

I began the process of unwrapping myself from the layers of sodden winter gear so I could disarm. Mom was scared of someone getting in the house but she wasn't about to let us all wander around armed and looking for a shootout like it was the "gosh darn O.K. Corral." Her words. Repeated many times. Sometimes very loudly. Directed at my father who was somehow after almost twenty years of marriage to the woman still under the impression he could ever, would ever win without her letting him.

"I think he's downstairs."

She danced back to the kitchen table presumably to do more calculus. I descended into the basement to seek guidance. He'd done more death notifications than I ever would. I needed to break this to Aja as gently as possible.

I found my dad arranging canned goods on the wire shelves in the pantry. "Do these look natural?"

What? How in the hell were cans supposed to look natural on metal shelves? "Yup, just like they grew there."

"You're not funny." It was an old game.

"Yes, I am. I'm hilarious. But, seriously, what did you expect? It's a crazy question."

The question wasn't the only thing that was crazy. My dad had gone full on prepper in the wake of the attack on me. He'd had the storage room walls and doors reinforced with metal plates in order to turn the long space into a makeshift safe room. A separate energy source, WiFi hotspot, bedding.

"I meant, are they arranged in a way that you'd naturally search for them if you were stuck in here for an extended period."

"I'm never going to be stuck in here for an extended time, Dad. I would rather battle zombies than be trapped in here with my family for longer than twenty minutes."

Even Seth had tried to talk them out of these crazy plans. They'd told him to get on board or get the hell out of their metaphorical way, that he didn't have kids, and that one day he'd understand.

The therapist has explained to me that it helped them feel in control in a situation that was even scarier to them than it had been for me. She told me to let it go, and I had. Once I stopped trying to get them to see how silly it was, they had scaled back their plans considerably.

What had once been planned as a full-on panic room the envy of any celebrity looking to lay out some disposable income on the latest high-security bunker able of withstanding anything short of nuclear attack had become a much simpler hiding spot with its own separate hotspot for communication. I was relieved.

Their first plan had been to sell the whole place. A mostly hilarious time waiting at the airport (the double-takes were enormously entertaining when I began remarking "rough flight") to pick them up from the cruise last fall had turned into a scene rivaling the most dramatic telenovela (watch one of those without the sound and try telling me it's not every teenage fight you've ever had with your parents but with better-looking people) as my parents had gotten a full look at me.

Mom had alternately cried and grilled both me and Seth for details of my injuries. My father clenched his jaw the whole trip, and when we pulled into the driveway there was a realtor waiting for us. My quip that I was sure I'd be able to pack even with my arm in a sling saw the woman in the too-large blazer quickly shooed off. My recovery dragged on and the *sell the place* rhetoric turned to talk of renovations to accommodate a more robust security system. Then we'd "downscaled" to the basement shelter-in-place plan. I think if I'd managed to drag it out a little longer I could have gotten away with a flare gun and some mace. Or maybe a mace.

My injuries hadn't put off my father from weaponry though, and as soon as I could hold a gun and squeeze a trigger we were at the range daily. Shooting practice was the last thing I needed, but that too was an emotional thing the therapist explained. Hell, I spent more time talking about other people's feelings at some of my sessions than I did working out my own. Mine were pretty simple—I was scared and pissed that I was scared. I'm not the most complex individual. Nor am I great at managing other people's feelings.

"I need some advice. I have to talk to Aja about this guy that's been bothering her and—"

"If I ever get my hands on that punk, I'm going to teach him a lesson."

"As you've said on more than one occasion ranging from a boy being late to pick me up for a dance to the kid who made fun of Ben for being a genius."

"Those kids were—"

"Yeah, yeah, you're a scary dad. But back to my point, a body was found in a pond near Aja's house. He had the card I gave her and we think it might be her stalker ex."

He'd bent down to pick up more cans but stopped and stood back up. "Dead?"

"As they come. Initial reports are beaten to death. I checked her place this morning and the locks had all been damaged. He was likely parking somewhere near and hiking through the wooded areas so no one saw his car."

I purposely did not mention the altercation I'd had with the masked British history fan. He didn't even glance at my ripped jeans. Clothing damage had stopped being a topic of conversation the same year I'd moved in with him. I was an active kid without an ounce of Leila's grace or poise.

"That's probably what he did the other day when your windshield got the carnival game treatment."

"Yeah, well, he won't be doing it anymore. I want to warn her before Jan gets here."

He started on the cans again. He was under the impression that he thought better if he was working. Mom had once told him that and he'd clung to it. Once upon a time, she'd wanted some yard work done and he had demurred because he was trying to puzzle out a particularly difficult case. She'd then told him of this study that showed you were able to make more headway with a problem by directing your mind to menial tasks. End result was the lawn got mowed and she got an end run around him that she could use forever. Ben got his brains from her.

"Being straight with her won't work. She needs more coddling than you or I are built for, my girl."

"Yeah, I'm aware of the genetic defect that you've saddled me with, pops, but I can't exactly recruit Mom or Ben for the job," I said.

"Why not?"

"Hey, dear brother, do you mind interrogating our new houseguest to see if this dead guy is the one who's been terrorizing her? I'll give you my dessert like when you did my algebra. Cool, thanks."

"I knew you were having him do your homework. Just coloring, huh."

"It was just algebra and I only got a C."

"He was six, Willa."

"He's also supposed to be a genius. So what's up with the C?"

He started to laugh. "You can never tell your mother."

I doubled over laughing, tears instantly coming to my eyes. He was so clueless.

"Oh, Dad. She's known for years. Ben ratted me out the second she found him with chocolate pudding all over his mouth. That kid couldn't keep a secret from himself."

Except that he was an elite white hat hacker, but that was really more a secret we were both keeping. And Seth. The three of us. And the ATF. Which meant all the federal agencies knew. So it really was only a secret from our parents.

"That is a discussion for another day. I was really thinking more that Mom could sit with the two of you. She's tougher than you think she is, Will."

For her to be tougher than I thought she was she'd have to be damn near indestructible. I knew who was the real badass in the family and it wasn't anyone with Pennington genes. I just didn't want to put any more on my side of the scale. Yeah, I measured our relationship like that. Yeah, it's fucked up. What part of being in therapy was confusing?

"It's ... you're right." There was no point in arguing with him about it. He was right like he always was when the subject was Mom.

He shoved a can of green beans into my hands and pushed me toward the stairs. I set the can down on the floor just outside the door to the storage room. My mother would never serve canned vegetables—BPA lining.

CHAPTER

10

I SPIED ON AJA and my mom in the kitchen and my heart twinged.

"Hey, sweetie." They saw me spying on them and my mother motioned me into the room. I tried not to think too hard about what all had gone down in that kitchen. A new tile floor that replaced cracked and stained, long-past-its-expiration-date linoleum had helped. The cheerful yellow paint to cover the spots of blood that had been washed off before they got home helped too. But home improvements weren't going to erase the memories. I was always going to see that night.

"How's it going?" Mom asked.

I looked over at Aja. "We'll see."

She got my meaning instantly and put down the spoon she had been using to stir whatever healthy and amazing smelling dinner she was making. We flanked Aja at the table.

She looked at me, then my mom, then back to me. "Uh oh." She placed her pencil on the seam of the book and shut it. "What's happened?"

"Aja…Damian, what's his last name?" I still held out a sliver of hope that the dead kid wasn't someone she'd once cared about.

"Murphy. Damian Murphy. Why? Did they arrest him?"

My mother put her hand on Aja's back and the girl seemed to melt into it.

"I have a friend who is a police officer and she needs to come talk to you about Damian. Okay? She's a homicide detective."

Jesus, Willa, that was the best way you could break it to the kid?

Mom pulled Aja into a one-armed side hug and reached out the other hand to me, placing it on my arm. In between gentle murmurs of consolation, she looked up and gave me a sad smile, mouthing that I did fine.

My phone blipped. Jan was on her way. I got up to call her from the foyer. My mom had the Aja situation under better control than I could. I had no idea how they taught people to be a mom, but she must have been the valedictorian.

"Hey, Jan. Aja confirmed the ex's last name is the same as your victim."

"What did you tell her?"

"Nothing. I just confirmed the name and told her you wanted to talk," I replied. "She's prepared though. She's tough."

I sounded a little defensive, I knew. Jan didn't let it phase her. Like she hadn't blinked at any of my rants about the police hiring someone who'd used their resources to send a killer after me.

"Good to know. You made any progress on our other case?"

"I've perused it. I'm getting back to it tonight. I got pulled away to deal with a floater today." My voice was light. If she wanted a rookie partner to hand down her wisdom to then she was getting the real me and not some earnest, scrubbed suckup.

"This is the job, kid. Learn to multitask like a grownup detective." Then she hung up on me.

I walked back to the kitchen. "Hey, Aja, my friend Jan is on her way. You just need to be honest with her. Tell her what you know and she'll do the rest. Okay?"

She nodded, biting her lip. While I was trying to figure out words to be comforting or some reasonable facsimile of it, Mom had taken over again. It was more her area anyway. I decided to check out the dinner situation and I felt a look burning the back of my neck. When I turned my mother was staring at me with a nervous expression. Fine. A case could be made that I was inept in the kitchen and my mere presence had the ability to ruin food. I raised my hands to show I wasn't wielding a dangerous spatula or spoon.

"We've called Aja's parents but there's an issue with their charter plane company." She rolled her eyes and I almost laughed. It was rare that my mother took an attitude, but she was fully capable of it.

"Aja, do you have any questions?" I asked

She looked at me and I knew that I had made a rookie mistake. I figured she'd ask some pointless questions about what Jan would ask her but, like a normal human person, she was concerned about the fate of the person she'd once cared about. Lesson learned. You lead them where you want them to go.

"What happened to him? Like, I know it wasn't a car accident or anything because you said she's a homicide detective but, like, was he ... ?

I swallowed and shoved my hands in my pockets. She didn't need to see that they were shaking. My mother hadn't missed it. She softened her expression realizing that my reluctance wasn't because she'd done a terrible job raising me to be a person who gave a damn but because I was dipping my toe back into the waters.

"I didn't see him, so I don't know for sure." And the body being in the coroner's van before I got there suddenly made sense, as did Jan's bunt of my wild speed ball accusation.

"She did mention there might have been a fight." The vague terminology for someone being beaten to death wasn't vast.

"Where was he?"

How were we not done with this?

I looked at Mom again with the *rescue me* expression she knew too well. She shook her head almost imperceptibly. Now? Now people were taking the kid gloves off?

"He was found in a wooded area near his house." The address on the license had showed he'd lived farther from the spot than it was to Aja's house, but she didn't need to know that. Before she could ask for more specifics, I slipped in a question of my own.

"What did Damian do outside of school? Was he involved in sports?" Something besides being beaten that could explain bruises. And his sudden physical transformation.

"He was really into art like me but then over the summer he just ... stopped. And he started going to the gym with friends. New friends."

"Did he join a team at school? Football? Wrestling? Was he interested in the MMA club they tried to start?" What in the hell spurred on the change?

She shook her head. "No, and he dropped art. I mean, he couldn't change to a new course but he stopped coming at all. He failed it the first quarter and I guess the last two, as well."

She guessed? "Aja, how long ago did you break up with Damian?"

"November."

She'd been dealing with this for over three months?

"And how long had he been bothering you?"

"Um, it was kind of why I broke up with him. I mean, he'd be, like, super distant, and then totally overbearing, wanting to know where I'd been and who I'd been hanging out with. It was a bummer. And we didn't have anything in common anymore at that point."

"How'd he take it?"

She shrugged. I recognized the shutting down mechanism. Yay for partially functioning mental health. I didn't know how to short-circuit it but I saw it.

"He was probably angry?" my mother asked. It was leading the witness a bit but considering he'd been vandalizing her house, this wasn't exactly putting words in Aja's mouth.

Aja mumbled something. Even Mom seemed to have missed it the words were so quiet.

"What did he do, sweetheart?"

"He threatened to kill my cat."

Threatening to kill an animal wasn't normal. It wasn't close to normal. It was in a different state, an exceedingly long car ride from normal.

"He didn't. He said he would but … I gave her to my cousin."

So not that he didn't but that he couldn't. Three months ago. She'd been terrified of this guy for three months and her damned parents

107

were off doing whatever self-involved assholes who didn't deserve children did instead of staying home and, you know, parenting.

"Oh, sweet girl." Mom wrapped Aja in her arms.

Cat killing, even threats, had a way of getting your attention. I thought about Fargo and what I'd do if someone threatened to hurt her. I concluded that I'd beat that person until I got tired of hitting them and then hurting an animal wasn't something they would be capable of thinking about ever again. I had a lot of anger in general; they'd likely stop thinking about everything long before I got tired of punching them in the face.

Had Damian diversified his attentions? Maybe a new girl who was just as tuned into the crazy as Aja had been? Maybe one who confided in someone a hell of a lot sooner than Aja had? Someone less likely to follow the legal—okay, legal-ish—route? It was something to suggest to Jan.

The doorbell rang and I was grateful for the excuse to walk away from the emotional intensity for a moment.

I let Jan in and nodded her into the kitchen. I knew Nancy would stick with Aja and that allowed me to slip downstairs and grab the file on the cold case murder. Jan would fill me in on her interview with Aja anyway and I'd been ordered to multitask like a grownup detective.

I took the file and my laptop to the bed. The laptop was new and I was still working out my relationship with it. I wasn't sure about the touchscreen or what I did on the mousepad that caused the view to keep shrinking to Alice in Wonderland proportions. It was frustrating when all I wanted to do was type up a case file. I'd had Ben optimize (his word) the case management software for my more visual working style. That had been the whole thought process behind the touchscreen—that I could move and draw out my conclusions.

The reality was that I just kept banishing pictures and notes to some screen Neverland and couldn't find them again without listening to my baby brother harangue me about my lack of technical skills and pitiful hand-to-eye coordination. I was getting ready to drag his butt back to the dojo to give him a demonstration of my hand-to-eye skills. I'd make him hold the body bag during drills if he didn't get off my case and get me the file scan interface I'd been asking for these last few weeks.

I'd gotten barely a paragraph typed in when my phone lit up with a text asking me to come back upstairs. Five minutes. I just wanted five minutes to finish one task completely. If this was multitasking as a PI it blew dead bears and I would like to take a hard pass, thank you very much.

I smooshed all the papers in the file back in as quickly and neatly as possible. If a second text came in from my mother, I would be in trouble. And if you think staring down a neo-Nazi was the scariest thing I'd ever do in my life, I would show you her hard mom stare and you could tell me which you preferred. You'd choose the neo-Nazi every time.

I just needed to hit that first step—we called it the snitch step because it gave you up every time no matter where you stepped or how lightly you hit it—and I was home free, but when I rounded the corner from my room my father was standing at the foot of the stairs, one hand on the banister knob and one on the wall. Blocking me and smirking. Old game and probably his passive-aggressive way of getting back at me for liking Mom more than him. What can I say? She's a better cook.

If he wanted to play, we could play. I had dirt on him. I weighed using it or saving it. I still had some currency from my injuries. I could hobble into the kitchen claiming rib pain but I decided to lay down my ace. That didn't mean I wouldn't use the rib when I needed it (ribs took forever to stop hurting), but I was taking the old man down for the fake stakeout. He had a secret and he'd long suspected I knew.

"I have pictures, you know. Proof. And you know I'll use them."

He narrowed his eyes at me and the hand braced against the wall dropped. "You've got squat and you and I both know it, pie pop."

The old nickname burned, as he'd intended, but I kept my game face on. If he thought a little putdown was going to cause me to crumble, he'd raised the wrong kid.

"I've got distance and close-up. I've even cropped a few for the best details."

I felt him taking my measure. Was I bluffing? He knew my skills were impressive—hell, he'd taught them to me—and he was sure he could discern even the tiniest tell.

The phone blipped in my hand. Two texts. A third would be real trouble and we both knew it. I had no problem taking him down with me. I was loyal to a certain extent but if push came to shove, I chose me.

"What's it going to be, old man? Do I out you to your wife? She'd never trust you again, you know."

Real fear showed on his face and his hand wavered on the banister. One more push and I'd have him. He had too much to lose. "Your own father?"

"Versus Mom? You bet your ass."

He moved aside, defeated. I hit that step and it let out a squeal that sounded like victory.

I was winded when I turned the corner round the stairs and into the kitchen. Actually winded from the rush of the standoff. I had to watch my back now. I'd made an enemy. He'd know the proof was on my phone and he'd try to get it. I couldn't upload it to the cloud where

Ben would have access to it since I'd made sure I'd severed his wireless connection to my phone. I'd have to use one of the burner phones I'd gotten for just such an instance. I'd text myself the pictures of Dad in my stash of junk food, chocolate smeared on his mouth and fingers, as insurance. It was a flawless backup.

"Sorry. I was helping Dad. I told him you'd texted that you wanted me but he said it would take a second and you could wait."

Game, set, and match. Send me on another fake stakeout, I dare you.

Nancy merely nodded rather coolly and stirred the pot of, again, ridiculously delicious-smelling food.

"I needed to see you, kid," Jan said.

Lizard brain flicked out its forked tongue to test the air and found a crackle of danger.

"Big girl detectiving here, boss." I waggled the file folder at her, flinging crime scene photos onto the table and floor.

"Good to see you're taking this seriously," Jan said.

I restrained my eyes from rolling freely and picked up the errant pictures.

She continued. "I need to get a witness statement from you regarding the break-in at Aja's house the other day. The one in which your truck was damaged. The one about the intruder this morning seems less critical but I need it for the file."

That explained Nancy's frosty nod. I had neglected to mention that specific series of events to my parents. But, hell, I was presumably an adult and a professional buttisnky, at that.

"I began a sweep of the house using appropriate single-man floor-by-floor, top-down procedure. I had completed a sweep of the attic level of the domicile when, upon hearing a noise outside the residence, I discovered the front door and my vehicle had been damaged."

111

A perfect statement summary. I'd have gotten a gold star from my training officer for that succinct yet complete description of the events.

"Impressive recitation of the facts," Jan said. Her dry tone indicated that she was buying exactly none of the shit I was slinging. "Now can I get a few more details? In your own words, please. I don't need examples for the report writing manual."

I was already in trouble so I laid it out as baldly as possible.

"I freaked out. It was only supposed to be me helping her feel safer and possibly to convince her to get the hell out of Dodge and then she said he'd been in the house, that he'd touched her bed, slashed her pillows and it just started tumbling in my head so that by the time I started the search, which again had just been to make her feel better, I missed the signs. He'd been in her house. He'd touched her bed, Jan. And I felt so exposed. Like he was watching us at that moment. He'd gotten inside her head and he was in mine too."

The stirring had stopped. Jan, normally so reserved, reached her hand out to me and lightly brushed my knuckles. I had to get through it all before I couldn't.

"I hid her in the laundry room and forced myself to do the sweep."

Nancy came up behind me, close, but not touching me.

"I didn't want her to see me like that," I said, quietly.

"Willa, there's nothing to be ashamed of. You went through something traumatizing and suddenly, you were in a situation that felt similar. You're human," Jan said.

"She called me for help. I promised her I'd help."

Nancy did touch me then, kissing me on the top of my head, the smell of her coming down over me, bread and lilacs, and I let the breath out that had been squatting in my lungs. "It would help her to see that you understand what she's been through. Is it really all that different from what that man did to you?"

I bit my upper lip and forced the tears back down. "Yes. It is. Because I'm the lifeline she reached out for. And she wasn't safe yet. I wasn't doing my job."

Nancy stroked her hand down my hair then settled it on the back of my neck. I was embarrassed that I couldn't get through a simple witness statement without my mommy having to rescue me from the mean cop who made me cry. The fact that the two of them didn't see it like that made it worse.

"You made sure she was safe. First at her house and then by bringing her here. Whatever else you think you could have done or should have done is useless."

Jan gave me a look that said the matter was closed. I nodded and gave myself another second to pull it together.

"Did you see the damage Aja told you about? The pillow?"

"No."

"You didn't see anything as an independent witness until today with the sabotaged locks and the masked man lurking on the property?"

"Correct."

"Sabotaged locks?" Nancy asked. "Sorry, sorry. Finish your official stuff."

"As you indicated today, the location where the body was found was quite close to Aja's house, through the woods. Had she given you any evidence of finding mud or leaves in the house during these incidents?"

That was an odd line of questioning. It wasn't like we were going to be able to charge the exceedingly dead Damian Murphy with stalking Aja. He wasn't ever going to be indicted for breaking and entering so who really cared if he'd gotten the carpets muddy while he was skulked around her house trying to locate her kitty to pull a *Fatal Attraction* on?

I reminded myself that sometimes investigators have thought processes that don't always make sense to other people. Not even other investigators.

"No. To be fair, I didn't ask. I wasn't officially working for her so I was playing a little loose with how I did case intake."

My father wouldn't be thrilled with that admission. Luckily, he was still hiding in the basement waiting for the junk food inquisition to start.

"Okay." Jan put away her notebook. "I want to tour the house with you. You can point out the area you saw the person this morning then."

And just like that it was over. The tension I'd been feeling popped like a soap bubble and my senses returned to normal. The most annoying aftereffects of being the victim of a crime was how when your brain was stressed, it started to shut down stimuli it felt you didn't need, ready for fight or flight to kick in. You never even noticed until the birds started chirping again and you could feel your extremities. I whined about it now but that fight or flight had come through for me in a big way in the past so I was trying to be grateful for all that my brain did to enable it.

"Jan, please stay for dinner. I've made beef stew."

There was nothing Nancy liked more than a full house for dinner. With Jan we'd be six, a full table.

Fargo settled on my feet after we dished up, trying to avoid all the other feet crowding a space usually more open. Aja sat with one leg underneath her like a flamingo. The conversation swirled around the upcoming baseball season, a topic I knew less about than calculus and I knew nothing about calculus. Jan was surprisingly conversant on the topic and she and my dad had a spirited conversation, with Ben and Aja providing mathematical insights on statistical averages. Trying to follow it all was impossible so I let it wash over me without tuning in and just observed.

Aja's hair was starting to fade from the artificially dark black she'd been dying it and hints of auburn swished every time she turned her head to participate in the volley of words. My dad was excited to have someone to talk about his love of baseball and was animated in a way I hadn't seen in a long time. Nancy was quietly pleased watching her family—to her, Jan was family now too—being fed and enjoying each other. A flicker in her eyes let on that she was worried about me. I gave her a smile to reassure her that I was no worse than usual. I was no better but status quo was always a win over decline.

My phone blipped and I apologized my way into the foyer, Fargo bumping my heels as I hurried. The name on the screen surprised me.

"Seth?"

"Hey, Sunshine. It's a crazy story."

Ah, so he'd heard my twenty-two voicemails. They'd started out cogent arguments as to why running off without a word was not how adult relationships thrived and quickly degenerated into protestations of disbelief then just as rapidly into strings of curses.

"Uh huh."

It had gone silent in the kitchen. A table full of teenagers and detectives was going to be a nosy group in general, but my family elevated butting in to an art form.

"A spot at FLETC opened up unexpectedly. I didn't even pack. I got on a plane and showed up to make sure I got the chair."

The Federal Law Enforcement Training Center was putting on an annual course that Seth had been unsuccessful in securing enrollment in, despite his recommendation letters and the recent commendation in his file. He'd been deeply disappointed. Everyone, including past

FLETC instructors, had assured him he'd be chosen. The class wasn't in the regular courses in the catalog and was word-of-mouth only. He'd been allowed to tell me about its existence as generalities only and those generalities had been it was a class and it was this week. I didn't even know which FLETC location he was at.

"I see."

Remember when I said I wasn't complex? That isn't always accurate. My feelings regarding Seth are complex. Complex, contradictory, and wildly swinging. Current mood—deeply annoyed and exceptionally proud. He knew what he wanted and despite knowing his actions would cause problems with me, he did it.

"You're very angry. Still?"

I took a moment to choose my words. This situation had great potential to be turned to my favor and I wanted to make sure I got as much out of it as I could. Without alerting any family members there was juicy information to be had.

"I'm contemplative."

He was silent for a full minute, clearly trying to decide his next move. Ours was a love affair plotted out in strategic moves that would make a 3D chess player weep with frustration. He was trying to come up with an appropriate response and I was listening carefully for any background noise that would give away where in the hell he was in the United States. *When Spooks Fall in Love* will be the movie they make about us.

"Are you contemplating changing the feelings you've done an excellent job of expressing on my voicemail?"

"The circumstances would seem to warrant that, but I find I need more information to fully assess that course of action."

I was driving everyone nuts being so vague. The eavesdroppers were getting no satisfaction and Seth had no idea what to say or do. Perfect.

"Do you want me to come home?"

A bluff. He knew I'd never say yes and I knew if I did say yes, he wouldn't. Interesting attempt. He felt he'd nudged us into a stalemate.

"If you feel that's the best course of action."

Everyone's food had to be cold by that point. Good.

"I, uh, I want to know what you want."

Weak sauce, bud. Lobbing that crap over the net at me guarantees a blistering return.

"Really? Is that what you want? To know what I want? To tell you to come home? So despite how you chose to go about this, I'm the bad guy. Are you scared, Seth? Is this course intimidating you now that you're there? Do I need to be the bad guy so you can call it quits and then it's my fault?"

I could picture my dad dropping his head into his hands. *Don't lose faith, Dad. I got this.*

"No, Seth. I don't want you to come home. I want you to take this class because it's what you want. Even if it's scary right now. You can do this. I have faith in you."

He'd tried to goad me into a fight—our default setting for months now—and I'd just dropped a daisy cutter. Chopper incoming with reinforcement troops in three, two ….

"I really feel like you're where you need to be right now, Seth. And I have two cases all of the sudden so I'll let you go. Check in when you can. Bye." And I disconnected the call.

Five agog faces greeted me upon my return to the kitchen.

"Um, I don't know if I'm supposed to say something or not but…wow," Aja said.

"That was…something," Ben added.

"Willa, honey, you handled that…hell, I don't know, well?" Dad was at a loss.

Jan avoided my eyes.

"Pinned his wings right to the board, didn't you, sweetie? Two days without a how do you do and just calls acting like it's nothing. He'll be running that conversation through his head nonstop," Mom said. She smiled and put a big spoonful of stew in her mouth.

That was the cue for everyone to stop goggling at me and finish their dinners.

That's right he'd be thinking about it for a good long while. And I'd just bought myself a big old bucket of leeway the next time he thought I was being reckless and leaping before I looked. I'd supported him and treated him like an adult when he hadn't acted like one. He got on a plane and flew to who knew where and waited over twenty-four hours, two days of me leaving voicemails, to tell me where he was and what was going on. Screw that noise. *Choke on the support and understanding, Ace.*

CHAPTER

11

FARGO WHINED FROM HER bed on the floor. Apparently the ultra-deluxe, triple-layer, memory foam dog bed with the upgraded fabric in cow print wasn't as comfy as she'd like. Unfortunately, her better choice, my bed, was currently covered with crime scene photos from the homicide of Amanda Veitch. I was comparing the photos with the crime scene evidence log and my eyes were swimming at the tedious, painstaking task. It had to be done though.

Being a PI was not the glamorous occupation shown on TV. Or in movies. There were no sexy dames with gams for days, unless I counted Fargo's gangly puppy legs. There were no well-dressed men in fedoras staking out the hotel lobby bar, cigarette smoke heavy in the air while a torch singer moaned into an old-timey microphone about the man who done her wrong and at the end of the hour and a half, she and the PI would press into each other, a smoldering kiss almost upon them when the screen would fade to black.

No, being a modern PI was wearing a grubby t-shirt emblazoned with *Matt's Pool 'Que* and riddled with holes from said long-legged puppy's teething issues, sitting on a bed that desperately needed clean sheets (added to the obscenely long to-do list of chores ignored for far too long), combing through a hundred photos taken of every conceivable angle in a ten-by-twelve bedroom looking for the one piece of evidence a detective with more experience investigating than I had shaving my legs (something else for the to-do list) had missed in the almost twenty years she'd been going over the case.

It was midnight and I was exhausted. I knew I couldn't make the same mistake I'd made investigating Joe Reagan's murder last fall. I had to sleep and eat regularly. I had to interact with more people than my younger brother and the guy I thought was the murderer. I had to, at least, shave my legs on the reg. I had to use caffeine responsibly. More responsibly. Okay, not recklessly. Which was why I had not made a second pot of coffee after dinner even if I'd only had two of the ten cups from the first pot. Okay, three, but I hadn't finished that cup and it sat, more than half full, on the nightstand.

I needed to go to sleep and clear my brain out to start again in the morning. I needed more space for the photos. I needed to just put it all away and go at it again when it was daylight. I jotted a quick note about reworking the list by piece of evidence and noting which photos showed that piece then arranging them that way.

I pulled on a pair of pajama bottoms and went to check the locks on the slider. I peeked behind the curtain to make sure no one was lurking in the backyard. Locks were well and good, but those sliders were mostly glass and there were easy ways to bust them that didn't involve making a ton of noise. I checked the two windows to make sure that the window locks were engaged and the pins were in place. It had been a few days since I'd checked the storm windows to make sure no one had tampered with them. I added that to the top of the to-do list, pretty much ensuring my legs would have to go another day without being shaved.

I wasn't content with merely checking the security downstairs and decided to make a perimeter sweep of the upstairs. I hopped over the snitch step and weaved my way up the rest of the staircase, avoiding the squeaky spots on all the other boards. Fargo wasn't heavy enough to set off any of the noisy points yet so she slipped up behind me like a dancer.

Dad slept about as well as I did and I wasn't keen for anyone to get shot. I was pretty sure he wasn't stupid enough to hear a noise and come out guns ablazin' but you read stories about perfectly intelligent people being surprised in the middle of the night and shooting a loved one. It was probably why Nancy has instituted the Everyone Disarm in My Darn House Right Now and I Mean It policy.

I went to start with the office and the door was almost closed but I could see the soft glow of the desk lamp spilling out around the frame. Déjà vu struck me and I half expected to push open the door and see Seth rifling through the stacks of manila folders like I had months before. Instead, Ben was sitting behind the desk, fingers flying over the keyboard of Dad's laptop. I found it disconcerting he didn't even look up to see who it was. Had we not drilled being safety conscious into his head at every turn?

I opened my mouth to chastise him and he cut me off before I could start.

"I knew it was you before you opened the door, Will. Fargo's nails clicking on the kitchen floor gave you both away."

Wow. That was pretty observant. I had tuned out the sound of her paws days after we got her. And his hands hadn't even paused while he was talking. That was next level impressive.

"Don't get cocky, Benj. What if I was being held at gunpoint to get to you?"

He stopped typing. "You're the only family member annoying enough that someone would just kill them first."

"Um, thanks. But what if some extremist group managed to track you down and kidnap you to force you to hack into the NSA?"

Fargo, lacking any commands to sit or stay or do anything, trotted over to Ben and put her paws up on his legs. It was adorable so I was sure he'd tell her to stop, but he just rubbed her ears while he gave me a pitying look.

"One, no one is going to be able to track me down. I'd explain to you all the levels of encryption I use to mask myself online but we both know it would be a waste of my time. And, two, I can't hack the NSA so they'd just have to kill me."

I had no doubt Ben thought he was being reassuring but he had a long way to go if he hadn't seen the mistakes in his assurances.

"Okay, smart guy, don't be so sure no one can track you. There's always someone smarter or more determined. It's no comfort that someone will and I quote, 'just have to kill you,' and, finally, how do you know you can't hack the NSA if you haven't already tried and failed?"

He looked at me his eyes widening. "I didn't exactly try to hack them. I just ... um ... ."

"Let me guess, you could explain it to me but it would just be a waste of your time?" I cocked an eyebrow at him. Genius, my ass.

He was just outsmarted by a solid C student who'd had to get her six-year-old brother to help her with algebra. "Just finish up whatever fully legal, non-federal sentence resulting activity you're doing and go to bed. It's long past the time you should be asleep."

He opened his mouth and this time I got to cut him off. "I'm just checking the locks and then me and pretty girl are going to bed ourselves."

As expected, everything was double-locked and as secure as it could be. I led Fargo downstairs and we both climbed into bed to snuggle up for the night.

Two and a half cups of coffee weren't enough to overcome my need for sleep and the comforting warmth of Fargo's body against my back. We were both still asleep and dreaming when my alarm went off. I knew she was dreaming because Fargo's twitchy legs continued while I groped for the phone to turn the alarm off or, at least, down. I had somehow cranked the ringer volume way up from the usual low I kept it at. I was a light enough sleeper that I didn't need anything extreme to get me up so if anyone was thinking of getting me one of those clocks that you have to chase, you should forget that now. I'm cranky in the mornings and I'm a good shot even with sleep in my eyes.

I was tired. I was beyond tired. And I had interviews with Amanda Veitch's mother and brother in the morning. In the morning that was light as opposed to the morning I was in where it was dark and I was staring at the glowing red number of the clock.

Six thirty. Time to get up. I was extra groggy because I'd been woken in the middle of a dream cycle. That always threw me off. I gathered my hair and put it up into a messy whatever it was called when it was in a ponytail but not pulled all the way through. It wasn't a bun. It didn't matter. I jammed a pair of earbuds in to listen to the morning meditation both Leila and Nancy had sent me. I was supposed to be sitting in a chair, with my feet on the floor, relaxed and ready for brain bliss but I didn't roll like that. Meditation needed to be portable.

I shook Fargo awake and she turned her head toward me, yawning.

"Time to get up, Fargo. Time to go out."

I had some special morning command to give that told her to go to the bathroom in Dutch, but it was too complicated to remember in the early-morning hours. And who was going to try to break into her training to tell her to get up in the morning besides me? She understood the English version just fine if her reaction was any indication. She scampered off the bed and sat at the door waiting for me to open it and lead her to the slider.

The air chilled my bare arms and feet as I stood outside waiting for her, an icy fog hovering a few inches off the ground. She was barely a few feet away from me and I could only make out her faint silhouette. One of the first things we'd taught her was the perimeter of the yard, but she was still young and in training.

"Fargo, stay close."

She knew that command well. It was probably the two words she heard most. *Stay close.* She ambled back toward the door, still sniffing around, still not doing her business.

"Fargo, get on with it. I'm cold." She didn't care about the temperature. She had a fur coat. She had no concept of thin cotton shirts and flannel pants that did nothing to block the damn air creeping up the leg. She finally squatted and did her business. And like an asshole, I left it because it was going to be months before anyone was back here and it was unlikely anyone would ever be walking flush to the house. If someone was there, I doubted they had good intentions creeping around and, at minimum, deserved a sole full of dog crap.

The meditation droned on in my ears as we went inside. We both skipped the bottom step and went up the stairs in search of sustenance. I was trying this thing where I ate real food to make my moms happy and I didn't want to admit to either of them that I had more energy and felt better than when my diet was ninety percent fake everything except sugar. I just kept eating healthier and we all left it undiscussed. I hadn't even checked my stash in days. For all I knew, my dad had decimated it.

Nancy was at the counter, fiddling with the electric kettle Seth had given her for Christmas after finding the whistle of the manual kettle did something unpleasant to his hearing. I didn't even hear it but I'd lived with it for years. She didn't seem to like the new one much and I thought it was a crappy reason to give someone a gift, but she used it even if Seth wasn't around.

It was an early morning for me but she'd been up for an hour getting Ben and Aja off to school. It struck me how odd it was that Aja's seamless transition into our family wasn't being treated as odd. With Michael and Seth and Ben's friend, John, there were always kids that weren't hers in and out of the house, all days of the week, all hours of the day. It didn't matter to her if she had four mouths to feed, five, six, eight, ten. There was a space at her table and enough food. It was one of the things I loved most about her—her heart expanded out like the biggest sofa bed you could imagine, always room made for something to find shelter.

"Morning, Mom," I said, pulling my earbuds out. I laid my head on her shoulder and wrapped my arm around her waist. Times like this were the few I felt comfortable with physical affection. I'd never been touchy-feely as a kid because Leila hadn't really been a huggy-kissy kind of mom. When Nancy became my mom, she was always careful to go at my speed. She laid down firm rules, but my body was mine. I decided who touched it and when.

"Morning, sweetheart. Sleep well?"

That was my cue to yawn. "Actually, yes. Fargo is a good pillow."

Hearing her name so close to the proximity of her food bowl caused her ears to perk up. Nancy laughed.

"Yes, it's time to eat, puppy." Nancy bent to open the cabinet with the special food she bought when she saw the dry kibble Ben had brought home. No amount of explaining to her that it was nutritionally balanced, high quality, and expensive as hell could dissuade her. She took the inferior dog food to the shelter and went out to buy even more expensive food. For a woman who fought getting a dog so long, she certainly seemed to be enjoying all the tasks she swore she wanted no part of.

"I got it. Finish making your tea." She had another hour before she needed to be at the elementary school to oversee any of the maladies that grade-schoolers passed around like crayons. It was flu season so her tea was echinacea with a vitamin C chaser.

I scooped out the food and placed the bowl in front of Fargo. She stared at me in anticipation. I looked back at her. I let another few heartbeats pass before I said, "Paid for."

Fargo stuck her face in the bowl and made little sounds of joy as she crunched the bites of food.

"I wish that wasn't necessary," Nancy said.

"We'd do that even if she wasn't in training as a working dog. We don't want her eating just anything that smells like food. She could eat a dead, rabid animal carcass. That would suck."

"I know." She sipped her tea. I could see she wanted to say more.

Fargo finished her breakfast and trotted out of the kitchen to stand at the front door. Good girl.

I went to let her out again and she trotted out to sniff around a bit finding her favorite spots. I shut the door behind me so I wouldn't get yelled at for letting the cold air in. Or the warm air out. They were never too married to either point. They'd given up yelling at either one of us for not having coats on. Ben had pointed out that it was an old wives' tale and that you couldn't get sick from being underdressed. That had been about the same time he was doing my math for me.

Fargo finished her desecration of the grass and hurled herself up the cement steps toward me. I'd need to take her for a run as soon as I finished eating enough fuel for exercise. She was getting as antsy as I felt. We'd run; she'd avoid the zoomies and I'd avoid getting too deep inside my own head.

———

"We've interviewed them a number of times over the years so they know the drill. No question is off the table. Just be as tactful as possible."

I hadn't been offended when Jan went over the rules in the car, but sitting in front of Mandy's mother I reminded myself that tact wasn't my strongest skill. I vowed to treat her like I would my own mother if something happened to Ben.

"Mrs. Veitch, this is a consultant who works with the department. I've asked her to review your daughter's case to give us a fresh set of eyes."

The woman who stood before us seemed smaller than the pictures I had seen of her. She was painfully thin with skin that looked loose on her bones. I knew from the files that Mandy's birthday was coming up. She'd have been thirty-five. It didn't seem fair that she had to get through the anniversary of her daughter's death and the holidays all on top of one another only to have to face her daughter's birthday and then Mother's Day in a short interval. Not that any day was a day she'd have forgotten or put it behind her for even one moment.

"Willa Pennington, Mrs. Veitch. I'm so sorry about what happened to your daughter. I'm doing my best to help Detective Boyd give you a resolution."

She grasped my outstretched hand with one that felt as fragile as a bird's wing.

"You're so young." She stared at me, eyes dry and somewhat empty.

"Willa is a very talented investigator, Mrs. Veitch. I trust her completely." I'd never get such high praise from Jan directly. It would have felt good if I'd heard it any other time but as I stood in front of this woman who looked like she was dying slowly, it didn't give me any pleasure. It did make me all that more determined to find out who had killed Amanda.

"I'm sorry. I didn't mean that you weren't good at your job, Miss Pennington."

I smiled at her. "No offense taken."

She gave her head a little shake. "Please come in and sit down."

She ushered us into a small living room that seemed to be decorated as a technicality. It had the air of a room that had been staged for photos to appear on a realtor's website. The furniture looked as fresh as if the delivery service had just dropped it off. No magazines on the table, not even in a neat stack. Not one family photo anywhere to be seen. I knew from the file that her son was married with a daughter of his own, but there was no evidence this woman had a family of any kind.

"Can I offer you a beverage? I have a fresh pot of coffee."

I looked at Jan hopefully.

"Coffee would be great," Jan said.

I used the time she was in the kitchen to organize my files and review my questions. I made sure my notepad and pen were ready and available. I willed my hands to stop shaking. Nerves or caffeine withdrawal would be determined when the coffee was served.

Mrs. Veitch brought the coffee in on a tray so at one point she'd entertained. She set it down on the coffee table and handed out cups. Tiny cups. Infinitesimally tiny cups. Caffeine withdrawal for the win. Come collect your winnings.

"Sorry, I only have real sugar. I don't keep artificial sweetener."

I dumped a full bag of cookies' worth of real sugar in and smiled. "That's okay. I'm allergic to it."

Jan stared at me. "I didn't know that."

"It's never come up before." I shrugged, dumping in creamer.

We both turned back to Mrs. Veitch hearing a sniffle.

"Amanda was allergic to artificial sweetener. I've never met anyone else who was. It was always a struggle to keep it out of her way since they put it in everything back then, but I read every label. I still haven't broken the habit."

I nodded, blowing on the coffee. "My mom is pretty militant about it too. I'll admit, when *I'm* responsible for it, I've had some slips. It's not enjoyable."

Mrs. Veitch shook her head. "It's hard to watch your child suffer and not be able to do anything about it."

An awkward silence settled over the room. The conversation had gotten a little too real, but it didn't matter where it went at that point. I mentally tossed my first set of questions. I'd ignored the receipts with their time and date stamped. Those could be faked and I'd come into the house with the assumption that all suspects were on the table, but this woman hadn't killed her daughter. I closed my eyes as I took a sip of the now cooled coffee. One down, two more to go.

———

Kyle Warnicky—Amanda's boyfriend—had moved out of the area so we had plans to Skype with him later in the day. We drove straight from Mrs. Veitch's house to her son's. Kevin Veitch lived no more than a mile from his mother. Both had moved out of the house Amanda had died in within a month of the murder. Kevin transferred to George Mason to finish his degree and in short order married and became a father. His daughter was named Amanda.

"That's hardly the sign of a guilty conscience. You wouldn't want to be reminded of murdering your sister every time you talked to your daughter," I said, reviewing my notes, finally able to chat with Jan about some of the details. She'd been so insistent that her views not taint mine that, outside of generic talk about me working the case, we'd avoided the topic entirely.

"Could be penance."

I wasn't sure how that worked as we weren't a religious family but that seemed a pretty extreme way to punish yourself. I'd have cracked before now. Long before now. And I was damn good at compartmentalizing my feelings. Of course, I'd never murdered a sibling.

We pulled up outside a tidy brick Cape Cod. It didn't look like the Veitches made a bundle of money. I flipped to the financial report on them and saw they were a one-income family, Kevin being a high school chemistry teacher and his wife, Courtney, a stay-at-home mom. I reviewed the family demographic page again.

"Their daughter is fifteen. Date of birth is April twenty-second. She'll be sixteen soon."

I started to do the mental math but Jan interrupted my train of thought. "Yeah, the wife was pregnant when Amanda was murdered."

"Did that ever cause you to doubt that he was the guy?" It had to have. Jan was a great cop and part of that was being able to read people. She'd know immediately upon finding out that information if it made the suspect more or less likely. But that was now. This was then. She'd been a new Homicide detective. Just off Burglary on her first murder case. No second chair on other cases, like they do now. Deep end of the pool, copper, where you sink or swim.

"It was the piece I couldn't place in the puzzle. I thought I knew where it was supposed to go but always doubted myself."

"And now?"

"Now I've got you to look at it with fresh eyes, kid."

But when Kevin opened the door, I knew. I looked back at Jan standing on the cracked concrete step behind me.

His broad smile and sad eyes told me everything I needed to know about him. Two down, one to go.

"Come in, detectives. It's a teacher workday so it worked out well. I just put a pot of coffee on. Oh, maybe you'd like something else to drink. We've got water, juice, sodas, regular and diet."

He was nervous. That was understandable. He just didn't seem guilty to me. He seemed more eager than anything. Eager to help. Eager to find out the truth. Eager for it all to be over. If he'd done it and he'd wanted it over, he'd confess.

"Water for me, Mr. Veitch. My associate will likely want coffee," Jan said.

She was right. That itty-bitty cup earlier had barely dented my deficit.

"Come on into the kitchen then. Manda, my daughter, has got a science project all spread out in the family room. She and my wife had to run out to get some more supplies. The science fair is later this week. I hope you didn't need to talk to them."

Definitely eager. He was not our guy. I knew it soul deep.

"How do you take it?" he asked.

Too eager. I hated people who insisted on fixing your coffee for you. It seems considerate, but nine times out of ten I can't drink it.

Look, you wouldn't let someone adjust your car seat for you. Or determine what temperature your shower should be, right? It's not any different. I've been making my coffee since I was twelve. I know the exact pour. And if you can't afford to let me have all the creamer I need, don't offer me coffee. It was a testament to Jan's powers of observation that she got mine even more right than I did.

"That's okay. I'm happy to do it."

He looked up, guilty. "Right. I'm just … when I get nervous I get fidgety."

I shifted through the blue and yellow packets looking for the actual sugar. I found a single white one under half a dozen blue ones.

"Why are you nervous, Mr. Veitch? This is only routine. We've asked a consultant to review the case and we're getting her up to speed."

I don't know if Jan meant to sound like a hard-ass but her demeanor and delivery were worlds apart from an hour earlier with the mother. I shot her a look that basically read *cool it, already* and she shot me back a look that wasn't defiant but was annoyed. Tough crackers, sister. This was my interview.

The front door burst open and a flurry of bags and chatter swept into the small house. The wife and daughter had accomplished their supply shopping and then some, it appeared. Their first stop was the kitchen, probably looking to dump out the bags and organize the purchases. It was a familiar scene. Nancy and Ben had done it plenty over the years, though not as much recently. Lately all Ben's science fair projects were less supply-based and more cloud-based. Gone were the diorama days.

"Oh, sorry." The girl looked exactly like the pictures of her deceased aunt. I must have gaped because I felt Jan's hard look. I wiggled my eyebrows at her and she tipped her head slightly. Damn right she should have warned me.

"We'll get out of your hair, honey," the wife said. They must be fairly used to the drill.

The daughter dropped her bags in the hall and breezed into the kitchen with the air of a kid who didn't quite grasp the gravity of the situation. A dead aunt that she'd never met, even one she was named after, even with pictures she'd seen, wouldn't really register as a real thing. Cold cases, police interviews, these were not her real life. These were elements of a TV show or movie. She wouldn't maintain that naivete too much longer.

"Manda, Daddy's busy," the wife stage whispered. Right, like we weren't going to hear. She was trying to get us to excuse the kid's actions but it didn't bother me, getting to see the family interplay. I watched Kevin fix his daughter and wife cups of coffee with the practiced air of a man used to being surrounded by women—first his mother and sister, now his mother, wife, and daughter.

Kevin handed his daughter a white, no sweetener coffee and his wife a cup with cream and two packets of sweetener added—one blue, one yellow. I turned my back, pretending to look for a spoon as I gagged at how tooth-achingly sweet that coffee had to be. I was glad I hadn't let him make my coffee—I didn't want to spend the rest of the day in an allergy-induced haze of migraine and vomiting because he'd gone on autopilot and made me his wife's coffee.

The daughter practically danced out of the kitchen after getting her coffee, so much motion I feared for their rugs. Kevin just smiled indulgently.

"I'll get her to put in some headphones and do some quiet calculations while you finish up," the wife said. Courtney. I needed to think of her as Courtney.

"Thanks, dear." He sat only after his wife was completely through the door.

"Sorry about that. Manda tends to be a bit of a whirlwind. She may look like her aunt but her personality is exactly like my wife at her age."

Nice opening to the past, Kevin. Thanks.

"You've been together a long time?" I asked, sipping my coffee, appearing nonchalant.

He laughed. "Romantically, no, but she was my sister's best friend. They were opposites, kind of like we are." He'd grown wistful as he'd finished the sentence. "They were quite the pair—Amanda was more thoughtful, reserved, nose in a book. I guess Manda does take after her, and me, in that respect. She loves school like her aunt did. Courtney . . . she was always ready for an adventure. She'd never met a wall she didn't try to climb over or break down."

"Sounds like motherhood mellowed her quite a bit." That was usually the way it went. That it took my mother more than two decades to act at all mom-ish was down to her stubbornness. I came by it honestly and double-barreled. It was never any surprise to me that my parents hadn't worked out—both too stubborn with too strong of personalities. Courtney would have run right over Kevin.

"No. It was Amanda's death that did it. She changed when my sister died. It was like someone deflated her. I always thought she was paying homage to Mandy by trying to turn into her."

Interesting. People reacted to grief in so many ways. With the one-year anniversary of Michael's death looming, I was painfully aware of that fact.

He twisted his coffee cup back and forth on the table, looking down into the cup like it had some answer he needed.

"You're never going to catch the person that killed my sister, are you?"

I felt Jan stiffen beside me. She was determined to close this case, but I was beginning to feel like Kevin was right. I wasn't at all confident we were going to be able to find Amanda Veitch's killer and that thought, along with the look on his face, made my heart hurt.

"We're not stopping until we do, Kevin. That's my promise to you." I flipped open my notebook and picked up my pen. "Are you ready?"

CHAPTER

12

I PULLED THE CAR door shut. "Nothing except DNA is going to convince me that he killed anyone, let alone his sister. Did you hear how he talked about her? How he described her?"

"Yeah, I did. And they'd also had a violent fight two nights before her death which he refuses to discuss."

"He said he doesn't remember what it was about. If you asked me what Ben and I fought about two days ago, I could not tell you. The TV remote, the dog eating a shoe, my phone suddenly having a cartoon superhero case on it."

All real fights and all from some point within the last month or two.

"The mother said they never fought. You and Ben never stop fighting."

Okay, that was hurtful. We didn't always fight. We were just very different.

"You know how fights escalate. One minute it's about the laundry and the next you're yelling about how just because he's the baby he gets away with everything including hacking the school system's grades database."

Jan's eyes saucered.

"As a hypothetical example." I really needed to remember not to incriminate my brother for any felonies he's committed.

"And those arguments can escalate to murder if the person has kept it all bottled up for years."

"But that would make it premeditated. I can't see that. The way he talks about his sister—"

Jan shook her head. "It's not what he's saying, Willa, it's what he's not saying. If he'd tell us what the fight was about..."

———

Skyping with Kyle Warnicky was a bust as well. It took barely more time than we'd had to wait while the techs set up the system in the conference room. His story hadn't changed. He couldn't remember anything more and I could hardly expect him to, considering it had been the better part of twenty years. His relationship with Mandy had been more than casual and less than serious, both focusing more on school and family than each other. A high school romance that had been running on first-semester-of-college fumes. It likely would have ended over winter break and they would have stayed friends, was my conclusion.

He seemed like a nice kid who had turned into a nice man. I hadn't picked up signs he was lying or hiding anything. He wasn't overly devastated still or uncaring—his friend had been murdered a long time ago and he was sad. It all rang true and could have been utter bullshit.

It wasn't long before I was back at home in the basement family room with the Amanda Veitch crime scene photos spread out on the floor, cataloging them in the manner I'd noted the night before. I reasoned that a photo could be in two piles considering the angles but I just wanted to see if anything popped for me taking each piece of evidence singularly instead of as part of the whole. A trees for the forest method, if you will.

I kept shuffling piles and started to get confused about which item of evidence I was looking at. I took the log up to the office to make copies.

My father was in there, feet up on the desk, hands folded on his soft but not fat belly, head leaned against the high back of the leather chair, snoring. I inserted the papers into the scanner and set the output count for the total number of items listed and punched the button. The scanner/copier came to life with a beep just loud enough to rouse my father. He yawned, stretching.

Good to see one of us was earning money for the company, she said sarcastically.

"Whatcha doin'?"

I gave him a basic rundown of my morning, the interviews, and the case. I snuck in a quick dig about it being real work and not a fake case, but he sloughed it off.

We chatted about Fargo and Ben while I waited for the machine to spit out the requisite copies. Then he turned the conversation to Aja in a particularly rough segue.

"The kid doing okay?"

I shrugged, pulling out the stack of paper that was already done to let the small tray fill up again. "She seems okay to me but what the heck do I know about teenage girls acting normal."

"Your mom says she's upset but functioning."

I kept my eye on the machine. More often than not, it would crap out and start chewing up paper after a few dozen pages. It seemed to be behaving but, like all office machinery, it was evil and waiting for the chance to destroy us. When Skynet became sentient, we weren't going to be fighting off robots; it was going to be warfare with fax machines and copiers, I was convinced.

"She's been functioning for a while now on her own. I imagine with Mom and Ben by her side, *functioning* takes on a different meaning. She's a smart kid. She can, for the most part, recognize when she's in over her head and ask for help. So clearly, she's nothing like me."

I smiled up at him and then dropped my eyes to the printout tray immediately. I was not about to let this machine force me out to the library to make copies or, worse, the office supply store. First, I was home and comfortable in my sweats, and second, I didn't have clearance to be running all over the county with the file. I was sure the police department brass would frown on some kid doing a project on Gandhi ending up with an evidence report from a murder because I got distracted like I usually did at the library.

"You two have a lot in common. I'm surprised you don't see it."

I chuckled. "What do you find most alike about us? Our brains?"

"Damn, kid, I know growing up with a little brother who is an actual genius is hard, but you're smart."

I was smart and I did know it. I'd never felt insecure about my brains even with Ben next to me talking about crap none of us understood even as a little kid. Both of them in the house, though, with Aja also sporting a brain that seemed larger than most teens should have been a little intimidating. Considering I was on the trail of a murderer, I was doing okay self-esteem-wise.

"I'm street smart. Which in the suburbs means knowing which Starbucks gives the most whipped cream on a Frappuccino."

I cut off his protest as I gathered the last pile of the evidence report and combined it with the ones I was holding. "I'm not in need of a pep talk about how everyone is different and special in their own way. I promise I'm good."

I waved the pages at him and went back to the lair I had appropriated more and more of as the months went by. Fargo was sitting at the slider when I got back and I let her out, keeping one eye on her as I leaned on the door and highlighted each individual piece of evidence, one sheet at a time, going down the list.

Fargo began to bark frantically and took off around the side of the house, startling me into dropping the pile and lighting out after her, yelling her name and the command to stop. I made it around the side of the house in half the time it would have taken me a year ago when I still wore a uniform and supposedly had strict fitness requirements. Fargo was sitting at the edge of the lawn as the high school bus pulled up and Ben and Aja got off. Ben instantly began chastising me about being responsible and diligent about Fargo's training while Aja got down on the ground and pulled the puppy into her lap.

"Dude, you better take it down several decibels or I will drop you to the ground and pants you in front of that bus."

Aja laughed at the look on Ben's face.

"You wouldn't," he said.

"You know I would."

He looked at me to see if I was serious and must have concluded that I was. When he spoke again it was a normal conversational level.

"She can't be running loose, Will."

And I agreed with him. I had no idea why she'd run off unless it was part of the quirk that made her unsuitable for law enforcement work.

"I'm not disagreeing, Ben, but whether you like it or not, I'm an adult and you're not so you don't get to yell at me. I was in the back with her and she just took off."

He considered my words then looked at Fargo exuberantly licking Aja's face. It was free of the layers and layers of eye makeup she'd worn the first few times I'd seen her. It should have seemed incongruous and callous that she was happier now, after she'd been told someone she'd known and cared about had died, but that was the human brain for you. Aja was relieved she wasn't going to have to take care of herself or be scared anymore. She'd dip in and out of the five stages of grief at her own pace.

"It's you," Ben said in an accusatory tone. "You broke my dog."

Aja looked confused. "I've been here two days."

"She never did this before you came to stay." But he wasn't angry. He was thrilled. "We need to get you involved with her training. She clearly has a very strong bond with you."

Okay, that was going to make me insecure. They could have their big brains and a working knowledge of calculus, but I got the dog.

"We can expand her skill set to take her to hospitals or rehabilitation centers."

Who was this *we*? He was leaving for college in six months, as was Aja. That left me. Who hadn't wanted the dog trained to be anything other than a well-mannered dog. Ben was still prattling on about how exciting it would be if he could cross-train for both activities when I interrupted.

"No. Just no. She's a dog. She shouldn't be doing any of the crap you want her to do. Plus, you just got done whining about her training being broken by Aja being around two days."

I was more annoyed than I thought because I sounded really harsh. Nancy's timing was stellar as she pulled her minivan into the driveway.

"Why don't you two go inside and get a snack? Mom's going to be after you to start your homework the second she gets in the house so get the food while you can."

Ben picked up his backpack and slung it over his shoulder, a pout on his face. He might have been more than half a foot taller than me but he still had the pout down from when he was half my size. Aja and Fargo followed him.

"Why are you barefoot, Willa Elaine?"

Crap! One of her biggest rules: no shoes inside, shoes outside. There were many dangerous things that could be stepped on since people weren't at all careful—cigarettes (Want to see Nancy go nuclear? Discard a cigarette on the ground), metal, broken glass, etc. Wear shoes outside. So simple a child could understand it—as we'd been informed many, many times.

Plus, I'd totally forgotten the back slider was open with papers all over the floor. I hoped Fargo wouldn't get into them when she got back inside.

"Fargo's potty break turned into a prison break when her superior hearing picked up the bus."

She eyed me as if deciding the veracity of my excuse. Which was all posturing. We both knew I'd dance around the truth but I'd never outright lie to her.

"Maybe when you let her out in the future it would be best to have shoes on just in case she happens to bolt again. Also, I have to take Aja to review her statement for Detective Boyd so . . . ."

She sighed. Probably because she knew me well enough to know that while it was a perfectly reasonable request it was also likely one I wouldn't accommodate most times. As long as she wasn't watching.

I walked back around the house in the cold grass with more care than I'd took coming out.

The pages were just where I'd dropped them. I shuffled the few I'd already highlighted back into order and settled down to highlight the rest. A pack of sticky notes and I was ready to reorganize the photos by evidentiary display. It was the height of tedium but at least it sounded fancy. More non-glamour that was still yards better than driving around in a cramped cruiser waiting for something to happen.

I was surprised to see an hour had passed when I got up to stretch my tight back. I was spending too much time on my butt lately. I paced around giving my legs a good stretch when my phone blipped.

I'M AN ASS.

I replied with a terse agreement, no emojis. I wanted to stay mad. I just didn't have the energy. I sent another text letting him know we'd work it out when he got home and to concentrate on his training. In reply, I got a flower emoji. Damn, he was charming.

One final text back to him with a smiley face and I put him on mute. I needed to concentrate on the pictures. Most of the photos showed the body and its immediate environs, but there were photos of the dresser, the nightstand, bookshelf, closet. They all showed a normal teen girl's bedroom. Some of the angles could be considered arty if hung on a gallery's walls . . . and weren't showing a corpse. Who knew? That might make them even more arty.

I gathered the photos that showed the bottle of acetone on the dresser. It had been used to douse the carpet and bed clothes as an accelerant for the fire. The cap was found on the floor by the front of the dresser. No prints found on either, not even the victims, so they both had been wiped. No lighter or matches were found; the killer must have taken them with him. But left the acetone.

I suddenly wanted to see Aja's room back at her house. She was only two years younger than this victim. Would they have similar items? Even if they didn't, it would have the same feel. A smart young woman, college important to both. I could get into the victim's headspace.

I picked my phone up and texted Jan to meet me at Aja's house. I had gotten an email from the locksmith earlier in the day that the locks had been cleaned out. The attached bill had another set of digits on the left side of the decimal high enough to make Snoop Dogg vow to give up the chronic. I reminded myself that Aja's negligent parents were paying the bill and that made me feel warm and cozy.

Jan replied to my text asking if I wanted Aja to come with us. I pondered it for a minute and replied that I did. She could help me see things more clearly. I stuffed my feet into shoes, gathered up my file minus the photos, and grabbed a jacket. It was a quick drive to Aja's house even taking a slight detour to wind my way through the streets closest to the route I assumed Damian took through the woods.

I was in the driveway a good ten minutes before Jan arrived with Aja, so I made notes on what I wanted to look for. It was more a feeling and less a cataloging. Just getting the lay of the land I hadn't lived in or visited much.

Jan's headlights lit up the rearview mirror as she pulled in behind me. It was much lighter out, still late afternoon, but the gray gloomy weather we'd been having in the late winter kept it feeling almost timeless all day long. I'd begun to rely on my stomach to tell me the time of day and it was not a reliable indicator. Especially when I ate disproportionate amounts of food at one meal and none at the others.

Jan and Aja seemed surprised I was sitting in the truck waiting for them. I handed Aja the keys.

"It's your house."

She gave me a tentative smile. I knew she was nervous about what she was going to find. I felt confident that the house was in the same condition we'd left it. The locks were high quality and damn near unpickable even by the experts. It was why I had splashed out the extra cash on them. That and it wasn't my money. What did I care how much they cost? They were higher end than the ones we had at our place but we also had less expensive items to destroy or take and multiple reasons why a burglar would think twice about targeting our house.

Aja led us into the house, her shoulders tense. She swiveled her head to take in the foyer. Jan did the same thing, her hand hovering over her holster. Aw, she liked Aja too.

"Everything look cool?"

Aja nodded, her body posture relaxing. She smiled. "Yeah, it looks fine."

I remembered that her car had fared about as well as mine had the last time we were here together.

"Listen, about your car—"

"He did that at school. That's why I haven't been driving it."

"Oh."

I really had no other response. It was a baller move. It's not like the parking lots were ghost towns during the school day. They had a school resource officer and teachers that came and went. Buses flowed in and out of the lot at all hours for field trips and to make the circuits of the middle and elementary schools. Heck, kids came and went for appointments and I knew seniors could arrive late or leave early if their first or last class wasn't needed for graduation credit.

"So, um, why did you want to come?" She stood fidgeting with the keys and rolling out her ankle like she had the first night I met her. Christ, it hadn't even been a week.

"I was hoping you could help us with a case we're working." Jan frowned and I made the tiniest wait motion with my hands. "I need to see a teenage girl's bedroom."

Jan's frown disappeared. "Of course you do." She sounded incredulous.

"I can't go back to Mandy's bedroom but I can see Aja's; get a feel for her space."

Jan smiled and nodded. I felt an absurd amount of pleasure that she thought it was a good idea. I had problems with authority but I craved approval. I had a complicated psyche.

"Who's Mandy?"

And just like that Jan's smile disappeared. "She's a girl who's waited entirely too long for me to figure out what happened to her."

It wasn't just about closing an open case file. It was a personal failing to Jan. She was responsible to Mandy for a resolution. She was that kind of cop. We had that in common. Badge or no, I wouldn't stop until I got to the bottom of the case.

"Just like you're going to do for Damian, Detective Boyd?"

People really sucked, in general. As a group, you could count on them to do stupid, selfish, mean things. Individually, people were these amazing concoctions of deep generosity and bad ideas, staggering strength and breath-taking vulnerabilities, like every crayon in the box all melted into one pool where you could still see the separate colors.

"Exactly like she's going to do for Damian, kid. He did terrible things but he didn't deserve to die like he did. It's literally the principle that gets her out of bed every morning. She won't stop until she knows."

Jan had turned away after she explained about Mandy. When she turned back, her eyes were dry but red. She nodded. "Mandy and Damian."

Awesome. We were all girl-powered up with integrity and shit.

"Lead the way?" I motioned toward the basement stairs, but Aja led us upstairs. Okay, that was confusing. I was sure she slept in the basement. Had she told me that or had I just assumed it? I tried to think back and could not remember. I had been intent on listening to her story and then checking the house to make sure the little asshole—who'd been murdered, so I probably should stop thinking of him like that—hadn't found himself a hidey-hole that he was waiting to pop out of and go all The Call is Coming From Inside the House.

"The basement?" I was getting a little nervy going back to the upper floors of the house. My being-watched feeling from the other day returned in force and even Jan being with us didn't seem to cause it to abate.

Aja turned back while we wound our way up the curving staircase. "I crashed down there after the pillow thing. I figured it would be easier to get out from the basement. He'd never really been down there."

Plus, the whole space was a giant exercise in optical illusion where Aja would have home court advantage. I had to give the basement's all-black color scheme credit for, at least, being a good place for Aja to camouflage herself.

We'd reached the top of the stairs and went left down the narrow corridor between the open railing and the wall. I had gone down the hall on the other side of the opening of the staircase the last time. There was a door that I assumed had been a closet because it looked narrower than a regular room door, but that had been an optical illusion. Aja opened the door and entered but Jan hung back, leaving the doorway open for me to walk through.

"I thought I'd check out that loft space you mentioned. I haven't had the chance you've had to see the house and the effects of Damian Murphy's behavior here."

I followed Aja into her room and marveled at how different her official bedroom was from the basement where she'd been staying. Whites and pastels dominated. Soft charcoal drawings of flowers covered the walls. Her bed, a massive carved white wood four-poster affair was a fluffy mass of downy bedding and pillows. She had one wall of built-in bookcases jammed full of books, stuffed animals, and snow globes. It was a dream room for many girls.

Aja, her arms wrapped around her body, twisted back and forth. She was uncomfortable here or she was uncomfortable with me being here.

"It's pretty different from my room, huh?"

"A little," she said softly.

"It's really lovely. I'll be honest, it's not what I expected." I walked over to the nearest drawing. The ragged edge made it obvious it had been ripped from a notebook. They all had. Her name was in the corner of all the ones I could see. The dates varied, but there was nothing from the current year.

"You're really good, Aja. I've never been good at anything like you're good at drawing."

She sniffed and rubbed her sleeve under her nose. "You think I'm good?"

"Oh, kiddo, don't you know? Can't you see?" How could she not know? Her talent was literally on the wall for everyone to see. But who had been here to see? No one.

"I have an idea. Let's take some of these down and take them home with us. I'll bet my mom would love to see these."

She nodded. "Okay, so what do you need me to do to help you figure out what happened to Mandy?"

God, she tugged at my heart. A few days of anyone paying attention to her and the hard shell had just dissolved. Good. And it hadn't even taken that much. Just a few family dinners and some hardcore momming like only Nancy could mom. I couldn't ignore the prospect that knowing her tormentor wasn't ever going to bother her again helped a great deal. Looking at her room, I was starting to realize the transition to the black hair and heavy eye makeup had come at the same time as the transition from scrawny teen to bulked-up stalker was occurring in Damian. I knew why she had morphed from butterfly to emo girl. What had caused the change in Damian?

"Just talk to me about what you'd do in here? Drawing, I'd guess. Talking to friends? Doing your hair? Just regular Aja stuff."

She began to walk around the room pulling down pictures that looked random to me but I could see the consideration in her face as she chose. Once she'd gathered the pages she wanted, she started pointing out her favorite things and why they were where they were. She pointed out how some items could be seen from the bed or the chair that sat under the window, perfect for reading. She talked about the books she'd saved from when she was child.

I interrupted her recitation of her favorite books to ask her if she'd like to bring some of them back with her. Her eyes got big.

"I should leave them here since I'm only going to be at your house for a little bit longer, right?"

"I don't know if Mom is ready to let go of you just yet. She gets attached easily."

Aja seemed to grow a little larger. "Okay. So I definitely need this one and this one." She kept up a running narration as she stacked books in her arms. If I wasn't careful it was going to be me who wouldn't be able to let go of Aja when it came time. Gone was the hard girl with the go-to-hell attitude; in her place was an earnest child who drew flowers and had four copies of *Harry Potter and the Philosopher's Stone*, different editions that I was assured were all critical to her emotional well-being.

"Maybe we should get you another bag to bring this stuff back with us," I said.

She set the books down on the chair and opened her closet. I walked over and peered in behind her. There hadn't been any pictures of Mandy's closet. Why? Because it hadn't been part of the immediate crime scene? Clothes hung neatly, cute stuff that seemed more in style with the pastel room and flower pictures. I saw Aja run her hand down a few dresses. She was obviously longing to get back to who she'd been before. What was holding her back? Worry about bringing too much back with her? I decided then to make Ben take my truck to school the next day and subtly convince Aja to get whatever she wanted. She deserved to be herself. She hadn't done anything wrong.

Being in her room with her helped me understand Aja better. It didn't give me as much insight to Mandy as I'd have liked, but I was sure that the killer was someone she knew and trusted. A person's room reflected their true nature. Aja's was, mine was, Mandy's would have been too. You didn't invite people you didn't trust to view your true self. There had been no signs of disarray, no violent altercation. There was just that small amount of blood on the corner of the night-stand. It had been a shove or fall; that was all it took. The fire was the coverup. It might not have been murder at the beginning. Once that fire was set though … Once the person tried to cover it up instead of calling 911 for help, it became murder.

None of that cleared or incriminated the brother, though I understood why Jan had just those two people as suspects. Most murders were committed by someone the victim knew—usually a family member or romantic partner. And women were predominantly murdered by their husbands or boyfriends. Those were the facts. Brother and boyfriend, neither with an alibi that could be confirmed. I opened the file and flipped through the pages for their alibis. Nothing.

I heard a knock and looked up. Jan stood in the doorway.

"How's it going in here? Did you get what you needed, Willa?"

I nodded. "Yes and no. I wanted to get a feel for a teen girl in her room. Who she'd let in, who she wouldn't, how it was set up, what she had, how she treated what was important to her."

"Uh, you were a teen girl. How come you don't know what one's room would be like?" Aja asked.

I could dodge the question with some excuse about being old now or I could tell her the truth and deal with the discomfort that came with people feeling sorry for me. I dodged.

"Oh, sweetie, I needed to see a *normal* girl's room." I winked at her. She laughed and went back to packing up the suitcase she'd dragged out of the closet.

Jan didn't laugh. She just looked at me, her head tilted slightly, like she was trying to decide something. "Let's wrap it up here. I promised Nancy you two would be home for dinner."

CHAPTER

13

WE WERE HOME IN time for Aja to be put to work helping with the salad. I got a pass to take a shower and change into clean clothes. Nancy's subtle suggestion was that maybe I needed to think about getting some new, more professional clothes. She was right, as usual. I took a quick shower and dressed as tidily as I could in jeans and a t-shirt then headed upstairs.

They must have missed the whine of the step because Nancy and Aja were talking about me when I hit the top of the stairs. Chopping sounds erratically clicked through under the words. I stood at the top of the stairs eavesdropping, like a good detective does.

"No, I don't know that I'd use the word *normal* for Willa, either. She's so much more than normal." Moms rock.

"Yeah, but it was weird. I thought it was just a joke until I saw this look that Detective Boyd gave her. It was kind of sad and kind of proud at the same time."

"Okay, this isn't exactly a secret but it's not something we talk about all that much. When Willa was little before she came to live with her dad, they didn't have a lot of money. Acting is a really rough living. They were always moving as Leila chased work. They moved a lot. One day while they were at the theater they got locked out of the apartment because Leila hadn't paid the rent for … a while. The landlord put their stuff out on the street and when they got home most of it was gone. Including a baby quilt Arch's grandmother made when Willa was born."

"Oh no," Aja said.

I pressed my head against the wall. It was shitty having a seventeen-year-old pity me.

"Willa loves her mother and she's too loyal to admit it, but she's never forgiven her for that. Willa's mee-maw had died earlier in the year and Leila wouldn't let her fly to South Carolina for the funeral because Arch couldn't afford to fly both of them. So … anyway, it wasn't too long after that Willa decided she wanted to live with her dad."

"How old was she?"

"Not quite ten. Arch and I were engaged then. She had some birthday and Christmas money saved and put herself on a bus headed east. Leila was in a panic when she called Arch to tell him about the note Willa had left her."

"That's so horrible. She was just a little kid."

"Sweetheart, Willa has never been a little kid. That's what I'm trying to tell you. Chronologically, yes, but emotionally, no."

"I guess she got here okay. I mean, obvi."

"Arch lived at that bus station until she arrived two days later. She said she'd stuck close to a woman and I guess everyone assumed they were together. We got this story as she sat at the table eating. Her little legs didn't reach the floor, and it took everything in me not to cry in front of her."

I heard her sniffle and I fought back my own tears.

"The next day Arch started searching for the perfect house for us and we've all been here ever since. She's lived here with us almost twice as long as she lived that crazy nomad life with Leila, but she's never really put down roots. I guess once she lost that quilt she decided that she couldn't count on things being hers. She has things, but nothing special that she could lose. It's why losing Michael hit her so hard, I think."

I heard a throat clear quietly and saw Dad standing in the opening between the dining room and living room. I knew he'd heard it all too. I shook my head. Nancy would feel bad that I'd heard them and worry about my feelings. I slipped back down the stairs halfway and made a big production of coming up.

Aja was setting the table when I walked into the breakfast room and she avoided looking at me. I breezed past her to turn the L into the kitchen proper, where Nancy stood tossing the bowl of salad. She too avoided eye contact.

"What's for dinner?" Dad asked, coming in through the doorway from the dining room. It was choreographed to seem like we were arriving at the same time by chance. We were well-practiced at it.

"Um, chicken, brown rice, salad, and green beans," Nancy replied, focused intently on the salad bowl. Sheesh, maybe I should have given them extra time to compose themselves. I made a face at Dad to convey my uncertainty. He gave me a slight nod then dropped his eyebrows. Excellent. He was going to take care of it.

"Shoot. I forgot to wash my hands. I'll be back." I fled the room for the office's bathroom and heard Dad muttering behind me. Then he was practically on my heels, racing me for the office door on the other side of the dining room.

When we were alone we started talking over each other.

"I thought you were dealing with them," I said.

"I thought you were going to get them off on a different subject," he said.

"What subject was that? Our scintillating menu?"

"Don't you have a case you can talk about? I know you're working with Jan," he replied.

"Yes, I have the murder of a teen girl from almost twenty years ago and Aja's ex-boyfriend slash former-stalker's beating death from a few days ago. Which do you feel will sufficiently lighten the mood?"

I glared at him while he stared back at me, confused. "Good point."

"I suppose I could talk about my stakeout waiting to get the goods on a cheater at a sleazy motel," I said. "Maybe you'd like me to tell that story so Mom and I could both get angry with you again. Or I could bring up Seth being adopted and you knowing and not telling him or me."

I heard a bark from behind the closed door. I opened it to find the family assembled. Apparently Ben had wandered into the kitchen when his stomach's timer had gone off, having heard me and Dad talking.

"Dinner's on the table," Mom said.

"Be right there," Dad said.

I left with them while he stayed behind in the office. Maybe he really did need to wash his hands. I'd just showered so I felt mine were clean enough for eating. We were all finished distributing the food onto our plates when he finally arrived. He placed a file folder next to my plate and sat down in his spot to my left.

"You can decide what to do with that information, Willa."

I left it sitting where he'd placed it. Mom was pretty loose with us talking about work while eating, but I knew she'd be upset if I buried my face into paperwork. We kept conversation light, mostly about what Ben and Aja were doing in school and the college acceptance process. Ben had heard back about all his applications and had been accepted by all the colleges he'd applied to, naturally. Aja had her acceptances from her top two choices but couldn't decide. She'd asked me how I'd chosen where I attended and I'd answered honestly that I went to the only school that accepted me—Mason. I told her a bit about Michael's deliberations. She was interested in him and our history. It was, as far as awkward dinners go, enjoyable enough.

Ben volunteered to clean up with Dad so I took my folder downstairs and locked myself in my room. I got comfortable on the bed before opening it. I was curious but stalling because I was nervous about what the folder contained. I was right to be nervous. The three single pages in the folder told a whole story. One page each for Michael and Seth's birth certificates with parents' names. The third page was a death certificate that had been issued by the Arizona Department of Corrections for the man on the birth certificates.

"Dammit, Dad."

———

I woke up after a night of fitful sleep. Those three pieces of paper weighed less than an ounce, yet the information on them was a burden so heavy I could barely stand to think of it. I stumbled up the stairs vowing to buy a coffeemaker for the basement. I could hole up down there and avoid my family entirely.

Through the open front door, I saw Aja and Ben's bus pulling away from the curb with my mother waving goodbye from the porch. A senior in high school and she still watched him wait for the bus. I could only imagine the sadness she'd feel on the first day of school next year when there was no bus to watch for anymore. It probably wouldn't feel as bad as it would if you learned your biological father was a violent criminal who'd died in prison.

My father stood in front of the coffee pot. He had a cup he'd clearly just prepared if the steam wafting off it was any indicator. Even sleep-deprived I was a master detective. I got a cup down from the cabinet and moved to the pot, but Dad didn't budge.

"We should talk," he said.

"We *should* talk. If you'd like me to be coherent, you might want to step aside."

He moved enough so that I could reach the pot and pour myself a cup. He was stubbornly stuck against the counter, giving me enough space to access the pot and nothing else. I had to ask him to move twice more to get the sugar and half and half from the fridge. Mom had come in while we'd bantered about access to the pot but watched the exchange in silence. Finally he sat at the table and I joined him. If he thought a night's sleep—assuming you could call two hours a night's sleep—was going to have changed my mood toward him, he was very much mistaken. I would have been annoyed enough without the bombshell those three pages had contained.

"What do you think?" he asked.

"What do I think about you keeping the secret of Michael and Seth's parentage from me … and him? Or what do I think about you deciding, once you'd been found out, that you were going to dump the information in that folder on me at the dinner table? Please clarify."

"Oh, honey. I know you're upset—" my mother started to say.

"Their biological father was a violent felon who died in prison serving a thirty-year sentence for rape and mutilation of his victims."

Nancy's hand flew to her mouth.

"You knew I'd look it up, Dad. You didn't even warn me what I was going to find. I have to decide what to do with that information? Are you serious? My choices are don't tell Seth and live with him possibly finding out that I knew or telling him. Those are not choices, Dad."

"Yeah, they are, Will. They're just not good ones, but that's life. That's love. Making hard choices to do the best thing for the person you love." He was looking at Mom over my shoulder when he said that.

This was the thing he wanted to use to give me some kind of lesson about love? Was he nuts?

"Arch, this isn't fair. She's right. You can't ask her to take this on. Seth's parents need to be the ones to tell him something like this," Mom said.

I didn't know if that was a better choice of who to hear this from, but I knew I didn't want to do it. Not that it mattered who told him. If Seth was going to go off the rails because of this, he was going off the rails no matter what.

"I have to be the one to tell him. I'm the only person he trusts now."

Dad nodded. "Exactly, Will."

Dammit. I hated it when he was right. I mean, I didn't hate it when he was right most of the time but it would have been good right now.

Seth deserved to know the information and he deserved to hear it from me, someone who loved him enough to put themselves second. That was love.

I put the mug down and rubbed my eyes. "What do I say ... I mean, how ... ?"

My mother put her arms around me. "You don't do it now. You wait until he's home. You deal with the discord from him going off without telling you first. This information isn't going to change in the meantime."

She was right, of course. Kicking the can down the road made sense.

"Willa, he's going to be mad that you looked into it behind his back. Make it clear that I found it after Barbara and the Colonel came to us. He can be mad at me. I can take it. Then he knows he can trust you."

Oh, the irony of us worrying about him trusting me considering his Casper act at the moment. But they were right. I had time and Seth needed to trust me of all people. I was pretty much the only one he had left.

"What about the woman?" I couldn't call her his mother.

"No current info on her that I could find. I've got skip traces scrolling for any mention of her but she dropped off the radar about five years ago. No one that I contacted, old neighbors, coworkers, knew what had happened to her."

"So she's alive and off the grid. Good. At least for the time being. One mess at a time."

I picked the mug up and took a swallow. The coffee was surprisingly still extremely hot. It felt like ages since I'd poured it, though it hadn't even been five minutes.

"Let me make you breakfast, sweetie," my mother said.

"That'd be great, dear," Dad said.

"You can have cereal, Archibald."

Looked like Dad was in the dog house. Dog. Where the hell was Fargo? In all the stress, I'd forgotten all about her.

Mom noticed my sudden searching gaze. "Adam came by and took Fargo for a long run. He said he'd take good care of her." My mother always knew what her kids were thinking. It was kind of eerie.

I tried to enjoy the eggs and bacon she made me. I knew the food was delicious, but my stomach roiled from the knowledge I was failing to put to the back of my mind.

Nancy rubbed my back. "It'll take some time, hon. You're still processing."

Still processing, indeed.

———

I was showered and sitting cross-legged on the basement floor arranging and rearranging the photos when my father clomped down the stairs. I invited him to sit with me and offer any thoughts he had about how to look at the information in a different way. I would get credit for my work with Jan and the FCPD but, technically, he was still the supervising investigator for my apprenticeship.

"Is this all Jan gave you?"

"No, I have the autopsy file and the evidence log. She held back her notes and the witness statements. Said she wanted my eye and my own interview notes without hers intruding."

He nodded. "It's not a bad idea. Show me how you've been working the photos."

I handed him several of the copies of the log with each item of evidence highlighted and my handwritten notes on which photos showed the item.

"Good thinking. Take each item and look at it separately within its context in the scene only. Are you making any progress?"

I took the pages back from him and stacked them back on the piles of photos where they went. "Maybe. I don't know. It's why I wanted to go to Aja's yesterday; see how she lived in the room, how she moved amongst her things, give myself some idea of how to build the scene and the vic's movement through the scene. Like a movie. Then running the movie backwards from the moment she hit that nightstand."

"It's clever. Would the witness statements help with that?"

I shook my head. "No one was home with her in the hours before she died. Her mom was shopping ... Black Friday with the receipts to prove it. The brother said he was visiting a bunch of different friends but he can't be sure about the times he was at any given house and neither can any of them. Best friend hadn't even seen her in months." At this odd look, I added, "College."

"Okay, well the brother's story is totally legitimate and would leave him under suspicion."

"He's one of two suspects Jan had. Him and the boyfriend."

"Just the two?"

"No one else fit any of the usual criteria. The victim and the brother had been fighting the day before and hadn't been getting along in the months before. The boyfriend ... well, he was the boyfriend."

"Friends? An ex?"

"Nope, she had only arrived home a few days before. She was going to be catching up with friends that afternoon. You know, if she'd survived to see it."

"And your interviews with them?"

"Nothing. I can't see any of them killing her. It's so frustrating."

He got up, slowly. I could empathize. Getting up off the floor was a chore for me and I was thirty years younger and had better knees.

"Here's a thought. You've been looking at what's there in context. Maybe look for what's there out of context."

What in the hell was that supposed to mean? I had no idea, but the man had been solving crimes longer than I'd been alive so it must be good advice. What's there but out of context? I knew what was there. I had a list. But the list wasn't everything in the room. What was there but wasn't there? What was out of the context of the evidence in the murder?

I grabbed a sticky and started making notes of what I saw in the photos but wasn't on the evidence log. I started putting them on the back of the photos, in some cases overlapping there were so many items. I was going to need a master list. And some lunch. It was going to be a long day.

I hadn't realized I'd dozed off until my phone woke me to the darkening sky through the slider. It was the alarm company with an alert to a breech at Aja's house. The back door into the basement, the operator informed me and did I wish for the police to be called? You bet your ass I did. With one hand, I texted Jan to meet me there as I shoved my feet into boots and grabbed my jacket.

I called for Aja as I hurried up the stairs. She met me at the top of the stairs.

"Is there any reason someone would be at your house?"

She shook her head, eyes big, lip in between her teeth.

"I'll be back. Text anyone you think might have tried to visit you to double check, okay? If you find someone who said they stopped by, call me immediately."

"What's going on?"

I didn't want to worry her, but I didn't want to lie either. "The alarm company just called to let me know the basement slider alarm has been set off. I'm going to meet the black-and-white."

"But...if Damian's dead, who tried to break in?" Aja asked.

My guess? The masked man.

CHAPTER

14

Shattered glass and soil littered the floor of the basement surrounding an upended planter.

"They had to have been strong. It's not one of those foam ones made to look real." Jan gave me an exasperated look and I held up my gloved hands. "I gave it one poke to see and I have on gloves. I'm not an idiot."

"It had to have been loud too, but Mr. Busybody said he and his yappy dog were watching *Jeopardy*," Jan said.

"You've been over twice now. You see a wife either time? I mean, he could have killed her and stuffed her in one of those big freezers. Won't our faces be red if he sells that house and goes on the lam before the new owners find her trussed up like a Thanksgiving turkey."

"Don't you have enough cases on your hands right now, Pennington? And, yes, I saw the wife. Her cookies aren't as good your neighbor Susan's."

Nobody's were. They needed to come back from California. I wasn't at all enjoying their new plans to winter in sunny climes. I missed the cookies, sure, but they'd been over more often in the wake of my injuries accumulated in pursuit of the killer I'd stumbled over during their granddaughter's case. It had been like when Ben and I were younger and they'd acted as surrogate grandparents. It was nice for them that their relationship with their son was repaired in the wake of all they'd done for his daughter, Violet, though.

Wayward parents and daughters reminded me of Aja. And the question of the hour: If Damian Murphy was lying in a tray in the county coroner's office twenty miles away and we weren't seriously considering zombie apocalypse, then who in the hell had picked up a planter that weighed at least forty pounds and flung it through a glass door hard enough to shatter the door and launch the planter a good five feet into the room?

"No drag marks from its previous location on the patio, which is ten feet from the door?"

"Easily. And since we know it's real, it wasn't picked up and used as a battering ram. It was thrown."

We stared at one another. *Strong* was an understatement. The person had to be really built up to be able to pick up that planter, carry it close enough, then gather the extra force needed to throw it.

"Damian's physical transformation is making more sense, huh? Dimes to dollars the coroner finds steroids in his system."

"Makes sense. Wait, dimes to dollars? Is that another one of your grandfather's sayings?"

"What do you think?" I squatted down to view how far the glass and dirt had spread into the room. "Y'all have some kind of program that can calculate the force and velocity?"

Jan shrugged. "Considering this isn't a television show, I'm going to have to say probably not."

"That would have been cool."

"We already know the person had to be extremely strong. The exact strength it would take seems unnecessary."

"No, but it would still be cool."

Ugh. All the talk of calculus must have infected me.

"The uniforms cleared the rest of the house, right? I'd like to take a look," I said. I was dying to take the gloves off. They were itchy and my hands were hot.

"Yeah, let's take a look around. They said there was some ransacking."

I tried the knob to the other half of the basement space and found it locked. I made a note to ask Aja if that was the way she left it.

"At least we'll have an idea if anything is missing. I mean, I won't know if some painting was expensive or a statute is historically significant, but I'll notice the space," I said.

"Aja's parents have to be notified, you know? We have to do it now."

I started up the stairs to the main floor. "I know. I told her. She's freaked out about the break-in but seems unfazed that her parents are going to be called."

"She's a smart girl. She's probably worried that Damian Murphy wasn't her stalker."

We reached the foyer, lights out, and I kicked myself for leaving my flashlight in my kit in the truck. I slid my feet along the floor to make sure I wasn't going to trip over anything and made it halfway to the door when the wall was illuminated in a beam. The circle of light located the switch panel and held steady until I'd flipped on all five switches. At least Jan had her tools with her. I walked to the other side of the door and turned on all the outside lights. With the black-and-whites leaving, I wanted to make it abundantly clear that the building was still occupied.

Burglars sometimes came back after triggering alarms. Sometimes they triggered them on purpose, waited for the cops to come and clear the location after seeing nothing and then proceed to make entry. Stealing shit was just so much easier when the cops had already told everyone that nothing was wrong. Whoever had the ability to heave that planter wasn't someone I wanted to run into. Not since he'd probably beaten Damian Murphy to death.

"Split up?" Jan asked.

Gulp. I didn't think there was a way to say no without looking like a scaredy cat so I nodded. I stripped off my right-hand glove and shoved back my jacket, unsnapping my holster. I watched Jan stroll into the formal dining room with its plush carpet and acre-like polished wood table. The gun was a reassuring weight in my hand. I didn't feel any less scared, but I was at least more prepared. My dad always said being brave wasn't not being afraid but being afraid and doing something anyway.

I reminded myself that the uniforms had cleared the place. I just hoped they'd done as good of a job as I would have with Jan Boyd on the way. Up the winding staircase I went for the third time in a week. The bright lights from the foyer and first floor followed me only so far. As I got to the top, deep shadows slashed the walls. I took the turn to the right, heading toward Aja's room and losing almost all the light. There didn't seem to be a hall light switch accessible from that side, so I pressed my back against the wall and leveled the gun at the wall.

My stomach fluttered and I stopped my advance to take a few steadying breaths. There was something about this house that had my panic button on a hair trigger. I reminded myself that the uniforms swept for an intruder, knowing that other cops were going to be wandering around with the expectation they were safe. I mean, Fairfax County wasn't exactly Beirut or Saigon in the seventies, but there was sweep protocol for a reason. I just wish it was done with every light in the joint blazing and not flashlights.

I continued inching toward Aja's room, a trickle of sweat rolling down my spine. My armpits were damp and cold, another sure sign panic was creeping up on me. I reached inside the open door and turned the light on. Breaking the first rule my training officer had drilled into me, I stepped into the doorway without looking first. I only realized it after I'd done it. I was well and truly spooked and that was causing me to rush.

Luckily, there was no one in the room who wanted me dead or otherwise incapacitated. In fact, there was no one in the room at all. It wasn't in disarray and the only missing items I noticed were the ones she'd taken with her the day before.

I heard a scuffling noise at the door and jumped, whipping my gun up. Jan stared at me, startled.

"Dammit, Pennington, I've been hollering 'clear' at you for the past five minutes. Didn't you hear me?"

I lowered the gun, engaging the safety as I did. It had been five minutes since I'd started up the stairs. How long had I taken to make it down the hall from the stairs to Aja's room?

"Sorry, the house is so spread out and with this room tucked back here … ." The excuse sounded lame to my own ears so I could only imagine what Jan thought of it.

"We should have held at least two unis at the scene. This place is too big for just the two of us to sweep and secure."

I nodded. "This room is clear. Nothing moved or taken that I can tell, and I got a pretty good look last night. If there was a search, it was professional and that breach in the basement was anything but."

Jan nodded. "I agree."

The two of us searched the remaining room on the floor together. Jan remarked that she'd thought a house that size would have more bedrooms. I mentioned that I was sure they'd had it customized. Nothing seemed amiss anywhere we'd looked, which meant that if the uniforms had seen signs of burglary beyond the basement, it was in the attic loft space.

Jan waved me up first and I knew she was remembering me pulling a gun on her a few moments before. This way if someone got shot in the face it was going to be an intruder and not her. It was a smart strategy from every standpoint except paperwork. My nerves stayed down knowing Jan was at my back and I made it up the stairs without a *why the hell are you taking so long* poke from the flashlight. We hit the top and swung the flashlight over the space.

Ransacked was one word for the condition of the room. Our mystery guest had hulked out on the room. Even the daybed was flipped. That thing probably weighed as much as the planter.

I turned on the overhead light to see the full extent of the damage.

"Jesus, how could he have done so much damage in such a short time?" She flipped open her notebook to consult the times. "Twenty minutes from the moment he slung that planter to the first cop stepping through the opening. He got up here like he knew exactly where he was going and then tossed this room like a grenade had gone off."

The scant furniture in the room had all been tossed around. Holes were punched and kicked straight through the drywall. Even the carpet and underlay had massive slashes in them, ripped open to expose the subfloor near the outside wall.

"He was looking for something. He knew exactly where to come and he was pissed that it wasn't here," I said.

"Something worth enough for him to beat Damian Murphy to death," Jan said.

Good for me, I'd made the same assumption Jan had. Take that, house search jitters.

"And Damian screwed him over."

"Or Damian screwed Aja over. He may have sent the guy here knowing *it* wouldn't be here but Aja would. His last bit of revenge."

Or Damian hadn't cared enough either way. The more I found out about him, the less sad I was that he'd gotten himself beaten to death. The only part of his demise I was starting to regret was that I hadn't gotten to him first.

Jan's phone went off.

"Crime scene's here. Let's let them do their thing. I've got some stuff for you in the car anyway." She looked at the gun still in my hand. "You can holster that now, you know."

———

I found that the pictures had been picked up off the floor and a long, folding table sat in the same spot, neat stacks lining the far edge. Thank god I didn't have to spend another moment sitting on the floor. It had gotten to the point that all I had to do was think about working the case and my back would start hurting. Not that I thought about much else.

The snitch step squealed and I saw Aja standing in panda pajamas at the bottom of the stairs, Fargo at her feet.

"Hey, pretty girl." I knelt down and the dog came at me so fast she knocked us both over. Another reason she wasn't cut out for law enforcement work—she loved too hard. It worked just fine for me though.

Aja hadn't moved. That *screw you* expression back on her face. Unless she was mad at me, and I couldn't imagine why but I pissed off a lot of people without knowing it so it was possible, she was upset about her parents.

"Why aren't you in bed, Aja? You have school tomorrow, right? It's a weekday, isn't it?"

I honestly didn't know what day of the week it was. The days had slid into one another like I was back on the painkillers again. Cases were like that for me. And with the cold case and the stalking/break-ins and Damian Murphy's murder, my brain was extra full.

"My parents will be here tomorrow."

"Excellent. They should be here to support you."

She walked to the table and tried to rifle the pile of photos but I put my hand on her wrist, stilling her motions. "You don't want to see those."

She planted her hands on her hips, attitude coming off her in waves, like she was ready to fight. "Maybe I do. Maybe I want to be a cop like you."

Like she was ready to fight … a fight. I had danced around that earlier when I was running and thinking, but there was a way to find out. We knew Mandy hadn't been in a fight because there were no defensive wounds, but had Damian fought back? Had his knuckles been bruised?

171

"Aja, we'll get back to being a cop later but now I need you to think for me. Damian ... the last time you saw him, what had he looked like?"

She stopped rubbing Fargo's head and looked at me. "Looked how? I told you he was working out more, he'd gotten really built."

"Yeah, but was he bruised up like he'd been in a fight or something?"

She nodded.

Anabolic steroid use jacked up the normal testosterone. Testosterone, what Adam and I had joked was the stupidity hormone, was already at messy, mood-swing levels in teenage boys. Then we packed them all together in small rooms, sat them at desks, forced them to read instead of letting them out on the basketball court or football field to get out the energy and caveman tendencies. I'd been an idiot to forget that. Damian had been possessive, threatening, breaking into Aja's house, destroying her things, dominating the weak, so there was no way he wasn't going to react physically and violently if someone pissed him off.

I held up a finger asking for a minute while I dug out my phone.

DID DAMIAN'S BODY SHOW DEFENSIVE WOUNDS OR THE SIGNS THAT HE'D BEEN A FIGHT?

Jan would get back to me when she had information from the coroner.

"So you want to be a cop, huh?"

Where the hell had that come from? Was she under the impression that this was all just some extended career-day presentation? It wasn't as if I had put some sexy, movie-PI gloss on it. She had gotten the no-sleep, busted-windshield, family-fight version so I was pretty sure she didn't mean it. She was frustrated and scared, looking for an outlet. She just looked at me belligerently.

172

"Fair enough. You want to be a cop, then your first step is to declare Criminal Justice as your major. I'd take Psychology too because it comes in handy dealing with the spitting angry guy you've just pulled over in his more money than sense, midlife crisis sports car going ninety down the parkway trying to impress a girl young enough to be his daughter."

She giggled. That was better.

"Seriously, kid, you don't want to be me. You've got brains to spare. Do something good with your life that doesn't involve chasing the people who cut corners."

She fidgeted. "Ben says you solved a murder last fall."

"I did. Along with Jan ... Detective Boyd, that is, and another friend. It was most definitely a team effort, eventually."

"That's cool."

"Even with help, it wasn't easy, Aja. I hit a lot of brick walls. The friend, Seth, he didn't want me involved. He wanted me safe at home while he did it all single-handed. Sometimes people are like that. I'm like that. This job can do that to you."

"I know."

But she didn't know. She felt small and scared and thought taking charge and being the person tracking down clues would make her feel safe and strong.

"Do you? Because I think you see this family and it's not like the one you have. And with your parents coming back, that might be pretty appealing. You saw the pictures of what happened to me. Is that really what you want your life to look like?"

She bit her lip. If this was being a mentor, I sucked at it. Royally. Like I could win an award at sucking at it. Then it hit me.

"Just so I'm clear, you're a part of this family now. You don't need to be a cop or a PI. You can just be Aja, okay?"

She flung her arms around me and I stiffened for a second then wrapped my arms around her, feeling the bones of her rib cage, nubby under her pajama top. Just as quickly as she'd hugged me, she darted back up the stairs.

Mentor I wasn't great at, but I had big sister nailed. And I had a long night ahead of me with the full file notes Jan had just handed over plus the case files on Damian Murphy's murder and the break-in at Aja's.

A long, long night.

After my third trip upstairs for coffee replenishing I vowed to go to the box store in the morning and get a single-serve coffeemaker and mini fridge for the basement. Those were items I could take with me when I moved out eventually but would make working cases easier when I needed to not share a small space with my dad.

I had finally finished the photo array project of marking what was there but wasn't there—aka the crap in the room no one considered evidence at the time. I had most of the furniture and closet items and a can of soda on the desk. The desk sat on the opposite side of the room from the crime scene and while a date book had been logged the can had not. It was unopened and it had likely been written off as something Mandy had brought down intending to drink. Still, it was there and even if it didn't have official evidentiary value it was a part of the whole.

I slid over to the middle of the table and picked up the file on Damian Murphy. I flipped past my own witness statement and picked up Aja's reading it over twice before I took a highlighter and started pulling out the sentences that had to do with his transformation from regular artsy kid to muscle-bound stalker. Someone at the FCPD technical unit had accessed Damian's social media and I used

Aja's statement as a timeline to match up the photos, working out what looked like his physical progression.

My phone showed it was four thirty. Adam had been up for thirty minutes if he wasn't shining me when he said he got up at four every morning to meditate and, blech, ground himself. It was wrong to be judgmental of his new age-y approach to mornings, especially considering my process was to throw cold water onto me and coffee into me until I resembled something close to human whereas he was a successful business owner with two percent body fat who'd taken my dog out for a day of frolicking and left me a nice note when he returned her.

Ugh! The guy was annoyingly perfect. Kind, ripped, hot in a Muppet/refrigerator/bear kind of way.

He'd said thirty minutes to meditate, which meant he was making his crazy buttered coffee at four thirty and change.

"Hello?" Theo, Adam's husband answered my call. Also kind, ripped, and hot but in a decidedly *prettier than anyone human had a right to be* kind of way; his face fine-boned but masculine, the exact opposite of Adam's. Also an early riser and he made a killer brisket. Like, slap your mother good. I wish I were kidding, but I would seriously slap both of my mothers for it.

"Hey, Theo, sorry to call so early. I have no manners."

"Nonsense. You know we're always up at this hour." God, the voice on the man. It was just not fair. I was starting to realize I had a thing for voices. Hands too. Fatigue was making me loopy.

"Of course, you've probably run five miles and made a soufflé already."

He chuckled. "Six miles and it's eclairs today."

Man, I really loved them. Adam made sure I was in top fighting form and Theo plied me with food.

I heard Theo call out for Adam like a four-thirty in the morning phone call was totally normal. My phone rings at that hour and I'm out of the bed and on my feet arming myself before I even get a "what" out. If I managed to make it to the point that a pre-dawn call didn't engender panic, I could maybe get to "hello" like a decent human person.

"Hey, Will. Good morning."

"I'd like to send you some pictures and see if you can confirm for me that a guy was taking steroids."

I heard him draw in his breath sharply. Adam and Theo weren't exactly *my body is my temple* kind of guys—the brisket and soufflés and eclairs would have made that impossible—but they were definitely *steroids are bad and if you want muscles, apply lots of hard work* kind of guys.

"I'm happy to help you, Willa, but can you bring him in?"

I blamed the excessive not sleeping for that mistake. "No, the guy is … not with us anymore."

"So I guess there's no way I can talk him out of taking them anymore?"

I felt like crap. Adam always wanted to help. I should have seen that coming.

"No, but you can help me figure out what he was involved in and maybe that will lead me to who he was involved with and that might ultimately lead to who killed him."

"He was killed?"

"He was beaten. Probably by someone who was also using steroids."

And right on cue …. "You know, not that I don't want to help you, but Seth can probably tell too. We've both seen enough of steroid abuse to pick it out from a few clues."

"Seth is, uh, off on special assignment at the moment."

Adam was a smart guy, he'd pick up on the vagueness I'd just thrown at him.

"Huh. Okay, well, I'm happy to help. Do you want to come over now?"

I desperately wanted to drive right over knowing that Theo was likely already baking and the thought of warm eclairs was making drool puddle in my mouth. However, I was in no condition to be on the road, especially in the dark.

"Brunch? I need more time than you do to look presentable. Plus I've been up all night, so who knows how long it will take to be coherent enough to drive."

"You've been up all night?" As if both of us were reading from a script, Adam's mama bear tendencies kicked in.

"I'll be fine. I've been sleeping when I lie down at night but I've got two, two and a half cases right now."

"Two and a half? Willa, I know you think you can get by without sleep, but it's terrible for your central nervous system."

The reminder that a body acts funny when its deprived of rest made me realize that my eye had been twitching for hours. One of those supremely frustrating micro-spasms designed to make you willing to do anything to get it to go away. Everything except put down the paperwork and go to bed like a normal person. But I wasn't normal. I was a detective and there were two people dead.

Logic told me they'd still be dead even if I got a full night's sleep, but my sense of justice told me that was another night two murderers were sleeping in comfortable beds when they should be sleeping in prison. It didn't take two guesses to figure out which thought process I always indulged.

"I know. I just ... there are people who deserve answers, Adam. I'm just wired wrong, I guess."

He sighed. "Oh, Will, I've never met anybody wired more right. I'll see you later. Please get some sleep."

I disconnected the call and felt a wave of fatigue wash over me. Fargo hadn't stirred from her spot on the floor next to me the whole conversation, but her doggie ESP kicked in when I started to contemplate lying down next to her. She got up and stretched her body for a moment before trotting over to the couch and leaping up. Circling at the foot, she then laid down and stared at me with her head on her paws. An hour or two on the couch wouldn't kill me. So I followed and, wriggling my feet under her, fell asleep within moments.

CHAPTER

15

ADAM AND THEO'S HOUSE was a well-kept post-WWII bungalow settled in a gentrified neighborhood full of other ridiculously good-looking couples and families. It was like the whole area was a set for the Young, Successful, and Good-Looking movie series. I felt bad dragging my unkempt ass into the place and ruining the aesthetic.

Theo greeted me at the door wearing an apron over his (inappropriately named) wife-beater and khaki cargo pants. He was the work from home half of the couple, with a crazy successful blog and social media empire in the making. Cornering the Hot Guy Baking market without even trying, Theo made his baked goods on-camera unapologetically and drew in every demographic. He was literally the marketing unicorn.

He gave me a hug and ushered me inside. The house smelled amazing, like always, and I vowed again (a vow I knew I'd break) to become more proficient in the kitchen. It seemed to provide Theo with a calm oasis in the midst of any turmoil that might go on in the outside world.

Every flat surface was covered with pastry shells. Dozens upon dozens. They looked picture perfect to me, but I knew Theo evaluated and discarded a piece based on some criteria I didn't understand.

"Adam has brunch ready for you two in the dining room." He wandered off back to the kitchen, a ding marking his perfect timing.

I wandered through the tiny living room. The house was really not designed for two muscle-bound men over six feet tall, but it never seemed to bother them. They liked the place and the neighborhood, not noticing how the architecture or the almost-dollhouse sized furniture seemed dwarfed by their bodies. Adam's commute alone must have been annoying but he never complained.

The table was laid with delicate china and crystal that I knew was not for my benefit. Had they set out plates and glasses more consistent with their guests, there would have been red plastic cups and paper plates. Adam was placing the finishing touches on a small round, glass bowl of daisies and I marveled, not for the first time and hopefully not for the last, at how both men seemed to know everything about their friends. I could have told you Theo's favorite color or the football team Adam rooted for, but I was a detective. It was my gig to look for that kind of stuff. For the record, Dresden blue, which I'd had to look up to find the name for the exact shade, and the Panthers. You should be impressed.

Two plates loaded with steaming veggie omelets and whole grain toast sat across from one another and the drool returned to pool in my mouth. I hadn't eaten anything except a sleeve of saltines, one of the small ones, since dinner the previous night. I'd have been willing to bet that if the meal had been scientifically analyzed, it would be found to be exactly the perfect percentages of lean protein, vegetables, and carbs. A meal designed to combat, in some small way, all the bad habits both men knew I indulged in regularly—too much caffeine and sugar, not enough sleep or water. Not that I was complaining. Free food expertly prepared by a professional chef who looked like a male model? Please and thank you.

Adam and I chatted about innocuous topics while we ate. Theo practicing the narration for his latest video was a pleasant hum interrupted occasionally by the kitchen timer's ding. He'd begin filming after Adam left for classes at the dojo. They had it worked out to a science and that made me jealous. Seth and I couldn't figure out how to coexist long enough to watch a movie without fighting and they managed two businesses and a life in this tiny house.

I caught Adam smiling at me in concern and realized I was frowning thinking about Seth and his stubborn refusal to not act like a jackass in response to my stubborn refusal to not act like a jackass first. "What are you thinking about? Your poker face is usually better."

"I don't have a poker face where Seth is concerned. I've never had one," I said.

It was true. I had a stoic, take-no-shit face for days on any other topic. So much so that the district attorney had brought in a consultant to teach me empathetic facial expressions while giving my testimony on my last case. The concern was I looked more like the sociopathic defendants than a victim of their actions.

"You're upset with him?" It was phrased as a question but we both knew the answer.

"I can't really get into his special assignment because I literally know nothing about it other than it's special training and it's not here."

He nodded. "Let's look at the pictures you brought." That was the best thing about Adam—he didn't expect you to go around and around on a topic.

We began clearing the table until Theo shooed us out of the kitchen, taking the plates from us, giving Adam a soft, loving smile. Jeez, was everyone determined to prove how much healthier and emotionally stable their romantic relationship was compared to mine? Thinking of the photos of Damian Murphy reminded me what real dysfunction looked like and I felt better.

I spread out the photos on the table as best I could then shuffled them into monthly piles, oldest on the bottom, newest on the top. Even as crappy as the selfies were, they showed a clear, steady progression that to my untrained eye did not look natural.

Adam pointed to a photo. "There's an unmistakable sign. His skin. In the older photos, his skin is really clear but in this later photo, he's got obvious cystic acne. He's at an age that acne wouldn't normally be kicking into high gear. That alone would be a tip off to me if I saw it in the gym, but the musculature is indicative too."

I didn't know anything about steroid use other than what four years in high school would give one.

"His personality changed too. A normal guy to a moody, secretive, angry, we're pretty sure stalker."

Adam nodded. "Anabolic steroid abuse has physical and emotional effects. I've seen all of those behaviors in individuals using."

And that left me with no idea how to proceed. I had a maybe confirmation on a semi-professional basis that Damian Murphy had been using steroids, but that didn't give me anything I didn't already have except an ego boost that I had good hunches. Yay, me.

Nevertheless, I texted Jan about my conversation with Adam and I couldn't resist bragging about my doggie bag of eclairs, which was actually a gorgeous turquoise blue box with Theo's logo on the side. He'd insisted I was helping him by testing out the new merchandise before he offered it on his website. I agreed because I'm a giver.

Then he pressed an actual doggie bag into my other hand. It was full of organic, homemade dog biscuits for Fargo. Clearly, the day she'd spent with the two of them had gone well. I wasn't sure, but I thought he teared up a little when he told me they were a special recipe he'd designed with her as his inspiration. He'd never teared up over me. I was slightly disgruntled, but then I strapped the box of eclairs into the passenger seat and thought about having them later and all was right with my world again.

Aja had periodically texted me throughout the day and I'd ignored it because kids should pay attention in school. And I was tired and busy. When I got home and pulled them up I saw that she'd been investigating at school, trying to track down people Damian had still been friends with when he died.

I was alternately proud, because it was a good lead, and pissed, because it was a dangerous lead. We had no idea who he'd been getting his steroids from and criminal enterprises—especially drug dealers and manufacturers—got testy when you started poking your nose into places they'd rather stay nose free. I penciled in a lecture about Nancy Drewing without training and reluctantly placed the box with eclairs in the fridge. I thought better of it and put a note on the side of it that it was for dessert and no early snacking was allowed. I slashed the W on the note at the bottom as a warning. If I could resist, then everyone could. I was, by far, in possession of the least amount of self-control in the family. Yes, counting the dog too.

I grabbed the laptop Ben had set up for me. It had the case management software, solitaire, and a single internet browser. When my brother gave it to me and insisted on doing a training session, I was disabused of any notion that he thought I could handle anything more technical than microwave popcorn. Humbling to say the least. The less on the machine, the less I was likely to break anything, he said. I reminded him, only half jokingly, that I was more than capable of breaking bones.

He reminded me that I'd already broken two laptops in less than a year. Which was stupid because I'd dumped over a cup of coffee on one of them and that had nothing to do with the programs. I had given the last one a virus while investigating one of those cheating spouses hookup websites. You know, those spam emails for the hot, bored housewives in your area looking for action. It was so serious that he'd had to scrap the machine's operating system and quarantine it from the other computers. He said, but I don't think that's a real thing.

I uploaded my notes about Damian's suspected steroid use and flipped over to the cold case. I'd reviewed Jan's notes from her interviews with the family. The mom was understandably distraught. Mandy had been home for her first break in her freshman year of college. She'd likely worried about all kinds of things happening to her daughter at college and never once thought she'd be in danger at home.

The boyfriend had seemed sincere. He was unsure about his alibi, which was sleeping in until he didn't know when and then hanging out at home. As alibis went, it was vague and totally normal. That was a normal life. He'd never expected to need an alibi so he'd turned down a movie with his friends. A movie wasn't a great alibi either, so at least he'd saved the ticket price.

The brother had been hiding something, Jan's note read. She couldn't pinpoint what her issue was with him during the interview, it was just a feeling that he wasn't being entirely honest. His alibi, like the boyfriend's, seemed organic but was totally unverifiable—people had seen him, they just couldn't say when.

I sensed Jan's frustration with the lack of clarity in the case. She was a young detective on her first homicide case, which felt all-important. I'd lived with the insecurity and hunger that first case generated. Never knowing if you were doing it right and desperate to make sure you did it all by a book that doesn't exactly exist. Sure, there were legalities that needed to be adhered to, but how you got from point murder to point arrest was a moving target.

I could see why she wanted me to go without the statements at first. She was a new detective and wanted to see if she'd done it right. A newbie reviewing a newbie's case. Except I had an advantage she never got in her career—the ability to learn from her.

Fargo picked her bored head up from the floor and heaved a great sigh. How the dog had learned to guilt me so effectively I had no idea, but I was being a bad dog owner. I swept all the paperwork into the correct folders on the table and saved the case files. I shut the laptop and the click caused Fargo to jump up and run at me.

"Yes, puppy girl, we're going out. Do you want to run?"

Fargo stretched her whole body out, long front and back legs splayed, then popped up and ran to where her leash was hung up.

"Okay, just let me get changed." I dribbled off clothing as I walked from the table to my room, collecting them as I went. The basement wasn't by any means a private suite what with the pantry and laundry room, not to mention the panic room work Dad was having done, but during the day when school was in session and Dad and I were home alone, it might as well have been a deserted island. Still there was no reason it needed to look like a crime scene, or worse, porn.

I quickly put on workout gear warm enough for the day but nothing that I'd need to take off. I grabbed Fargo's training vest and leash. She began to jump when she saw them come out and I had to give her the command to settle down. So much energy that needed to be run out each day—from both of us. While I was thinking about it, I texted Adam that I'd see him at the dojo that evening and got back a smiley face emoji in response. The man was totes adorbs, as Aja would say.

I couldn't do a hard, exhausting run with Fargo like I probably needed to do so I jammed earbuds in and found a running mix moderate in tone and beat. That'd give me enough motivation to keep us moving and still allow space in my brain for turning the cases this way and that.

As we ducked into the trees and onto the pedestrian path, I caught sight of Seth's parents' house. I wondered for a scant second if they knew where he was and then pushed my angsty emotional crap to the back where it belonged. Seth was in training and we'd deal with what we needed to when he got back. I wasn't exactly counting the days. I missed him but not having to deal with our emotional mess, part of my own emotional mess, was a nice break.

In Damian's case I had a possible motive to consider in that he was likely involved in at least one criminal enterprise. In Mandy's case, there was no motive that seemed good enough. The sudden enmity with the brother was so vague and unremarkable I had a hard time imagining it escalating to murder. There was still the element that it was an accident and maybe he panicked. I just didn't know enough about him, but my gut told me no.

We had reached the county park and I stopped at the bathrooms. Fargo sniffed around the trees and the sidewalk separating the parking lot from the building. I dug the travel bowl out of her vest pocket and filled it at the water fountain. We both slurped water, her from the bowl and me from the fountain, then flopped down on the grass. It must have been naptime because the swings and play equipment were empty. There were a few elderly couples meandering from their car to the paved path in the opposite direction from the dirt packed path I intended to take around the lake. I calculated that it was a little less than five miles and decided to only take it halfway then cut through the woods back to the bike path and home.

I checked my laces and shook off the bowl, collapsing it and stowing it away again.

"You ready, girl? No yanking the leash to go after vermin, okay?"

She smiled up at me, her tongue lolling out of her mouth. She looked eager to get going so we set off at a slow trot until I saw how the path had fared during the winter. The county wouldn't have gotten the chance to inspect the whole trail and it was likely one of the snowfalls we'd gotten could have dislodged weak tree limbs. I didn't want either of us tripping and getting injured. I decided to take her to the dog park instead, so we turned back and headed for home. I mulled while we trotted along at a slower pace than either of us wanted.

Damian Murphy had been beaten to death and while he'd been a bigger guy than most his age, we didn't have any information that he could defend himself. It could have been ridiculously easy for someone to kill him despite his size. That person didn't even need to be amped up on steroids either. Not that I believed his death wasn't related to steroids.

The search and destruction at Aja's house was all I needed to know that Damian had gotten involved in something more than just personal use. That was a *where the hell is my product* search if I'd ever seen one. I mean, I hadn't, but I was smart enough to get the basic gist of it. Say I'm a bad guy and I've gotten bad guy stuff hidden I need to pick up from bad guy partner or henchman—I tear the place apart until I find it. Unless I knew where to look. Then I waste no time getting that spot accessed and when I don't find what I expect, I throw a hissy fit and punch a hole, or half dozen, in the wall.

Maybe I needed to check out this attempted MMA club first hand. Which meant I needed to visit my old high school. Oh, joy. I could revisit all the fun times I had with my now dead best friend and the boyfriend who I am currently angry with and who wasn't my boyfriend at the time despite the fact that literally anyone who watched us together—including actual people we were dating—couldn't deny we wanted to be together. We even got an honorable mention in his senior superlatives as Best Couple ... even though, again, we weren't dating. I mean, the yearbook staff saw it.

Mr. Kelly was still the principal and he would have been the one who shot down the MMA club. Rightfully so. A club that endorsed teenagers hitting each other in the face would not have gone down well with parents. Which begged the question, how were these kids explaining their injuries to their parents? I got plenty banged up just sparring with a partner who was either inanimate or professionally dedicated to ensuring I remained uninjured. So how was Damian Murphy explaining his bruises and injuries and failing grades his senior year to his parents?

More questions than answers was the gig. Didn't mean it didn't piss me off.

Instead of entering the house when we got home, I piled Fargo into the back seat of the truck, clipping her harness to the seatbelt.

"Wanna go for a ride, puppy? Let's go see Ben and Aja."

Her ears popped straight up at the sound of their names and just as quickly sagged back down. We were told we could tape her ears up but I liked that they were floppy. Her ears matched her goofy smile. She was going to be a big dog and as much as Ben wanted her to be the perfect guard dog, I wanted a running companion and snuggle bug. Yes, she could be both but either way I wanted her to look innocuous because scary dogs were scary. And she was a sweetheart.

I texted Ben and Aja both, a group text they'd jointly set up on my phone at dinner the previous night, and told them that the dog and I would come to pick them up. I managed to be only minorly hurt when Aja's reply indicated she might be more excited about showing Fargo off to her friends than me. I mean, how many teen girls have dogs? Tons. How many teen girls have their own crime-fighting, near-ninja, decently-IQed private eye? That's a pretty small club.

Student parking was fairly empty already. Seniors had priority over the lottery-based spots, and they were anxious to be anywhere but high school. Wait until they hit college if they thought high school was a drag.

Ben would have had his own car, too, if Seth hadn't gone behind my back. Instead of fixing the cut coolant line in my old car, he had it crushed into a brown cube. He'd argued that there was more wrong with the car than the plastic tubing—that it had over two hundred thousand miles on it and should have been retired long before; that it had bad memories. I was just miffed that I had to go shopping with some ATF smarty pants to get Ben some technical whosiwhatsit when I had a perfectly brilliant, free, present to give him—a very used car.

I pulled into a spot and got Fargo out, technically breaking like four different health code violations about animals on county property, and slapped her Working Dog vest on. You didn't even need any kind of special certificate or license to get the vest online. Then again you could buy just about any kind of weapon you wanted to so I didn't feel much guilt about fudging my dog's bona fides.

She trotted happily with her tongue lolling out of her goofy mouth, ears flopping as we picked up speed.

Aja had gathered a group of girls to adore Fargo and, puppy princess she was, lapped up the attention and affection.

Ben had been talking with a kid through the window of the only bus still on the grounds. I didn't think much about it until I heard the shouting.

"Screw you, Daniel," Ben yelled

As the bus pulled away, Daniel or someone, hollered out the window, "Dude, get over it. She's doable."

Aja rolled her eyes but Ben dropped his backpack like he was going to go after the person. Who was on a bus. That was driving away.

"Teenage boys, ugh, all hormones, no brains, right?" Aja said.

"Testosterone is the stupidity hormone."

I knew the kid had been talking about me. I wasn't under the impression that I was some kind of model but I was older and I had a fit and toned body from the months of intense workouts. I was also wearing workout clothes that left only the shade of my skin in question. I hadn't even thought about the workout clothes when I made my impromptu decision to visit my little brother's school.

A regrettable faux pas on my part. I always tried to minimize the embarrassment I put Ben through publicly because I remembered being his age and just how easy it was for the hot red flush to rise up the face, something we both got from Dad. Once Ben had become a teen having a much older sister, especially one who was a cop, had been a hard pill to swallow. He loved me, he just didn't always like his friends and me in the same place.

I leaned in close to him. "Sorry, Benj. I needed some info on the MMA club and I didn't think."

He nodded.

I pulled back and gently punched Ben on the shoulder. "And here is a prime example of it. Can you imagine if that kid had used a word other than *doable*, Aja?"

I figured I'd get him some White Knight mileage with the gathered group of teen girls. Just because I wasn't into a guy riding to the rescue and saving me from the evil of the world didn't mean others didn't or that it was even a bad thing.

"Oh, he did," Ben said, pushing me back, a little rougher than I'd punched him. Good. He needed to work out the aggression in a positive way. A more positive way than running after the bus and trying to start a fight with another dumb teenage boy.

"So, you're, like, what, Ben's aunt or something?"

I cocked an eyebrow. Aunt? Or something?

"Or something," I said, trying not to smirk. Her mangling of the English language didn't deserve the encouragement and I'd already embarrassed Ben badly enough. I'd let him decide what he told these girls.

"Aunt? No way. She's way too young to be his aunt. She's his sister and she's totally a badass PI," Aja said.

"Shut up."

"No way."

"Oh my god, that's so cool."

I didn't dare look at Ben. Showing up in spandex was bad enough, but to be outed as a PI was an especially painful blow. He harbored his own spy hero fantasies and no teenage boy, no matter how evolved, wants to be shown up by his sister.

"You needed to meet the assistant wrestling coach, Willa?" Ben asked, his teeth close to gritted.

I handed Fargo's leash off to Aja and allowed Ben to drag me toward the building. After we were out of sight, I pulled my arm out of his grasp. "Ow, dude. I said I was sorry. You don't need to yank my arm out of the socket."

"This is my world. I don't jump in the middle of your cases, do I?"

I stopped and raised an eyebrow. "Yeah, you wouldn't do that. It would be wrong for you to insert yourself into a case or even worse my boyfriend's job. How'd that ATF internship go, Ben?"

He looked away from me, down the hall. He'd forgotten I could go toe-to-toe in the You Got Your Chocolate in My Peanut Butter routine.

He continued stomping down the hallway looking entirely like a pissed off flamingo. Which meant one of the accumulated girls was one he was interested in. Poor timing considering they were all running off to different colleges in six months. Unless ... I texted Aja.

I'm deputizing you. Figure out which one Ben's interested in.

She replied with a laughing emoji.

I had followed Ben through the large gym and then back through a hallway with a set off series of classrooms and offices.

We arrived at the door of a room full of equipment, a desk shoved in a corner. The room was empty. That was a bust.

"Can I help you?" A tall, balding man was standing at the opening of the hallway, coming out of the gym.

"Yeah, we're looking for the assistant wrestling coach. I have some questions about the MMA club he was sponsoring this past summer."

Another moment a badge would have come in handy.

"Well, ma'am, you don't have to worry about your son joining. The club wasn't approved."

Okay, I'd only missed a night of sleep. I wasn't looking haggard enough to be mistaken for the mother of an eighteen-year-old.

"Yes, I understand, but I wanted to talk with him about why he applied for one."

The man sighed, like I was deeply wounding him for even wanting to talk to another human being about something.

"The administration understands it was ill-advised."

I thought I'd recognized him when he sighed, but his use of the phrase *ill-advised* confirmed it. He'd been my ninth-grade gym teacher. The guy who kept us outside while it was sleeting because it was one degree above the limit for what was too cold for outside gym. He'd said it had been "ill-advised" when my mother came barreling down to the school, demanding to speak to the principal, the vice principal, my counselor, and all the gym teachers. That had been one crowded meeting. People could not apologize fast enough.

He didn't recognize Ben, which meant he hadn't been Ben's gym teacher. That wasn't a coincidence if I had to guess. I decided to torment him.

"Mr. Hayes? Wow. Willa Pennington. I was in your freshman gym class. Man, that would have been fifteen years ago."

He literally cringed away from me. He remembered. My mother is a lovely woman but if you put one of her kids in danger, she was going to verbally flay you alive.

He regained his composure, likely honed through two decades of working with teenagers and their parents, and smiled. "How is your mother, Miss Pennington?"

"She's great. My brother here wanted to talk about the MMA club because he wanted to see if that group would be willing to take a class at a local dojo. If they get enough interest, they'll add MMA to their roster."

Ben was used to my methods so he just nodded, sullenly, as I gave the man a bright smile.

"Oh, well, I suppose that would be okay. Ramsey will be here in a few minutes."

He scampered off, probably before any other family members arrived, and we lounged against the wall.

"I really am sorry, dude."

"I know," he said, sighing. "It's just there's a girl and she was there and Daniel … ."

I suppressed the urge to inundate him with questions. I'm genetically nosy and this PI thing isn't a coincidence. I did always try to be my best self with my brother, though. He'd earned it being my sibling, a rough gig by any standards.

A stocky, muscled guy shorter than me came around the corner and stopped. He scowled at us.

"You're not supposed to be back here."

Nothing gets my back up faster than someone being hostile for no reason. I shifted into a more assertive posture.

"Mr. Hayes said otherwise." An exaggeration of the conversation but let's call that a gray area.

"Oh."

He still hadn't moved.

"We're waiting for Ramsey." I had the sneaking suspicion the man before me was going to turn out to be the man in question.

"Yeah?"

What the hell was up with this guy's attitude? He worked at a high school. He should have been well-used to dealing with people, yet he acted like he'd been in the joint for a decade.

"Yeah. We wanted to talk about the MMA club."

"Yeah?"

Was I speaking English?

"Yeah." Ball back in your court, dude. I can do this all day.

"Well, there isn't an MMA club so there's not much to talk about."

"Look, my brother is interested in getting an MMA class added to our dojo and wanted to contact the kids who were interested. Can you help us?"

I could see Ben out of the corner of my eye, he's adopted my stance and was staring the guy down. He could get mad at me but no one was going to give me crap. He might have been a decade younger but he was typical brother from the toes of his Chucks to the very top of his shaggy head. He was also too many pounds shy of intimidating but it was sweet.

"Where?"

Ugh. Pulling teeth would have been enjoyable compared to questioning him. Even if they were my teeth.

"Carson's."

"That's the girly martial arts place, right?"

I gave him my not-so-nice smile, bared teeth and *go ahead and piss me off* eyes. "I go there so if that's what you mean by girly then yeah."

"He teaches little kids how to pretend to fight," Ramsey said.

He was one of those. The people who think martial arts should be all about kicking someone's ass in a bar fight like something out of an eighties action movie.

"He teaches lots of things and all different ages. Listen do you have the names of the kids interested?"

"What do you take there?" He was smirking now.

"I'm in private training. We do a little bit of everything."

I wanted the information but I had a feeling this was just him getting his ego stroked.

"Maybe I have the list. Not sure. Everything?"

"Yeah, jiu-jitsu —"

He scoffed. "You rolling around on the floor in pajamas. Worthless."

What the hell? He was the assistant wrestling coach and he ... nope, he was fine with rolling around on the floor. For guys. I knew if he had the list he wasn't going to give it to me. Sometimes leads panned out like that. It was time to cut my losses.

"Okay, well, thanks."

"I thought you wanted the list."

"Yeah, we're not really interested in MMA anymore."

I turned away, Ben hiking up his backpack.

"What? All of the sudden?"

I turned back to find him smirking at me. I gave him full-force cop face and his arrogant smile slipped a bit. "Yeah, all of the sudden."

I pushed Ben ahead of me and we walked back out of the school the way we came in, Ben muttering under his breath about rude guys and one day doing something about it. I hoped that girl, the one hanging out with Aja and Fargo, liked him too because he was a good kid.

CHAPTER

16

I KNEW I WAS right. It only made sense based on the behavior we'd seen. If Damian had been abusing steroids, and I was convinced now that he had, he'd have been a powder keg, strapped to C4, and wrapped in a thermite coating ready to be set off. So who'd been there when the fuse was lit? Who was the bigger bomb?

I went over the whole sequence of events while I'd showered and my theory held up. I grabbed new workout clothes and dragged them over my body. Aja had to prep for an AP exam and Ben was still bubbling like a lava pool so I dragged him with me to the dojo. The after-school classes for the littlest kids were still going on. We sat in the car for a minute and I shoved a handful of almonds into my mouth while

Ben went on and on about how glad he was he'd be leaving behind all the "idiots and losers at that stupid school."

"Even Aja?" I asked around a mouthful of almond paste.

He sighed. "Why do you always have to ruin a good rant? You get to do it all the time. Why can't I just once get a nice rage going?"

I swallowed. "Because you're not me. You're you and you don't rage. So some stupid kid made a trashy remark. It's not a big thing."

As the voice of reason, I wasn't terrifically experienced but if some guy getting mouthy was the worst thing he had to deal with, he was going to do pretty well in life. People hated me enough to try to kill me. Granted, I'm pretty annoying but I work hard at it.

"Willa, it's wrong and it's sexist. Sheesh, you're a feminist, right?"

I stopped digging in the bag of almonds and stared at him. I had clearly not given him the benefit of my years on the force and all the crap I endured. I loved him in all his idealistic earnestness, but he was veering into mansplaining and needed to be smacked down.

"Yup, I am a big ole card-carrying feminist but I'm also a realist and the day men stopped saying stupid shit because they're hot for some woman is the day the last man on the planet dies. Don't do it in the workplace, don't do it on the street, don't touch people without their permission, don't ever think you can berate a woman for turning you down. And don't think for one second I believe that this violates your feminist principles. You're squicked out because this kid wants to have sex with your sister. Your much older sister."

He shuddered, opening his mouth and closing it like a fish on a hook. Mission accomplished.

"If it makes you feel better, I remember guys at seventeen and they're not particularly picky so ....

I saw in the rearview mirror the toddlers and their moms empty-ing out of the dojo. We had a two-hour window between now and the after-dinner classes to work out and get some of the emotional unrest out of Ben. I needed the physical release. My muscles were bunched from too many days away from my regular workouts and poor sleep.

I jumped out of the truck and hauled my bag out of the backseat. Ben dragged himself out of the passenger seat like a kid going to the dentist.

"Do I hafta work out?"

For a health nut, he sure hated exercise. "Yes, you 'hafta' work out. It's good for you. Plus Boston has some rough areas. You need to learn some more self-defense before you leave for MIT."

"MIT is in Cambridge," he said, walking as slowly as possible, stopping for every minivan waiting to back out of a parking space.

"Which is kissing distance from Boston where I know you and the other geniuses will go to listen to that crap music you love."

"It's called nerdcore and it's very popular."

"White guys rapping about video games, super heroes, and *Game of Thrones* is literally the opposite of very popular."

I stood, hand ready to pull on the handle, and watched as he managed to appear as if he was moving in slow motion.

"You get your ass in here right now, Benjamin No Middle Initial Pennington, or I will tackle you and embarrass you in front of all these people," I yelled, as loudly as I could.

He laughed, like he always did when I used his lack of a middle name as a middle name, and picked up his pace. Adam pushed the door out from the inside, laughing, as well.

"No middle initial?"

"Our parents thought Benjamin Pennington was pretty long and couldn't come up with a short middle name they both liked so they didn't give him one. On forms, though, you have to indicate NMI 'no middle initial' because they all want it and you can't leave it blank. That's how the joke came about. He's Benjamin NMI Pennington."

Ben slung his arm over my shoulder, good mood restored, and ruffled my hair. I hated it as much as he did and he knew it. I was definitely not letting him leave the dojo without putting him in a headlock.

Adam looked at us, correctly gauging the level of sibling nonsense he was witnessing, and smiled an indulgent smile usually reserved for the littlest of his students. "You two are ridiculous. You squabble more than the kids in my classes."

I swept past him into the empty room littered with pool noodles and force shields. Usually he made the kids clean up before they left, which meant either class ran long or he was making us tidy up.

"Okay, you know what to do," Adam said.

We were cleaning up. Ben gathered the force shields and stacked them while I picked up all the pool noodles and smacked him a few times before putting them in the container. It took all of three minutes.

"Way to go, you two. Nice teamwork," Adam said. I resisted the urge to pull a pool noodle back out and beat him with it. Mostly because it was a pool noodle and about as good a weapon as you'd expect of something called a noodle and made out of foam.

"Can you dial back the 'hyper excited to work with kids' persona, please? I can only deal with one personality crisis at the moment."

"Force of habit. And who's having a personality crisis? Not you. You're pretty much the most solidly formed person I've ever met."

I gestured at my brother who had pulled his phone out of god knew where and was texting.

"Oh, Benjy's a little stressed because one of the boys on his bus would like to take me to pound town," I said, smirking, knowing the euphemism would crack up Adam and horrify Ben. Ben was indeed horrified but Adam was more sympathetic than amused.

"Oh, Ben, man, I'm sorry. I dealt with that too. Kids are jerks."

"Says the man who's devoted his life to teaching children? I didn't know you had a sister."

Adam hemmed and hawed. "Well, actually it was my older brother. Gay teen, gay friends."

I had a hard time staying upright when I saw the look on Ben's face. He desperately wanted to laugh but given his earlier outrage at the treatment I, and by that respect he, had received, it was difficult to laugh at someone else who had gone through the same thing. Check and mate.

"Okay, enough with you both feeling feelings of outrage and confusion on behalf of older siblings. Can we get to hitting each other, please? It's all I live for."

Probably because I was not sympathetic to either of their plights, I got stuck working solo running drills on Bob, the freestanding heavy bag with the human torso and head minus limbs. Bob was flesh-toned too … and only flesh-toned. Adam knew it creeped me out, so it wasn't something he made me use often. The kids, on the other hand, delighted in Bob's tough guy expression and Venus de Milo condition. I don't think we give kids enough credit for their morbid little minds. I know I was particularly gruesome as a child due to lots of unsupervised reading and late-night television horror movie broadcasts.

I hit Bob in the face a few times just because his beige-ness annoyed me. Then I hit him in the face a few more times because I was pissed at Damian for emotionally abusing Aja, a couple of jabs for the guy who'd beaten Damian to death, a great right hook for Ramsey's smirky disdain for real martial arts, and I straight up pounded Bob in the face for that stupid kid who'd bullied my brother.

I stopped punching Bob. "Okay, I'm a little angry about the kid making sexist comments."

Ben and Adam stopped their drills. Adam looked at me with as blank an expression as he'd ever given me. Ben didn't feel the need for restraint and rolled his eyes. "Duh! Of course you're angry. Did you just realize that? I thought you were just teasing me."

I shrugged. "Mostly. It's just … ." I struggled for any words that would make it make sense.

"It's just nothing. You're not an object, Willa. You're a person. No more and no less valuable than any other person. Not to be used as fulfillment for someone's desires or anger at the world," Adam said. His tone was neutral but all three of us knew he meant Mark Ingalls and his cohorts from last fall.

I gripped my hands tighter inside the boxing gloves. A sexist comment was different than a racial epithet and yet the same—it reduced me to a thing.

I renewed my attack on Bob, striking blow after blow for all the slights and disrespect I'd endured. Putting my hip into the blows, I watched as Bob rocked on his base, threatening to tip over, weighted as it was for less serious combat drilling. Hard rock began to pulse from the speaker in the ceiling covering up the slightly tinkling strains of some top-forty pop hit from the dance studio next door. I recognized the song as the beginning of my hard run mix, the one I used when I needed the release of pushing my body and lungs to the brink of what I was physically capable of.

I felt Adam behind me. He began to softly coax me to adjust my stance slightly, to lean into the attack more. The first song had cycled into the next and on into the playlist. Time seemed to stall as I lost track of the order I'd memorized, minutes floating around me as I gave in to the endorphins swirling into my blood. Bob's face morphed into other faces as I landed torso blows that would have broken ribs had Bob been real. I fell back to jabs to drop my breathing into a more manageable pattern. Adam's words felt like they were inside my head, almost seductive, as he proffered the most effective ways to harm another human without making it permanent. It was altogether too easy to do that without good training. Too many bar fights ended in the morgue. It was scary how quickly you could land just the wrong strike and kill your opponent. Especially if you were young, stupid, and jacked up on some substance or other.

I dropped my hands and began pulling at the fasteners on my gloves. I turned into Adam, bumping him, he'd been so close I could have leaned back into him at any point.

"Off," I said, panting.

He stripped the gloves from my hands. "What's wrong? Are you okay? Can you breathe?"

"Phone," I yelled at Ben, in between breaths.

The music stopped mid-downbeat and Ben tossed it to me from the audio system setup across the room.

I barely caught the phone and it took two tries with shaking hands as I unlocked it. I pulled up the frequent contacts and found Jan in the list.

"Fight club," I blurted out when she answered.

"Uh, it's an okay movie," she said.

"Bob doesn't hit back. It's not real." I got the words out in between breaths that weren't calming in my excitement.

"Are you having a stroke? Do you smell toast?"

Of course, she was confused. I wasn't making sense.

"Right, the movie. But a fight club. Bored suburban teen boys. Video games. Sanitized sports. Steroids. An underground fight club."

"How in the hell did you come up with that?" she asked. I heard the clacking of the keys on her computer. Either she was into the idea or humoring me while she filed reports.

"I'm at the dojo training. Adam was giving me instruction and it reminded me of a fight trainer like in boxing or MMA. Getting the maximum damage without really hurting the other person. The crowd cheering. The adrenaline and endorphins."

"But sanctioned fights do drug tests," Adam said.

I punched the speakerphone key.

"But sanctioned fights do drug tests," I repeated.

"So why do steroids if not for some physical test?" Jan asked. The typing had stopped.

"All fight sports do drug testing for competition. Football and wrestling coaches are trained in what to look for. Gym trainers too. Sure, the makers can change the chemistry, but not the results."

"And the results are the reason. You gotta show it off," Adam said.

"MMA is so popular now, Jan. They tried to start a club at school but the administration refused." I looked at Ben. "When?"

"Last summer. Some of the guys who were on the wrestling team."

It was all starting to gel in my head. I handed Adam the phone. He gave me a questioning look. I held up my finger to ask for a moment.

"Uh, Willa says she needs a minute," Adam said.

"Take your time, kid." Jan's voice came through the speaker.

I walked over to the front wall of windows and closed my eyes, pressing my forehead against the glass. The cold felt like I was rooting me to the building. I pressed my hands into fists over my ears.

Some members of the wrestling team tried and failed to start an MMA club over the summer. The same time Damian started changing.

He'd grown rapidly. He'd have to have known that someone would suspect the changes. The timing. But it was a big school and he'd started to change his pattern. So many kids. Thousands in that giant building. But there was one who knew him. One who'd been asking his other friends about what they knew.

"Aja. Ben, you need to call her right now."

"What's going on, Willa?" Jan asked.

"One more sec. Adam, your classes have students from the high school, right?"

"A few," he said.

"I need you to call them, ask them about this MMA club. If Ben knows about it then the kids who would be interested know. I need the details of who was involved in trying to start it."

"Willa! Can I get in a word on my murder investigation, please?"

"Jan, he can't tell them this is anything to do with a murder investigation otherwise their parents will get involved and lawyers—"

"The coroner says the x-rays of Damian's body show many old, healing injuries. He was involved in something that had him getting beaten up pretty regularly."

"We're on to something."

"We're definitely on to something. Great work, kid," Jan said.

It was an amazing feeling, putting the piece into the puzzle. To pull the string and have the knot unravel that first little bit.

"She's not answering, Will. Mom says someone came to pick her up, that she wouldn't be home for dinner but in time for curfew."

The feeling of success died instantly replaced with fear, acid sour in my stomach.

"Who? Her parents aren't supposed to be in town yet."

She wasn't answering her phone and she'd been poking around about Damian at school.

"Gotta go, Jan. I will call you back soon."

I clicked the disconnect button and took the phone out of Adam's hand. I called Aja from my phone, thinking she might answer for me if she wanted to ignore Ben. They'd fallen into a very easy sibling relationship, close but annoying each other easily. She'd be more likely to answer for me. I let it ring until her voicemail should have picked up and didn't.

I texted her. And waited. A minute passed. Then two. Then five. The fear deepened.

I pulled up the tracker app on my phone. I plugged in the number of her cell phone as Adam and Ben watched over my shoulder.

"Are you tracking the GPS on her phone?" Ben asked, his voice cracking. He was trying not to show me he was afraid but it was all there in his face. Adam put this arm around Ben and pulled him into his side. They both towered over me as I waited for the dot to appear.

The steady blinking reassured me. Her phone might have been off or damaged but the GPS still worked. I pushed out the screen's view with my fingers to zoom into her location. The app could give me exact location but I knew instantly where she was based on the surroundings.

I raced over to my bag and grabbed my keys.

"Call Jan and tell her to get me a black-and-white to Aja's house." I rattled off the number as I hit the push bar to the door at a run.

"I'm coming," Adam said, practically running over me to get to the truck.

"Keep dialing. I want the pressure on." The trip was interminably long as I tried to focus on driving safely, cutting it closer on yellow lights than was legal. I didn't have time to get pulled over only because that left me less time to get to Aja before the cops.

"What's the plan?" Adam asked. I could hear the phone ringing over Bluetooth.

"If the person she went with was involved in trashing her house or killing Damian, the cops being there might escalate things. I want to beat the uniforms there and use them as backup. If this goes hostage situation, I think I'm better positioned to deal with some kid with 'roid rage."

"Have you done hostage negotiation?"

"No, I'm a girl in a tank top and workout pants, Adam. I'm going to appear as threatening as a tree stump."

"That's a big assumption."

"That's literally the job of being a PI, man. Assuming you can handle what the cops don't. You think angry spouses caught cheating don't get physical?"

I was a block away when, finally, the phone connected.

"Willa?" Aja's voice was shaking. She was terrified. My fear dropped right out and rage rushed in. I had to keep my head.

"I'm close. Are you okay?"

"You're coming?" She sniffled. I saw Adam clench his fists. I wasn't the only one who needed to keep their head.

"Less than a block." I careened around the corner of her street, almost clipping the nosy neighbor and his yappy dog. His mouth was an O of surprise as I slammed into the driveway of Aja's house and threw the truck into park. I was out of the truck, pushing the driver seat up and out of my way, punching the code into the gun case. I checked the magazine and made sure there was a round chambered.

"Young woman," the old man was shouting, running toward me.

I jammed the weapon into the back of my waistband awkwardly— the elastic wasn't designed for a gun—and pulled the tank top down over it.

"Fuck off, grandpa, I do not have time for your shit," I said as I took off for the back of the house. Aja didn't have keys so they'd have to have gone in using the plywood-boarded up basement door.

I heard Adam trying to soothe the neighbor as I rounded the corner of the house as fast as I could holding the gun to the small of my back. I didn't even hesitate with my footing in the backyard even though it was unfamiliar.

In through the opening made by the plywood having been peeled off and up the basement stairs to the foyer. I made my way more slowly and carefully up the main staircase to the second floor. I was sure they were in the attic loft, but I didn't want to risk startling this guy. I didn't know if he was armed. I only knew he was desperate.

I eased down the hallway past Aja's room, the light on, but I didn't see anyone. I made my way up the stairs to the loft finally able to hear Aja's voice.

"I don't know what you're talking about. I keep telling you. Damian didn't give me anything. I hadn't spoken to him for weeks."

"You have to have it. If I don't get it for him, he's going to kill me too."

I crept up the stairs as quietly as I could. I heard the kid pacing around, his footfalls heavy even on the carpet.

"Cole, my friend can help you. Just talk to her."

"No. I don't need help. I need the package."

I had slowly slid around the end of the stairwell wall. The faint whine of the sirens now audible in the room.

"Are you sure I can't just try to help you, Cole?"

The relief on Aja's face was a gut punch. I hadn't gotten her out of the situation safely yet.

Cole startled and moved toward where Aja was sitting. I watched as she pressed herself farther into the corner. The look on his face wasn't calculating though. He was scared. He looked at her as if for help.

I held my hand up. "Cole. It's okay."

"Who are you?" He was no more than seventeen. He wasn't as muscled at Damian had been but I could see the growth, looking out of place with his slight frame and childlike features.

I smiled at him, forcing down the adrenaline-soaked instinct that screamed at me to rush him. "My name is Willa. I'm a friend of Aja's. I just want to help you. I promise."

"You can't," he screamed.

Aja put her hands over her ears and tucked her head into her knees. Good. If I had to shoot this kid I didn't want her to see.

"Don't be too sure. I help people for a living."

"You're a cop?" He moved toward Aja again.

"Stop," I said firmly. "I'm not a cop. I'm just someone who likes to help people."

I had been inching toward him as I spoke. I could see his face more clearly, his tears and terror. His desperation. Desperation was dangerous.

"You said you needed a package. Do you know what's in it? Maybe we can find a substitute." My voice was as soothing as I'd ever made it. I needed to talk Cole down quickly. Once the cops got in the house, everything got much more complicated.

"No. I can't tell you."

"Okay. That's okay. You don't have to tell me. We can figure out something else."

I began to turn my body, forcing him to turn too to keep me in view. I needed to get between him and Aja so that no matter what happened, she was shielded by my body. It was a sooner rather than later premise though.

"You don't understand. He killed Damian when he found out that Damian hid the package. He told us that's what happens when you get greedy."

My hands up waist high, fingers spread wide, I kept moving, easing my way to position myself facing the opening of the staircase. I didn't see that Cole was armed but I wasn't taking the chance. In the low light as afternoon turned into evening it was too easy for an amped up cop to see something that wasn't there.

"Was Damian greedy, Cole?"

I just needed to keep him talking, to trust me.

"No. He was just scared. He wanted out. I just want out."

"That's good, Cole. I want to help you get out of whatever it is too."

"How do I know you can help?"

I had succeeded in swapping our positions in the room. Me in the back with Aja and Cole with his back to the room's opening.

"Can you trust me? Can me being Aja's friend be enough to make you trust me?"

I heard the commotion at the front door. Cole heard it too, twisting around to look behind him. Dammit. I was out of time.

"Cole. Don't be scared. That's the cops, but we can still fix this. I can help you fix this."

"You can't. No one can."

He turned and ran down the stairs. I chased after him, doing the exact opposite of everything I'd ever been trained to do, running toward an unknown situation, no vest, no gun drawn. I did not need this kid suiciding by cop.

On the second-floor hall, I heard the reinforcement the locksmith had installed holding up against the donkey kick the patrol officer was utilizing. They didn't have a battering ram so I knew they would be kicking for a while.

"It's fine. It's under control. Don't shoot," I yelled as loudly as I could.

It was a mistake. Cole had been going around the banister to go down the stairs and he turned to look back at me, tripping over his own feet. The curved staircase was wide and he hit the wall then bounced around wildly as he tumbled, unable to get a purchase to stop himself. The sound of him hitting the wall was awful. He'd pitched head first and had caught it on an angle.

I pounded down the stairs after him, praying and yelling for the cops to stop.

Cole lay on the foyer floor. His breathing was shallow. I skidded past him and grabbed the key off the table.

"I'm opening the door. A boy is injured."

I opened the deadbolt and wrenched the door open. The uniforms pushed past me, guns drawn. They were both yelling.

"Who's in the house?"

"Get down on the ground!"

I dropped to my knees, hands on the back of my head. "He needs medical assistance."

"Where's the perp?"

"He's the perp and he needs EMS, now. He fell down the stairs."

"Keep your hands on your head," one of the uniforms said. I hadn't moved anything other than my mouth but I wasn't about to give him any excuse to get jumpy.

The radio popped and then I heard Jan's voice advising uniforms that a FCPD consultant was on scene.

The taller one looked at me. "That you?"

"Yeah, Pennington. EMS NOW!"

The one that wasn't trained on me called for a bus and holstered his weapon. The other guy eyed me, keeping his gun in my face, which was pretty fucking rude, if you asked me.

"Do you mind?"

"You got ID?"

"I do and I'm not even twitching until you take your service weapon out of my face." I flicked my eyes over to the more relaxed of the pair. "There's a girl upstairs, the homeowner's daughter. She's the one I called about. The guy on the floor is a friend from her school who got her out of her guardian's house under a pretense and brought her here."

That was probably the closest facsimile of the story anybody was going to get out of either party. I felt comfortable letting it be the official account of the afternoon's event. They could get it later when people weren't in need of medical care. Cop number two finally lowered his weapon and I dropped my hands.

"She been assaulted?"

I shook my head and scooted over to Cole on my knees, taking his wrist in my hand. His pulse was faint but I felt it. "She seems okay. Scared. Cole just wanted some property that is tied up in another case I'm working with Detective Boyd."

I heard the ambulance wending its way through the subdivision. I stood up trying not to even jostle the kid. I was sure he'd broken his neck the second he'd taken the header into the wall.

Uniform Tense and Scowly pulled out his cuffs and bent down. I pushed him away gently. "You can't move him. He could have a neck injury."

"Protocol states—"

"Does protocol state you paralyze a teenage boy on what could be as flimsy as a menacing charge? You wanna stake your badge and a fifty-million-dollar lawsuit against the county on it?"

He shook his head and put the cuffs away. "He's not going anywhere until they cart him out."

Tense and Scowly turned to his partner, Sedate and Laconic. "What do you want to do with the guys in the black-and-white?"

"You brought people on the call?" I asked.

"Nah, two guys were beefing in the yard when we got here."

That explained the extra time I'd had. Nothing like wasting precious time on a kidnap call by arresting neighbors fighting.

"Shit! One of those guys is the neighbor and the other is my backup."

Tense and Scowly snickered. "You have backup? You're a consultant."

"I'm a PI and that guy you cuffed and tossed into your cruiser is a five-time World Martial Arts champion, current record holder, sixth level blackbelt, and likely the most well-known and beloved living figure in the martial arts community besides Jhoon Rhee."

They looked at each other and then Sedate and Laconic beat feet out to make apologies.

"I'm going upstairs to get my friend. That cool?"

He nodded and I turned my back on him to go upstairs only to hear him choke out a strangled yelp. I turned back to see his hand hovering over his holster. "You're armed?"

At the reminder, I registered that the gun was digging into the small of my back with a sting. In all the running around and sweating the gun had rubbed a good four-inch abrasion into my skin. That's what I got for leaving my holster in the gun safe at the apartment.

"Yup. Sorry 'bout that." I wasn't sorry for him being freaked out. I was sorry I hadn't mentioned it because that shit is how people end up with a clip emptied into them. Sometimes mentioning is also how people end up with a clip in them. It was a crap shoot these days.

I took the stairs two at a time, holding the weapon to my slick skin trying to avoid a deeper wound, to get up to Aja. I called out when I was on the second staircase up to the loft so she knew it was me and didn't decide to start chucking lamps.

She was sniffling in the corner where I'd left her. I walked over and held my hand out to help her up.

"Where's Cole? Is he okay?" Jeez, the kid was either a stellar human or a right dumbass.

"He's got EMTs looking at him. He fell down the stairs and is unconscious. I'm actually more worried about you right now."

She stood and held my hand tightly, pressing herself into my side. I wrapped my free arm around her and tried to pull her deeper into me but all the space that was left was occupied by skin and muscle.

"I'm okay. He was just ... so scared." She hiccupped. She was going into shock. I wanted to get her out of the house and back to Nancy, who could deal with it better than I could. Adam was just as qualified and he was even closer.

I walked us both slowly down the multiple sets of stairs. The EMTs were carefully working on Cole and I skirted us both right past them and down the basement stairs, as Aja tucked her head into the crook of my shoulder. My heart flared a little. How had this kid I barely knew become so important to me in such a short amount of time?

I took us out through the broken slider, reminding myself to call my dad to board that back up again when we got to the truck. I was happy to see Adam and the nosy neighbor were out of the backseat of the car and uncuffed as we made our way up the side yard. Adam had a blanket ready for Aja and he wrapped her up in it, taking possession of her.

I turned to the old man. "Sorry about earlier. I was a little pumped up on adrenaline when we got here."

He nodded curtly then took off his jacket and offered it to me. "I don't approve of that kind of language but I see you were just worried about the young woman."

Well, didn't that beat all. He was actually gallant in a sexist, fusty kind of way.

"Thanks. I appreciate you accepting my apology. I know things have been kind of crazy here lately. You probably don't believe it, but I have been trying to calm it all down."

He nodded again and I wondered if it hurt his neck to jerk it like that. Then he turned on his heel in perfect military precision and walked up the yard to his own house. I saw the curtain next to the door twitch. So the wife was alive and her chain reached to the door.

I went to the truck where Adam had Aja sitting and disarmed myself. The scrape on my back was stinging more as the sweat seeped in. I settled the gun into its home in the truck's built-in case and set the lock, shutting it firmly and sliding it back under the seat. If I was going to go on anymore rescue missions in workout clothes, I needed a better system and vowed to suck up the cost for the torso bandage-style holster. It was a write-off, at least.

My phone rang and I saw that it was Jan. "Where the hell are you? You missed all the fun."

"Fill me in."

Was she serious? She wasn't coming.

"Seriously?"

"Something came up with the Murphy case that I had to handle here."

I waited for her to elaborate and she failed to do so. It was an awkward couple of minutes while we each waited for the other to speak. I finally caved mostly because I was freezing my ass off in the February evening wearing sweaty, abbreviated workout clothes and the old man neighbor's Members Only jacket. Where did one even find these things anymore?

"Aja was poking around school today asking questions about Damian and one of the other kids involved must have gotten spooked. He played the friend card and then forced her to come to her house looking for, and I quote, 'the package.' Whoever Damian got it from or was supposed to give it to is rather pissed off that it's missing. He threatened that if they didn't get it, he was going to kill them—and no, I don't know who them is—like he killed Damian. Said Damian paid the price for getting greedy."

"That's ... uh, complicated. Damian's parents were here wanting to know what was going on with their kid's murder case. Their lawyer had been stonewalling every attempt for us to get any answers from them about his life, activities, friends, health. Anything and everything we need to help us figure out what he'd gotten himself into."

"Can you get a warrant?"

"Done, but they've had time to sanitize. What about the kid?"

"He's not talking. He's pretty seriously hurt. Took a header down the stairs. I'm not sure ... he may not make it." I had turned away, putting my back to Aja, and lowered my voice. I didn't need her freaking out any more than she already was.

"I'll get a warrant for him too—blood test, home, car, phones. Seems like you're seeing all the action and I'm doing all the paperwork, kid."

I was starting to feel like I wanted to make the trade. Watching Cole hit that wall was going to be in my head for a long time. I had a feeling that whatever replaced it might end up being worse if this case went on too long.

"Don't worry. I've got plenty of paperwork too."

CHAPTER

17

A FLASHY BLACK SPORTS car sat out front of the house when I pulled up. Aja sighed heavily. "My parents."

It was not the response of a child who'd been terrorized repeatedly and only wanted her mom and dad. It was the weary declaration of someone who'd lived far too long with disappointment and had grown used to it.

"I'm sorry. I know you're not thrilled to see them but—"

"I'm just tired of it all. When do I get to come first with them? Do I ever?"

"Hey, they came back. They could have sent a lawyer, someone with guardianship papers to handle it."

"They're selfish. They don't care about what happens to me."

"You know, I'm not a parent but I think, even the ones who are wrapped up in themselves, care. They just don't necessarily know how to show it."

"But your parents—"

"Let's not set the bar too high to reach. My parents can swing too hard in the other direction, you know. It isn't annoying to you yet because it's new."

"I don't think I'd ever get sick of it."

"My dad sent me on a fake stakeout and everyone knew except me."

The look on her face as we climbed out of the truck was almost enough to make me forgive him. Almost.

My mother waved at me from the picture window in the kitchen and I motioned her outside. She looked behind her and then disappeared from view to open the front door and hurry down the stairs. I met her halfway up the walk.

"Aja's nervous."

"So are they. This seems to be their cross-country bus moment."

Of course she'd known I overheard them. Nothing got past her. At least she wasn't crying. That was the only thing saving me from it.

"It damn well better be. They owe her better than what they've been giving her, which is a whole lot of nothing," I said, quietly sniffing. It was misty and tree pollen was starting to cause budding. I wasn't crying.

Nancy reached up and cupped my cheek. "She'll be fine no matter what. She's got a friend to help her through it."

I sniffled again. Pollen. It was the pollen.

"Why don't you go around back and get some real clothes on?" She'd phrased it like a question but it was a motherly order, and I managed to get around the side of the garage before the tears trickled.

I swiped at them with the back of my hand. I was exhausted. I was stressed about Aja and the two murders. I hated to admit it even to myself, but I needed my partner and he'd abandoned me.

I yanked my cell out of my pocket and fired off an explicitly angry text to Seth. Damn him. You don't just disappear. He'd harangued me to make sure I didn't do it to him and I'd, technically, only run off in the most extreme walk of shame anyone had taken. I hadn't owed him anything at that point. I hadn't made him any promises.

I saw the bubbles of his impending reply. Then they stopped. I waited for the bubbles to return. Nothing.

Fine. That was the way it was. I stuck my phone back into my hoodie pocket and walked the length of the house to the back door.

I opened the slider and there was my baby brother, the one I'd abandoned at Adam's dojo to deal with the beginner's class, and my dog waiting for me.

"Hey, Willy Bean." He smiled. I was in such a wobbly place emotionally that I didn't know if I was going to actually start crying but I found a laugh burble up. Leave it to Ben.

I crouched down and motioned for Fargo, who came at me with all the force her puppy body could generate—a considerable amount—knocking me on to my butt and causing Ben to laugh. I was glad our parents had splurged on the extra plush carpet padding. In the months since I'd been working with Adam, the fat pad on my backside had diminished considerably.

"Crazy day, huh, Benjy?" I rubbed Fargo's belly while she arced on the carpet, shedding her thick needle fur for me to step on later when I was barefoot.

Fargo lost interest in me and stretched then got up and ambled over to her bed.

"You scared the shit out of me, Will."

My phone buzzed in my pocket. I ignored it. Seth could damn well wait his turn.

"Sorry, Ben. This is the job."

His sweet man-boy face contorted. "No, it's not. Dad's been doing it for years and it's nothing like this."

I opened my mouth and had no idea what to say so I closed it again. I closed my eyes to shut off the sad, scared look in his eyes. He was right. Of course. This wasn't the way Dad did the job.

"I'm not Dad, Benjy. I'm me. This is ... this is how I know how to do what needs doing. I wasn't about to leave Aja scared and alone. I had no idea who had her or what they were capable of. I did what I'd want someone to do if it was you."

"And last fall? That wasn't about me. You've been off the force less than a year and you've been in more danger than in the five years you were a cop. That's bullshit, Will."

It was bullshit because he really had no idea how much danger I was in as a cop. I probably had no idea either. It wasn't as if that was a safe job. I knew he wanted me to say something that would reassure him, like that I'd stop. I'd had the conversation enough with our father. Would I just look before I leapt? Could I weigh the possible consequences? As if I could calculate those with some kind of formula or algorithm. Even if that was possible, I wouldn't have been capable of the math.

"I know you're scared. I understand it. I feel it every time Seth leaves the house in a bulletproof vest. I felt it every time Michael missed a call."

"And you know what can happen. You know what happened to Michael. He's dead. He got killed. Seth could get killed. You seem to be trying to get killed. Why are you all so ready to die?"

God help me. I was related to the only seventeen-year-old boy in the world who had a fully developed sense of mortality.

"It's not that we're ready to die …"

He glared at me. I wasn't getting out of it without answering him. Ben was the most stubborn person I knew. He eclipsed me and Dad by miles.

"Michael died and I just … I was scared all the time. It didn't matter what it was. If my gums bled when I brushed my teeth I was convinced I was dying. And I gave in. It was easy. I pulled fear over me like a blanket. And I snuggled down into it and let it protect me. From everything. It wasn't Michael's death that started to change me. It was letting fear rule over me in the wake of it. And it almost killed me, Ben."

"No, what almost killed you was a crazy racist."

It was hard to argue with that. Except with the truth.

"And, yet, I'm still here. Annoying you."

"For how long? Until the next time you do something stupid and scare the shit out of me?"

He was really working the curses today. He was pretty mad at me. And he was probably upset about Aja. He got attached to people a lot more easily than I did and that girl had wormed her way into my cold, dark heart.

My phone buzzed again and I grabbed it, intending to quiet it, but I saw it was Boyd.

KID'S NOT GOING TO MAKE IT.

"Shit."

"What?

"Jan says that Cole kid isn't going to make it."

"Cole? What about him? Make it where?"

Wait.

"Do you know Cole, Ben?"

"He's a friend of John's, sort of. They worked on a project together last year. John felt kind of bad for him. He's not exactly good at social stuff. Bullied."

"Blond kid?"

He nodded. I hadn't seen John in a while. He'd better not be mixed up in this mess.

"How close are they? John hasn't ... changed lately like Damian, right?"

Ben morphed back into normal teen boy and twisted his face into such disgust and annoyance I feared he'd sprain a muscle. "Dude, no. He's not stupid."

"How much do you know about this going on at school, Ben? Is this a lot of kids?"

His expression turned to disdain, one I was familiar with, and pity, an even more familiar one. This was the *You're so stupid but I'm not going to say it because you'd kick my ass* face.

"Will, the school is enormous. I only know about Damian being in this stuff because Aja told me and Cole because you just told me. I don't hang out with people like that."

People like that. What did that mean exactly? High school was pretty different than when I was there. It seemed like with these giant secondary schools, cliques didn't really form. And this generation Z as they were called were supposedly more evolved and socially conscious. What did it mean when a good, kind, generous kid said *people like that?*

Us millennials were inconsiderate assholes so I put him on the line, cocking an eyebrow at him. "People like that?"

"Jeez, I didn't mean anything bad by it. Just that I'm not really in classes with kids that aren't in the AP and honors program. Look, I know that's mean, but kids like Damian are the kids that need the A in gym, you know?"

Stunned was a reaction I didn't often have with my brother. I'd got used to his brilliance when he was small but he'd always been kind about it. This sentiment was ugly arrogance.

"You meant something bad by it, Ben. And that you don't see it makes me really angry and sad. I was the kind of kid that needed the A in gym."

I stomped past him and shut the door to my room much harder than it needed shutting. Within seconds I heard soft scratching and I opened the door to find Fargo waiting patiently on the other side. Of course she was on my side. She'd failed out of explosives detection school. She trotted in and I shut the door again.

I took my time gathering my clothes and texting Jan back. The whole Cole thing was throwing me for several loops. I felt guilty for my part in him falling. I hadn't put him in the position, but I'd distracted him and that was going to stay with me for a long time. I knew Aja was going to take it pretty hard too and she'd been through so much.

CHAPTER

18

"COME ON, GIRL. LET'S go get cleaned up."

The adrenaline sweat had dried and it was not a pleasant smell. I took my clothes and the dog and showered as quickly as I could, trying to keep her out of the water. She acted like a water dog and was always trying to get in with me. It was cute and tiring. She was a smart, tricky dog and getting clean with one foot off the ground to keep her nose out of the stall was a balancing act worthy of an acrobat. I had tried locking her out, but that resulted in a door that needed sanding and painting. She was fine being separated from me as long as running water wasn't involved. Eh, I had personality quirks too.

I toweled off and twisted my hair up into a clip. That was as fancy as I got. Nicer jeans than I would have worn while working and a button-down that mostly fit but was too short in the sleeves (long arms are almost always convenient except where sleeves are concerned) and I was presentable enough to meet Aja's parents.

The parents I was already predisposed to not liking. This would be a test of my tact and grace, as far as those existed. I would do my best to be the grownup in the situation and not the angry young woman who'd just had to rescue their child, the one they'd abandoned to jet around the world and party, not once but twice (or was it three times, at this point?) from a situation that, had they only stuck around to be near, could have been avoided with maybe one less murder and a potential fatal fall down stairs for a scared young man. Ah, the soothing tact and grace was just welling up from inside.

I trudged up the stairs longing for a cup of coffee (and, yay me, for ratcheting down that addiction just in time for me to really need it to come through for me) and a stout bat to smack the living crap out of people I had yet to meet and already hated. I dredged down deep for something, anything, from the therapist—a calming mantra, the Serenity Prayer, a power object—and found nothing. All strength of will then. I settled as nonthreatening a look on my face as I could muster. Less *you're going down in a crumpled heap of pain and tears, mofo* and more *I can't do anything to you legally or physically but you will not enjoy my tone.*

The woman person had glassy eyes that damn well better have been from unshed tears and the man person looked gassy. My mood? Not improved.

Mom sat across from them in a body posture I'd best seen described as *on tenterhooks*. I had no idea what tenterhooks were but the fact that they were hooks didn't make them sound comfortable.

Dad had his patent-pending Face of Doom which made the unshed tears and gassy extremely understandable. Aja looked ... like a girl who would rather be anywhere else in the world having anything else in the world done to her. Ben looked clueless.

All caught up on the nonverbal communication, I stomped over to the parents, stuck out my hand, and played grownup.

"Willa Pennington, your daughter's private investigator." Damn how I wished I'd had the foresight to print up a bill and hand it to them. They were definitely getting one via email once I figured out how much to charge them for the services their daughter shouldn't have needed.

The mother person popped up and grabbed me in a hug that felt too weak and too strong at the same time. It was like Pilates had met WASP apathy and I just barely resisted curling up my lip and nose.

"You're an angel." Okay, dial it back a dozenty hundred notches and while we're at it too.much.perfume. I felt like I'd just been accosted by thirty perfume spritzers at the mall. I hated the mall.

"Heh." I gently pushed her away. "I guarantee my mother would quibble with your angel remark but..."

The father person didn't meet my eyes so I stared at him until even I was uncomfortable and his wife dug her bony, be-ringed fingers into his arms. Her appendages looked like giant chicken claws and I wondered how someone's fingers even got that skinny.

He stood up, a little taller than I was, looking shorter, and jammed his hands into his pockets. What a dick.

"Yeah, I can see how grateful you are too. No need to get mushy."

I felt rather than saw Aja roll her eyes behind my back and decided that I didn't care who had what legal leg to stand on, jump on, or cut off, she wasn't going any damn where with these people unless I saw her take a polygraph and say, "Yes, I absolutely cannot wait to go anywhere with these cold, unfeeling, assholes."

I rolled my head on my neck and Nancy popped up out of her seat. "Coffee?"

I stared down Aja's papa and grinned a very unangelic smile. "Love some, Mom. Maybe Aja and Ben would like to help."

My scalp tingled with anticipation and then the damn doorbell rang. Jan. SONUVABITCH. I had been about to release the Kraken. I stared hard at him and then blew out a breath. While it would have been such a great release to unload on this asshole who couldn't find a tiny bit of humility to offer to the people who'd taken in his daughter and helped her, Jan would cut him up one side and down the other and that would be wonderful to watch. Surgical and yet he'd feel every cut.

I ushered her in and she gave me an amused look. She knew me well enough to know I was full-on nuclear angry and she knew who it was directed at. He didn't dare not shake her hand and I watched with relish as he squirmed under her look-right-through him gaze. She'd sized him up in a moment and let him sputter and choke on his explanations of why Aja was alone for so long. Aja's mother twisted a tissue in her hands, little flakes of it floating down to the rug with each jerk. They were both extremely nervous, almost too nervous, in Jan's presence and I wondered if they were stupid enough to be holding. To do that knowing you were getting ready to meet a cop, one who had been handling a murder that was directly tied to your parental negligence, took a level of dumbass and arrogant privilege I knew existed in the world but hadn't personally witnessed.

Dad had gotten up and meandered into the kitchen as Jan was coming in. It was starting to get crowded in there, and then she looked at me with a tilt to her head. I was being dismissed? Just when it was getting good? She flipped open her portfolio to pull out Aja's combined statements.

"Being Aja's legal guardian requires one of you or a court-appointed guardian ad-litem representative to review her statements before we can make them official."

Her words hung ominously. The mother reached forward with a shaking hand to take the pages. My last view of her was her bent head studying the pages.

Four sets of expectant eyes turned to me when I walked into the kitchen.

"What's going on?" Aja whispered. Her face was screwed up in a half anxious, half tough girl look. I pressed down the anger it stirred in me to use for another day on another person.

"Jan's just having them review your statements. It's a pretense to make them see what you've been dealing with. She doesn't have to get their approval on anything."

Aja nodded. "I have to go with them, don't I?"

I opened my mouth but Dad cut me off. "You don't have to go anywhere you don't want to with anyone you don't want to go with."

That settled it. Dad had spoken. This was why he had been a great cop and was a good PI. He cared about people. It didn't always seem like it, he didn't always act like it, he'd deny it if anyone ever accused him of it, but he cared deeply. His duty was to other people. He served and protected in the truest sense of the words. I didn't. It wasn't about that for me. I was in it to solve the puzzle. I was still working on the people part of it.

Aja looked at my father and then my mother. "I think I do have to. Like I need to. Does that make sense?"

Mom hugged her. "This is always home to you, sweetie."

And that was why they were the perfect couple. They were both more interested in other people's feelings and needs than their own. And I was just like Leila. It was all about my own needs. That didn't feel good. At least I was applying it to trying to right wrongs. She taught people how to cry on cue. I know, mean and unfair. Chalk it up to cross-fire anger directed at the Peter Pan parents in the other room.

Aja asked Nancy to help her go pack up. I stomped downstairs ignoring Jan and Aja's parents as they all made serious and sober-looking faces at one another.

The files on the cold case taunted me from the table. All the pictures, all the reports, all the statements and I wasn't any closer to figuring out who the killer was. I contemplated sorting through them one more time but admitted that I was only hiding from how I felt about Aja leaving with those people. They didn't deserve a second, or whatever number, chance. Admittedly, I wasn't big on second chances anyway.

As if on cue, my phone binged. Seth.

I SCREWED THIS ALL UP. KEEP THE FAITH, PLEASE. I'M THE ONE HANGING OUT THE WINDOW THIS TIME.

Well, shit. If anyone deserved a second chance, it was Seth. Us. Or whatever number chance we were on at this point.

No MORE PICKING STUPID FIGHTS. No MORE KEEPING THINGS FROM YOU. I PROMISE.

Double shit. How could I say no? If it had been me … hell, it was me. I kept stuff from him all the time. So he didn't worry. So he didn't try to White Knight me. So he didn't make me think about someone else's feelings and needs.

Triple shit. I truly loved the asshole. Thinking about giving up on us made my stomach hurt. I wasn't good at picturing the future but when I tried, all I saw was my family, Aja included. And Seth.

QUIT BEING A DUMBASS. YOU KNOW I'D NEVER LET YOU GO EVEN IF IT MEANT WE BOTH BURNED TO DEATH.

I really needed to start giving those texts an edit before I hit send. I waited watching the dots cycle as he typed his reply.

I was a teenage girl. I was a stupid teenage girl worried about texting with my boyfriend. I should shoot myself right now and get it over with.

The dots blinked at me. Was he writing the Gettysburg Address? Jeez, how long did it take to tell me I was weird or stupid? Maybe he was being smart enough to not tell me those things. I didn't need context though. I just needed words.

But the dots hovered and disappeared.

Fargo had laid down directly behind me and as I took the step back, she yelped and I pulled short at the last minute, falling into the table and launching my phone into the brick fireplace surround five feet away.

It shattered, loudly. Eggs were sturdier than my phone model, apparently.

Ben was pounding down the stairs in a second. "Hey, what was that? Something break down here? Are you okay, Fargo?"

Nice that his concern was for the dog. Although she'd made a noise of distress and I hadn't. My phone was incapable of making any noises ever again.

I pointed at the debris. "My phone. At least it wasn't a wood chipper."

"Can I?" Pointing at his phone, omnipresent in his hand. He gave it to me and then examined Fargo from the tip of her floppy ear to the tip of her unhurt paw.

I called up his contact list and found Seth's entry.

HEY, FARGO KNOCKED INTO ME AND I DROPPED AND BROKE MY PHONE. BUT I JUST WANTED YOU TO KNOW THAT WE'RE COOL. OKAY? WE'LL FIGURE IT ALL OUT WHEN YOU GET HOME.

LOVE YOU.

I deleted the text conversation and handed it back to him. I was sure Ben had some way of recovering it but there wasn't anything in it I needed him to not read.

"Will? Are you okay? You don't look okay."

"I really liked that phone."

We had multiple sim cards for that model but not extra phones. Not that model anyway. Burners it was until I had time to get a replacement. Another insurance bill.

"Aja's getting ready to leave with her parents. Do you want me to send her down?"

Was today Make Willa Deal with Uncomfortable Emotions Day? I nodded, not trusting my voice. I had a hard lump in my throat and I knew from experience that meant my body was trying to force me to cry. I hadn't evolved that much that I was going to cry in front of people. People did not include my mommy and I was desperate for just a moment to let go. I was exhausted and overwhelmed.

Aja came down the stairs slowly. She was dragging out leaving. I knew she was only going because she wanted to give her parents a chance; for them, not for her. It hurt in a way that was all about me and understanding the feeling of wanting your parent to be okay when it wasn't your job to make sure of that. But it was a lesson she had to learn on her own. And she had a safe place just like I did.

"You may regret how this turns out but you won't regret giving them another chance, kiddo. And we're always here." I could be mushy and big sisterly when I needed.

She nodded and swallowed hard, looking away. She was trying not to cry.

"Don't do that, Aja. Don't push the feelings down anymore. You need them and they need to see them."

She nodded again and flung herself at me. I cleared my throat around the lump and closed my arms around her, hard. I heard her whispering "thank you" over and over. I nodded into her shoulder and tightened my grip a little more.

"It was my pleasure. You're a great kid. Don't forget it."

She pulled back, sniffing, and went to wipe her nose on the non-existent hoodie sleeve. That made both of us laugh and I did the grossest thing I'd ever done as an adult. I picked up my arm and wiped her nose with my sleeve. We started laughing harder, falling against one another. One of us snort-laughed and we both laughed harder. It felt good to lean into her and just let out the tension. We stayed like that for a few minutes until she smiled at me sadly and turned away.

At the bottom of the stairs, she turned back. "I want to be just like you when I grow up. Strong and brave and fearless."

I stared at her as she walked up the stairs and then was out of view.

Fearless? Ha. That was a good trick. I'd fooled someone into thinking I was fearless.

———

Nancy took a sip of her tea, staring at me over the rim of her mug. "What's going on with Seth? Have you talked since the phone call the other night?"

The coffee mug was a soothing warmth in my hands. A plate of cookies sat on the table between us, ignored.

"He texted, apologized for just taking off and being weird and annoying in general, picking fights and all."

"What did you say?"

"I responded that it was fine. That I got it. We were okay."

"And is it?"

I took a sip of coffee, stalling. I set the mug down and took a cookie, breaking it into small pieces and eating each bit slowly, one at a time. I finished and made eye contact. If she was feeling impatient, she wasn't showing it.

"Maybe. I'm upset he kept the adoption a secret from me." I considered for a second. "No, that's not really it. I'm upset he kept a big revelation in his life a secret but proceeded to act like a jerk for what seemed like no good reason."

And that was it. Everyone's got their own private stuff they don't want to share and if that was his thing or even just one of those things, cool, great, bottle that shit up. But don't try to provoke fights with me because you're mad and you can't or won't talk to who you're really angry with.

My mother knew me well enough to know I'd said my piece on the matter. Unlike Seth, I knew how to express my anger to the person I was angry with.

"How's the murder coming? Murders."

I recapped the cold case for her. How frustrated I was with the lack of anything concrete.

"No one had a motive. Not a good one, at least. Jan's fairly convinced it was the brother but even she's wavering on that now, I think. They'd had some fights but no one knows about what and everyone there's a statement from agrees that they can't imagine him hurting her."

"Boyfriend?"

"No motive as far as I can see. Alibi's shaky but that's not a surprise. It's a holiday weekend and people are coming and going. People can agree they saw him but not a solid time. The brother's got the same problem with his alibi."

"Mother?" Her voice didn't even waver. I was a little surprised. She had been a cop's wife though. And an ER nurse. She knew what people were capable of.

"Alibi is solid. She was Black Friday shopping and has dated and timed receipts."

"And this boy Aja knew? Anything on that case?"

I picked up my mug again, mulling over Aja and Damian. Damian and Cole. Damian and Cole and this mystery man in the Guy Fawkes mask who wanted back whatever was worth killing over.

"Steroids is all I've got on that so far. We're fairly certain Damian had been taking them based on his physiological changes and I assume the autopsy will confirm. Cole, the kid who came for Aja, was doing them too. And from what Cole said, Damian took something extremely valuable and hid it. It's a straight line from Damian's murder to Mr. X but other than that, we've got nothing."

I remembered that I'd wanted to pick up another coffeemaker for the basement in all the thinking and talking about the cases taking me round and round.

CHAPTER

19

THE STORE WAS BLESSEDLY empty as I grabbed a cart and headed straight to the appliances. There were a myriad of colors and sizes available for the single-serve coffeemakers. My brain was not in a place where I could deal with too many options so I self-soothed by detouring to the candy aisle.

I grabbed bags of fruity licorice twists and a ten-pack of candy that had mixed caramel, pretzels, and peanut butter all covered in milk chocolate. My rapid-fire synapses began to amp down and I made sure I picked up a half dozen boxes of breakfast pastries that deranged people toasted and sane people ate cold from the package just as god intended.

Another jag down the cookie aisle and two bags of the butter cookies that made me feel in control of an uncontrollable world. I grabbed a small bear-shaped tub of chocolate-covered animal crackers which I then swapped for a large. Hey, they were called crackers because they were mostly healthy.

I took a deep breath and forced myself back to the unnecessarily complicated caffeine delivery systems. I chose a dark blue one in the size determined best for "small offices and dorm rooms" reasoning that Ben could take it off to MIT. At the end of the aisle, as I was heading for the checkout area, there was a display of coffee pods and a box of Extra Bold caught my eye. Extra Bold was the existential choice I was craving at the moment plus it was likely to be Extra Kick in the Pants after another pointless night of reviewing a case I wasn't making a damn bit of headway on yet was too stubborn to turn back over and admit defeat.

Finally armed with more junk food than good sense (and both my therapist and mother would agree), I headed to the front of the store, mentally awarding a Nobel Peace Prize to the genius who came up with self-checkout. I was in even less of a mood than usual for dealing with people. That included friendly cashiers, all of whom looked entirely too perky and ready to assist. I scanned the items and bagged them, feeling another soothing rush of dopamine at the sight of all my favorite mood levelers. The total made me wince a little but I swiped my card and pulled the receipt from the machine without thinking too hard about it.

I hadn't spent much of the reward money both Jan and Seth had strong-armed the ATF into making sure I got. There had been some whining from the higher-ups, always trying to save budget money for stupid crap no one really needed to do their jobs, but a few carefully chosen words about all the press the story and I, in particular, had been getting ended up with a check being cut.

The parking lot was sparsely populated and the night sky dark against the multitudes of lights in the parking lot. I loaded the bags into the truck and cranked the engine to get the heat going. I checked my burner phone for messages from anyone besides Seth and came up with a big, fat blank screen. Damn. I scrounged in the glove box for the charger I knew Ben made sure was available and plugged it in to charge.

I didn't want to sit in the parking lot too long after getting in my car. I was sure no one in the big box store cared but I knew each of the dozens of light poles had cameras on them and I was leery of ending up on some footage that the chain's corporate security had running through filters looking for suspicious activity. As I pulled out and pointed the truck toward the back of the lot to exit, I saw a car parked in the farthest corner spot. It had been there when I came in. I'd noticed because it was in the weird corner that wasn't a spot. It had likely been designed with the intention of making it a cart corral but it had just ended up empty. It was also at the bottom of the steep hill coming down from the corner light so people would cross the street from the townhouses and use the corner to walk down.

The nearest light was pretty far back in the lot, as if the designer had also misjudged how many needed to be ordered. That meant the spot and the car were in a dark hole with the evergreen pines, the corner, and the lack of light being thrown from the lot. Who would park there? Surely a store worker would park in much closer. I was even fairly certain there was a back lot for them.

My headlights lit up the mud gathered all around the tires under the car. It had rained pretty hard the day Damian died and the hill was bared of grass thanks to the winter full of snowstorms, leaving a wash of mud. The car had been there a while then.

I pulled in a spot near the car, a black BMW, and got out to take a look. I was no longer worried about the corporate security because they clearly hadn't tipped to this car. Using the flashlight on my key-ring I looked inside. I saw nothing out of the ordinary. A gym bag on the back seat spilling out clothing. A fast food drink cup in the holder between the seats. The ashtray compartment was open and, like mine, sporting a phone charger.

I got down on my knees and got a good look at the dried mud and debris under the car. It had definitely been there too long for a cheap commuter not wanting to pay for parking at the VRE lot behind the store.

That got me thinking about Damian's car. They had searched the surrounding neighborhoods and had found nothing. Could this black BMW be the one the cops were looking for? Could it had been that easy? Could I have just found the possible linchpin of the whole damn investigation while on a junk food run?

"Jan, I've got a license plate. You ready?"

I read it off to her and waited while she ran the search. It wasn't Damian's but when I explained to her my thought she said she'd dispatch black-and-whites to local store parking lots, of which there were at least a dozen. I reminded her to get the high school's parking lot too. There was a massive amount of blacktop surrounding the building and, having gone to the school myself, I knew there were places to effectively hide a car. I didn't explain how I knew that detail and while she didn't ask I heard her smirk through the phone.

"I'll keep you updated since it was your idea, after all. How's Mandy's case going?"

I got back in the truck and shut the door before I replied, "It's no-where. I've got nothing, Jan. There's no way you could have solved this case back then."

I heard her blow out a hard breath. I knew she was frustrated. "I need to wrap this up, kid. I ... hang on a sec."

I heard her push back her godawful squeaky chair. A door opened and swung shut.

"Listen, kid, I haven't told anyone here but ... I'm retiring."

I froze, my hand halfway toward the steering column, keys in hand.

"What? Retire? Why?"

She laughed. "I've been in Homicide almost twenty years, Willa. That's a long time chasing murder and I was in Burglary five years before Mandy Veitch's death. It's time. It's past time. I should have left the game a long time ago."

I sat in the truck like an idiot. If she'd said she was a brain-sucking alien, I would have been less stunned. I'd never considered that Jan would retire. Ever. She was the cop. She was Homicide to me. I don't think I'd ever considered her life. I'd never even thought about what she did when she left the station. What she did when she went home. What her house looked like. Did she own casual clothes? Did she have a cat? I was a shitty person.

"I don't know what to say. I guess I just figured you'd always be there."

She laughed again. "I'm not going to drop off the face of the planet, kid. I'm still going to be around. We'll still meet for coffee." But her voice had taken on a hesitant note. She was unsure. And I'd been wrong. Jan Boyd being uncertain was the one thing that sur-prised me more than her retiring.

"You'd damn well better be sticking around, Boyd. I'm going to need someone to bitch to when my dad forgets he's my supervising investigator and starts acting like my dad."

"I can't wait."

Then she hung up on me. I guess it had gotten too mushy for her. I stared at the phone for a minute, my stomach churning. In case it was hunger, I grabbed the bag and tore into the box of peanut butter toaster pastries. I knew it wasn't hunger though. Things were changing, things beyond my control. I should have meditated instead of eating my feelings. I knew my therapist wanted me to, in her words, utilize more appropriate stress-coping measures. But I was tired and there were two murders I wasn't solving. And Seth was apparently having his own nervous breakdown. Aja had left. Ben wasn't too far behind her and I was still pissed with him. I didn't like change. I wasn't good at it anymore. I pretended I was, but I'd grown set in my habits. I'd become comfortable being able to control things. And people.

My phone binged and for a second I thought Seth had somehow figured out I was using the burner but picking it up I saw the text was from Jan.

Because I know you.

Then the make and model of the car registered to Damian along with the license plate number.

I had snacks. I could check a few of the parking lots too. And if that delayed me from having to have an uncomfortable conversation inappropriate for the text format then so be it.

I found Damian's car in the lot for the Asian market only a block from the school. It was a short walk to Aja's place too, just cross the road, duck down into the parking lot of the next business park, over the train tracks, and through the woods to the swanky neighborhood where people could afford the soundproofing needed to deal with the commuter train blasting through five times an hour. It was the only place for miles around open twenty-four hours. It should have been the first place I checked. Across the intersection in the other direction was the dojo. Adam mentioned shopping at the Asian market for Theo sometimes, but I'd completely forgotten about it.

I sat in the truck under one of the weird sulfur lights that bathed everything in a sickly yellow glow and waited for Jan, fiddling with my temporary phone.

A sharp rap on the window made me jump and drop the phone. Jan's face smirked at me through the glass. I glared at her for a second then unlocked the door. I got out and bent back in the truck to retrieve my phone from the floor of the driver's side.

"You were expecting me, right? You seem surprised to see me," she said, loping away from the truck faster than her, frankly, stubby legs should have carried her.

I scampered after her, trying to appear as if I wasn't a child chasing after her mom in a store. "I was thinking. I do that sometimes."

"Sorry I disturbed you, Einstein. I thought you might want to participate in the search since you found the car."

I swallowed my smartass reply and kept pace with her. I'd made sure I parked as far away as I could so when they marked off the perimeter I wasn't accidentally trapped inside. The uniforms get testy when they have to redo the tape, like it's some kind of damn art project they were having to alter.

She took a pair of gloves from the uniform and tilted her head toward me. The guy handed me a pair too. How I hated those gloves. The feel of them in my hands like a deflated balloon sliding on itself and the powder inside them drying out my skin even though my hands always sprouted sweat the second I'd snapped them on, making that noise that set my teeth on edge. Another thing I hadn't escaped when I tossed away my FCPD pension.

"You start in the trunk, Pennington."

The other uniform popped the compartment using a pry bar and I sent up a silent prayer, as I did every time anything I hadn't locked opened in front of me: *Please do not let there be a dead body in here.* Logically, and aromatically, I knew there was nothing deader in the trunk than probably some batteries, but it was something I did subconsciously and I doubted I'd stop any time soon. My training officer had once found a dead body in a community pool's equipment storage chest and that visual had stuck with me—the lifeguard, still in her uniform one piece swimsuit, folded in on herself, bruises almost black on her face and neck, murdered for the small amount of cash still left in the snack bar's lockbox.

I braced myself as the trunk popped open. Body-free, just like I wanted. Otherwise, it was a mess. The space lit up and I looked to see the cop next to me holding his regulation flashlight up. I dug my keys back out of my pocket and added the meager light stream from my keychain light. I heard him chuckle.

"I have a real flashlight in my truck. I just didn't think I was going to get to search too." I was a little too defensive, apparently, because he dropped the smile and nodded curtly.

"Sorry, ma'am."

See? Shitty. Person. I was a shitty person. He'd helped me and enjoyed poking a tiny bit of fun at my tiny flashlight and I acted like a prima donna because I hated looking unprepared for a job I was just learning how to do. I sighed.

"No, I'm testy. I haven't been sleeping well."

"Well, I think that's to be expected, Miss Pennington."

Great. He knew who I was. And that's why he'd dropped the friendly attitude the second I'd acted like a whiny baby.

"Murders to be solved. No time for me to be a five-year-old. Thanks for having my back with the light, Officer."

"If you're done winning friends and influencing people, Pennington, maybe you could get your ass in gear and look for some clues."

I didn't need to see Jan to hear her words yelled from inside the car. Knowing the trunk lid blocked any view she'd have of me I risked pulling a funny face at the uniform. The cop covered his laughter with a coughing fit that was remarkably convincing.

New friend won, I settled into the trunk with my stupid latex-covered hands sweating like I was breaking into the damn thing.

There was a car kit full of the usual crap parents made sure their teen drivers had just in case they were ever stranded in the wilderness where the WiFi was sketchy and it might take them an extra three minutes to get the GPS signal solid.

Backpack full of textbooks that he hadn't been using, notebooks with only a few pages used, pencil bag full of brand-new supplies.

The gym bag was more interesting. There were one … two … six packages of unopened hand wraps. Okay, that was weird. I had two pair just to give them a break to dry out and let the elastic rest, and I worked out every day. They weren't the most expensive fitness equipment but they weren't cheap either. Not the good ones, anyway, which these were. So why would the kid need this many?

"Can you bring the light down a little? I want to dig in this bag and don't want to find any surprises the hard way."

He obliged as I tugged the opening of the bag wider. Since we were fairly certain Damian had been using steroids, I didn't want to end up on the business end of any used sharps.

I pulled out the packages and dropped them on the trunk floor. Underneath the fresh packages was an unraveled hand wrap. I pulled it and its mate out.

"Uh, Jan? Found one."

"One what, Pennington?"

"A clue. And it's covered in blood."

Her head popped around the trunk lid. "That beat the microSIM card I found?"

MicroSIMS went in phones. I knew this because I had several for my phone. Ben insisted that it was the best way to go incognito. I preferred the burners because they were easier than popping the little tray out and then trying to fumble the tiny cards out of and into place. Not only did I know what they were, I knew Ben had a tool for reading them.

But while blood didn't beat data, it still was evidence so I held up the wraps and Jan bagged them. I had one more fun little detail to add.

"Blood's on the outside."

Jan held up the baggie and looked at the wrap dubiously. "You sure?

"Positive. You wrap them around your hands and secure with the velcro on the wrists so there is an inside and outside. The way the blood's soaked in closer to the ends with the velcro means it's on the outside upper layer of the wrap. Unless Damian was wrapping his hands and then hitting himself, this is someone else's blood. We should take an unopened package for comparison."

She nodded and bagged a new package too. "Good job, kid."

"And I think I can help with the microSIM too. Ben has a reader. I can grab it and we can pull the data."

"What does that mean? Looking at zeros and ones is not how I want to spend the rest of my night."

I laughed. "But we could make popcorn and braid each other's hair."

Jan's horrified expression convinced me there were no movie nights in our future. Not even a shoot 'em up action movie.

I let her off the hook. "Nope, the reader is COTS but the software is all Ben."

"I'm afraid to ask ... COTS?"

"Sorry, common term in our house. Commercial Off the Shelf. So that any slob can buy one and use it. I'm sure the Computer Forensics Section has their own. You think any of them are on shift right now? Because we can wait until morning if you'd rather."

I cocked an eyebrow. It was Pennington Investigations listed as the official consultants to the FCPD. Therefore, Ben was included in the consultation agreement as our official IT resource. That meant it didn't matter if anyone was on shift with the CFS. And my house had cookies. Hell, my truck had cookies.

"We can break in my new coffeemaker too."

"I draw the line at braiding your hair, Pennington."

CHAPTER

20

AFTER SITTING THROUGH A lecture from Ben about the differences between mini, micro, and nanoSIM cards and the correction that what we had was a nanoSIM card, which was the standard in current cell phones and a bunch of other stuff I, and I hoped Jan, tuned out, the reader was handed off. We loaded the itsy-bitsy card into it after only dropping it three times and plugged the reader into my laptop. It was so easy to use I was a little worried about how many idiots were running around with these things and realized that regular people were probably more worried about the cops and people like me having them. If they even realized things like this existed, which was unlikely. Technology ruled our lives and we had no idea how deeply it reached.

The program sifted through the data, windows popping open as it segregated the data into classifications. Contacts, IP addresses, photos, and texts all flew from the bottom of the screen to the windows that popped up when a new category was found and created.

"This is creepy," Jan said, watching the screen while I fumbled with getting the new coffeemaker out of the box and then freed it from the additional packaging.

"Why do you think I'm doing something else? It's easier if you don't think about it all."

"And he just knows how to do this kind of thing?"

I stuffed the wrappings back in the box and kicked it out of the way. "This kind of thing was something he threw together for my dad a few years ago when he was lamenting getting locked out of his cell phone. He won some kind of tech fair with it. He was twelve, maybe. We've been offering it as a cheating spouse forensic deep dive service. If you think they're cheating, bring us their phone and we'll take a look, no charge."

"I'm so glad I don't have to deal with cheaters."

"Yeah, at least not until one of them ends up dead."

"That happens less often than movies would have you believe."

I handed her a cup of coffee, black, and doctored mine to perfection. My mother hadn't blinked an eye when I walked in carrying bags of junk food and a coffeemaker trailed by Jan and merely watched as I awkwardly fumbled it all to steal mugs, creamer, and sugar.

I knew she had an opinion about the sugar-laden empty calories. She just wasn't going to waste her time talking to someone who wasn't going to listen. I had reached that point of stress where I had to self-soothe—like an animal escaping to its den to lick its wounds. She knew me well enough, in fact, to not even offer to help me carry anything. A cornered animal often bit and was capable of worse. As I escaped with my loot, in my peripheral vision I had caught her smiling at Jan, adding a little shrug.

The program gave a helpful chime, indicating it had read all the data and finished categorizing it all.

I gulped down a mouthful of coffee and settled down to make Jan printouts of the text data, call logs and contact list. The pictures, of which there were only a handful, went onto the flash drive Ben had left waiting for me along with the card reader. It pays to call ahead and get your IT resource working before your mom sends him to bed.

I pulled up the pictures and found that most weren't well-focused and several were downright blurry. Most were taken at night in low-light and seemed like the phone had been held at waist-level.

"It looks like he didn't want anyone to know he was taking these pictures," Jan said.

"These are fairly worthless. I can't tell really anything about the people in most of these at this resolution."

I opened one up full screen. The blurriness was worse but at least I had a better idea of the subject. I pulled back a foot from the table to bring it further into context.

"They're fighters. Shirtless, two men in the middle of a space with a line of people behind them. I can see the hand wrap on one of the fighters."

Jan squinted at the computer then got up and took a step back. "Why would he be taking a picture of that?"

I rolled in and opened up the next photo in the sequence. Similar imaging, the fighters were in slightly different positions but it was obvious it was the same pair. I had an idea but wanted to see if I could find confirmation in one of the other pictures. I pulled the next several up in quick succession, scanning for the suspected activity until

I found one that, while it couldn't be used as legal evidence, was good enough for me to share my theory with Jan.

"If I'm right about the underground fight club, it's proof. It seems Damian was a budding blackmailer." I pointed to the screen. "And this looks like there might be a side of illegal gambling."

Jan leaned forward, looking at the area I was circling with my finger. "If you say so."

I nodded. "The pieces are there that make it make sense—the steroid use, the coroner's statement of healing bruises under the skin and the microfractures on Damian's hands and face, these pictures of the fighters. If I go through them from first to last, they change a little from one to the next. He was likely using the rapid shot function, holding down the button, which adds to the poor quality of the images, because the subjects are moving quickly."

I went back to the first image and put my finger on the screen next to where I wanted her to look. "Watch as I click through all of them. These two figures to the left of the fighters."

I cycled through the pictures again. If you paid attention to the people in the background, like a stop-action movie, you could see something changing hands.

"It's something changing hands, probably," Jan said. "It doesn't prove anything though."

"It doesn't. Not exactly. It's proof that something was going on that Damian was documenting. Why was he documenting it and hiding that he was doing it? Plus, he's perfectly positioned to record those two people and not the fighters. Do you go to a legitimate sporting event and take crappy pictures of the players in order to frame the picture around other spectators?"

"It's a direction to go in. I'll need more."

"You've got his contact list. Run them for priors."

She stared at me, her hard-ass cop look. "Thanks for the advice. Good thing I've got such a crack investigator to learn from."

"No more caffeine for you. You're getting cranky."

She scrubbed at her face. "I am. This is good stuff, kid. I may not totally buy your theory but I keep forgetting that you have the luxury of choosing a theory to chase."

"Isn't that why you ask for my help sometimes? I mean, as you point out, I don't have the experience like other people you could loop in."

She turned to go to the stairs. "You're a fresh set of eyes with good instincts. You just need to remember, getting married to one line of inquiry can lead you down the wrong path. You've got one theory about Damian's death that comes from some blurry photos and the remarks of a disturbed teen boy we can't interview. Keep your eyes open, kid."

And she left. That was gratitude for you.

Her remark about getting married to a theory got me second-guessing myself. She was right, of course. It was better to keep an open mind and let the evidence fall where it did. Pushing a theory meant you tried to find a way to fit the evidence into that theory. Worse, you went looking to fit your theory. It was one way innocent people ended up railroaded for a crime they didn't commit.

———

I eased away from Fargo's warm puppy body and she snuffled. I really didn't want to wake her up and have her harass me to go outside. It was still cold and damp out. The weather people had been predicting an early, hot spring but it was still winter and snow, even a blizzard, was a possibility. As damp and misty as it had been, a snow storm would roar in with heavy, wet snow, snapping tree limbs and dragging down power lines. An ice storm was even more likely and would wreak even more havoc. I beseeched the universe that no children were performing the time-honored bring-on-the-snow traditions of flushing ice cubes and wearing pajamas backwards. I had too much to do. Cops and PIs did not get snow days.

I successfully removed myself from the bed without waking my shadow and dared another moment to grab my sweatpants from the floor. I slid out a crack in the door big enough for my body to fit sideways but not enough for the light to fall across her snout. I wasn't that careful sleeping in the bed with a person. Of course, Seth was capable of sleeping through shelling, so me removing my 130 pounds from a high-tech mattress made of space-age, patent-pending, chemical-whatnot wasn't even a blip on his radar. That was in Seth's bed, though. Mine was stuffed with straw, kindling, and cans of pennies. At least, that's what it felt, and sounded, like. I began to rethink my insomnia problem and wondered if the reason I slept so well when I was with Seth might be the mattress that cost more than a used Ford Focus.

Thinking of Seth and his mattress and his regular requests to move in brought me back to my conflicted feelings about our future. I had overheard Ben remarking to Aja that if Seth was ghosting me, he would break into the Social Security Administration's system and have Seth declared dead. I had smiled. His more grownup, and federal offense, version of trying to protect me. It wasn't as funny, mostly because he was actually capable of it now, as opposed to when at seven he'd declared he was going to "kick the hiney" of a guy spreading rumors about me at school. I had kept a straight face and thanked him but assured him that I would take care of it. Which I had. A tube of engine block epoxy and a scramble through an open sunroom to pop the gas tank access door netted said bully with an un-twistable gas cap and a four-figure mechanic bill to punch a new gas tank access in the trunk. Mess with the bull …

I armed the new coffeemaker with a pod of Extra Bold and doctored my cup while I waited for the water to warm up. I yawned wide enough that my jaw popped, a souvenir of my previous case, and punched the button to get sixteen ounces of dark, rich, hopefully extra-caffeinated coffee. I pondered if the coffee thing was becoming a problem again when the time between the launch button and the cup being full seemed like the interminable wait between Houston asking Apollo 13's *Odyssey* for response and the silence yawning out as a nation held its collective breath. The fact that it felt more important than the historical event confirmed that suspicion.

When it had finally finished, with its satisfying hiss, I waited another lifetime for it to cool enough to drink. I sat down and pulled up the file I'd started on the Damian Murphy murder. I'd added all the data from the microSIM and the other evidence we'd logged from the car. I kicked myself for not getting pictures of, at least, the hand wraps. Not that a picture would have helped me formulate another theory. Were there other possible explanations? Yes. Did any of them line up quite so nicely? Who knew. But to me, this looked like a computer program did to Ben. I knew it when it made sense. Last time, I'd been too far behind the curve and it had cost me stitches, broken ribs, and sprained body parts. In addition to the new fighting skills, I'd learned how to think better and put the puzzle pieces together faster. I didn't have a name yet, but the contacts in Damian's phone were sure to have him or someone who knew him. Jan would unravel that and I'd be proven right.

That was a matter I had to put to the side, though. Amanda Veitch and her family deserved a resolution. Even though I knew the contents by heart, I opened the file for what felt like, and likely was, the hundredth time and flipped through the statements again.

I looked down at the blank page. I'd stayed old-school with this case, using notepad and pencil. If someone had told me I was trying to channel my dad or even my days in uniform, I wouldn't have disagreed. It just felt right, though. Old case, old methods. Too bad feeling right and investigative genius were not one and the same. Jan's notes didn't have her questions—merely the answers. They weren't a training manual for new detectives. They were, as far as I could tell, the same we'd learned in the J academy about what was important when getting the facts at a scene—who, what, where, when, how. The why? That was my job.

I heard stirring upstairs and checked the time on my phone. The morning was upon me again. Another Extra Bold into the coffee-maker and several scalding sips in my mouth before I went upstairs.

"Again?" Nancy asked. I could only nod.

"Again, what?" Ben asked, his mouth wrapping itself around a spoonful of something healthy and metabolism-friendly. It made my mouth water for the fake food in the bag downstairs. I'd bought it and brought it home, but I wasn't nearly stupid enough to eat it in front of my mother. She'd heave a sigh, giving me a disappointed look, and I'd find my inbox full of articles about type 2 diabetes and how excess sugar contributed to sleep issues.

"Just through these cases, Mom. I promise," I said.

"Oh, the stupid coffee thing? You know, studies show that four cups a day is actually fine," Ben said.

"How many?" Nancy asked me.

"How are we counting the start of the day? Midnight?"

"The last time you slept."

I put the cup down and closing my eyes, tried to count on my fingers, but swayed and had to lean against the counter for support. I felt a hand wrap around my upper arm and I opened my eyes to find my sneaky father steering me toward a kitchen chair.

I kept my mouth shut as the mug of Extra Bold was dumped down the drain. I wasn't stupid and I sure as hell wasn't suicidal.

"I've got two murders that Jan is counting on me to help her with. She's … under a lot of pressure on this Damian Murphy one." I'd almost mentioned the retirement thing. I'd never promised to not tell but I knew she wanted to keep it a secret.

"Your health is critical, Willa. You're still not fully recovered from your injuries and—"

"What your mother is trying to say is please try to be a little more cognizant of the choices you're making and remember that there are long-term repercussions possible."

We all gaped at Dad. It wasn't that he'd spoken up, as the voice of reason, or that he'd used big words, or even that he's strung that many words together. He'd done all three of those things before. It was that he'd done it all at the same time. The lectures that sounded like they belonged on C-SPAN were Nancy's gig. Dad was the indulgent one who snuck downstairs …

And I knew how to get the heat off me. I hated to waste a good secret, but I needed a door out and Dad was the key.

"You mean, like sneaking into my candy stash?" I took the coffee cup Nancy had just handed him and took a long, extra hot, swallow. counting down for the info grenade to blow up in his face.

He nodded, taking his cup back. "Yes, just like that. I confessed to your mother the other day and we both agreed that I needed to set a better example for you. The additional coffeepot for the basement was the wakeup call I needed."

Fargo whined at my feet, pawing gently at the cabinet with her special crazy expensive, super healthy food. *Et tu,* puppy? *Et tu?*

I flung open the fridge and grabbed a bottle of water. "Fine. I know when I'm beaten."

I twisted off the cap defiantly, devising my exit strategy. There was a coffeemaker and plenty of cabinet space over at Seth's and the apartment allowed pets, as long as no one knew about them. I could get dressed, pack up my junk food, and be there in under an hour. Maybe an hour. It was coming on bus hour—the time that was even worse than rush hour because once you got caught behind one of them or, god forbid, had to travel through a school zone, you were screwed.

I left Fargo to eat breakfast and crept down to my lair to shower. A quick rinse—I could wash my hair later—and I was dried and in grownup-ish clothes before Ben had finished thoroughly chewing his last bite of toasted, organic, sprouted grain bread slathered with grass-fed butter and sunflower spread. I hauled my laptop bag and gym bag crammed with workout gear and corn-syrup-laden foodstuffs that didn't fit anywhere on the food pyramid.

"Let's go out, Fargo."

She raced to get her leash.

"Honey, don't leave angry."

Dad just grunted from behind his newspaper. He'd likely run out of words for the day. I hope he hadn't planned any client meetings. He may not have felt this fell under our previous agreement that he not shanghai me anymore, but I did.

"I'm not angry, Mom. I'm just tired of not being treated like an adult."

"I'll treat you like an adult when you act like one." Well, it appeared he wasn't out of words. Bully for him, growing as a person.

"Arch!"

Great, now they were going to get into a fight. I didn't have time for it anymore.

"This is my point. Everyone's been acting like I'm the only one who was affected by what happened, but you're all worse than I am. Fargo's in crazy killer dog training, you two are installing a panic room and fighting all the time, people are monitoring my food intake and caffeine consumption. For god's sake, he sent me on a fake stakeout."

"You needed the learning experience."

"Arch, stop."

"I did need the learning experience and you could have chosen to send me on a real stakeout. Instead you made a decision to go behind my back, involving the whole family, and lied to me."

He slammed the paper down. "You were almost killed."

I dropped the bags on the floor, narrowly missing Fargo's snout. She yelped and ran out of the room, laying down in the foyer.

"I wasn't almost killed. I got the shit beaten out of me and I handled it. I healed. I learned I needed more training and went off to get it. I went to a therapist. I dealt with it like a grownup. You didn't. None of you. And I'm done being the only one handling it. Call me when you get your shit together and want to discuss this like grownups."

I picked up my bags, Nancy staring after me, and stomped out. Damn that had felt good. I had a nice rebellious buzz going when I grabbed the leash from Ben.

I pointed at him. "That shit from yesterday, Captain Superior. We're not done with that. Not by miles."

I slung my bags in the truck, belatedly worrying that I might have already damaged my laptop, and snapped my fingers for Fargo to get up into the cab. Another after-the-fact thought settled into my brain that I needed a place to park a rambunctious giant puppy and changed my destination from the substation to Adam and Theo's. A quick text confirming that they'd puppy-sit and I roared off, righteous indignation, or indigestion from an overnight of dumping crap cardboard substitute food and dark roast coffee down my gullet, burning in my chest. It felt good. I tossed back some antacid just in case.

CHAPTER

21

THE APARTMENT FELT STALE. I cracked open the windows in the bedroom and, like always when I was alone, I checked the arsenal we kept around the place. Partly because I felt exposed in the apartment building, people all around but none in my space, none I knew or trusted. I didn't feel as safe as I did at home. And that was the reason I had to get out. I needed to not be choking in the cocoon anymore. I needed to not feel safe all the time.

I started a pot of coffee with a satisfaction that was unseemly, took off my jacket, and sat down at the dining room table with my laptop. I had notes to transcribe and a lot of alone time to fill.

I worked for an hour and then took a break. Three cups of coffee insisted. Bladder appeased, I grabbed the bag of clothes I'd packed and dumped them on the bed, sorting through for workout clothes. I found a few of the appropriate articles of clothing and pieced together a reasonable facsimile of my usual garb, augmenting with stuff I'd left at Seth's. I vowed to not pack angry again. Or I just needed to move in once and for all.

I sat on the floor in front of Michael's now empty room and tied my shoes. I hated seeing it empty. I knew I needed to get over this feeling that people were trying to erase him. I just wanted a little more time I knew I was never getting.

I needed to move my body, get some of the caffeine jitters and all of the maudlin feeling sorry for myself out of my system. I would have taken Fargo out but she was with Theo getting to taste all the food he made for the videos. Lucky bitch. Dojo it was.

———

Adam's eyes were on me so I twisted a little more to the left and I couldn't see him in my peripheral vision anymore. He probably wasn't angry about getting cuffed yesterday. And even if he had been, that wasn't my fault. I punched Bob harder on his flat nose. He looked like the manufacturer had made the mold from a 1940s comic book villain who'd had a nose transplant from a Persian cat. I whirled around.

"Dude, I'm sorry, okay? I didn't realize the stupid uniforms were going to waste their time on people who were obviously not kidnapping a girl."

He tossed a pair of Muay Thai gloves at me. I pulled on the weighted gloves, biting down a groan. I saw Adam glance over like he was changing his mind. Being a badass meant you paid the bill when it came due. I'd slacked and now I had to grit my teeth and fight through the pain. Literally and figuratively. A lesson it would be nice if you only had to learn once.

"Sticky hands."

A kid's exercise designed for them to learn focus and connection. For me, a sop to my leaden muscles and need to warm up.

A good ten minutes of sticky hands and I was as warm as I could get.

"Water break and knuckle ups."

Knuckle ups in the weighted gloves were going to be torture. I took a minute too long with the water break and heard my workout playlist kick in, drowning out the horrid pop music pumping in through the open back door. The dance studio had the same problem as the dojo—crap ventilation. It got humid and hot and even worse, the pizza parlor on the other side of the dance studio was a constant waft of baking bread, which made the dancers and the martial artists crave carbs.

I did knuckle ups until my arms started to shake and Adam called time.

He'd set Bob up and we began to run drills with him yelling out the change ups. Faster and faster until I wasn't hearing and reacting so much as I was absorbing them and they became an extension of me.

When the music cut off, I saw that there was a crowd of elementary age ballerinas and moms watching through the plate glass window. Most had a look of disdain on their faces, especially the moms, but a few shined with delight. Those girls would be out of tutus and into gis before the month was out. I smiled and waved, sweat covering me from hair to ankles. One girl pressed her hand up against the glass. She was the tiniest of the bunch, and I motioned her in.

She ran and pulled the door open, her body a triangle to the door and ground as she leveraged all her weight to get it open.

She smiled at me shyly from where she leaned against her mom's leg while the skeptical woman talked with Adam. I motioned her over again, stripping off my gloves. I showed her the basket of the smallest sparring gloves, multicolored. I looked down at her teeny sneakers, no fancy cartoon characters or sparkly gems, just plain Chucks, black.

"I have a pair just like those." Nodding at her shoes. Her eyes got wide as I dug into the pile, pulling out a pair of black gloves.

I fitted just one on her, slipping her little fingers through the opening and then out the top. The sparring gloves left the fingers free to make the ridge hand and spear hand movements.

"Make a fist like this," I said, flexing my hand open and closed. She followed my motion and made a tight fist.

"Awesome."

"I didn't know girls could do hitting stuff," she said, her voice surprisingly strong for her delicate features and limbs.

"Well, it's not just hitting. There's a lot that goes into martial arts. Like learning how to stand and do forms. Hitting is called sparring, and you only get to do it when you've learned how to not hurt people first. Sparring is about learning self-control and working with a partner."

I saw Adam nodding. He and the mother had been watching me interact with the little girl.

"Having a partner is important. Sometimes you have a partner at school, sometimes you have a partner when you play."

"Why don't you have a partner?" she asked.

"I do. I have lots of partners. I have one at work. It's my dad. And I have a partner when I train ... a real one, not just Bob." I gave the workout dummy a gentle push. "Adam, he's the teacher here, is my partner."

261

And Seth was my partner. Except we weren't acting like partners. We didn't seem to know how.

The little girl waved to me as she left, her other hand in her mom's, tutu bobbing. The mom held a pamphlet and a few forms.

"Have you ever thought of teaching here? I'm always looking for part-time teachers with the right skills."

I shook my head. "Not even for a minute. I'm terrible with kids."

"That little girl would disagree. You didn't talk down to her. You read her to figure out her personality. Those are the best ways to deal with kids. And having a woman teach some of the classes gives the girls someone to look up to, someone to aspire to be like."

That would be a lovely addition to the community—a bunch of little girls with emotional walls who cursed like obscenities were being outlawed and had deeply codependent relationships with high-fructose corn syrup.

"You became a cop because you want to help people. Kids are just little people."

UGH! Why did he have to be so logical and level-headed all the time?

"I'll consider it," I said, "but don't hold your breath."

I was easing my hoodie back up my arms, trying and failing to not move my shoulders. The muscles were burning from the workout.

Adam handed me a protein shake with the cap undone. I tilted it to the side to check the label for any artificial sweetener.

Adam shook his head. "I can't imagine what it's like having to check everything you eat or drink to make sure it's safe. Or having to look at everyone as if they might be a bad guy."

"I once told Ben that the job was seeing people on their worst days. That's true. And not everyone is a suspect."

"Still."

I got the point he was trying, clumsily, not to make out loud. "My walls have nothing to do with the job. I'm not on the lookout for people to hurt me, Adam. I just … I know how easy it is for other people to not be who you want them to be. And how quickly you can lose someone who means more to you than your own life. Some people I don't have the choice to hold them at arm's length. But I get up every day and I get on with my life. And sometimes that means helping people learn that they trusted the wrong person."

I gulped down the protein shake that was rapidly warming and becoming more metallic tasting.

"Thanks for the workout, Adam. And the advice."

He smiled but he still looked unsure. "Drive carefully."

I had no idea how I'd garnered so many caregivers in my life but there was no denying it.

I tossed my workout bag into the backseat of the truck and cranked the engine to get the heat going. The winter's weather had been weird, mild for stretches then cold enough to bloom into two two-foot blizzards in one week. As we headed toward spring, it had turned rainy and the temperature had hovered in the mid-forties. While I'd been in the dojo, the temperature dropped and with the near constant drizzle, Adam had been right—the roads could have a good sheen of black ice. I was opening the weather app to check the temp when a text from an unknown number came through.

U HAVE SOMETHING I WANT I HAVE SOMETHING U WANT I'M WILLING TO MAKE A TRADE.

Just my luck to get some kind of weird espionage sext.

WRONG NUMBER.

I dropped my phone into the cup holder and began to put my seat-belt on when another text blipped through. I almost ignored it, but espionage sexts made for funny stories.

BITCH GIVE ME BACK MY SHIT OR ILL KILL YOUR BROTHER

My stomach bottomed. I could feel the adrenaline begin to surge in a swirl up my torso and down my limbs, my sore and fatigue muscles hummed to life.

Ben's scared face appeared on the screen, his mouth covered in duct tape.

WHEN? WHERE?

ILL GET BACK 2 U

I turned off the truck and shoving my phone into my hoodie pocket, I clenched my fists tight, struggling to control the panic I had no immediate means to expel. Deep breaths in and out helped amp down the fight or flight, allowing my brain to take back over. I dug the phone back out of my pocket and called Jan.

"Turn the recording on, Jan."

All police phones had the ability to record calls for evidentiary pur-poses. I was going to use the functionality to cut through a shit ton of red tape.

"Detective Boyd, this is Fairfax County Police Consultant Willa Pennington. A moment ago, I received a text from an unknown num-ber. The text indicated that the person sending it believed I had some-thing of theirs. It's my supposition this is related to the Damian Murphy murder. The text also stated that whoever sent it has my brother and that he will be killed if I do not return the property in question. As you are aware, my brother, Benjamin Pennington, is a minor. I give you permission to track my cell phone and obtain all records you deem necessary to trace the text back to the sender."

I paused, listening to Jan recite her badge number and all kinds of other authorization codes before cutting off the recording. She then began yelling orders to the bullpen of detectives who weren't daring to complain, especially when hearing there was a minor involved. That was the magic word—minor. I doubted the idiot who killed Damian knew or cared, but he'd bought himself a lot more trouble getting my brother involved. This was a straight kidnapping now. He'd demanded a ransom and the rules I had to abide by changed.

"What do you need me to do?"

"I need you to have plausible deniability, Jan. I don't want you to do anything to jeopardize your record or your retirement. You do the by-the-books stuff and I'll do the rest."

I was a hair away from pressing the button to hang up when I heard her say, "Be careful, kid."

But careful was the last thing on my mind. I'd been careful. I'd played by the rules. I'd been a good cop and a good PI. I was about to be care*less*.

I left the warmth of the truck and walked back through the door of the dojo.

"I need your help, Adam. I don't need a teacher or a conscience. I need a soldier who won't ask any questions. Can you dig that guy back out tonight? Ben's life depends on it."

"I've always got your six, Willa" he said.

CHAPTER

22

WE SAT IN THE truck in the parking lot of the big box store where I had picked up supplies. I was eternally grateful for suburbanites who needed nearly anything their minds could decide on and didn't want to wait for the one-day shipping it took on the internet.

Adam had suggested his more than impressive firearms collection but neither of us wanted to risk Ben being collateral damage. I hadn't seen any signs that these people had guns so I made the calculated decision that we'd do this the old-fashioned way—unarmed combat. I had no idea how many people we'd be dealing with when it all came down, but we had cop back up if shit got ugly and, frankly, having a former Special Forces, five-time world martial arts champion as backup, a six pack of energy drinks, and a rage like I'd never felt before just waiting to be unleashed meant I was confident I had the upper hand.

I looked at Adam. "Want to go on the offensive?"

"I'm generally not fond of it. I'm concerned about how calm you are, Willa."

"I have to be calm, Adam. I'd love nothing more than to lose my shit but that puts Ben at risk."

He sighed. "What did you have in mind?"

I lifted my phone. I had a handful of numbers memorized. Most I used daily but this one, it was for special occasions.

"Gordo, you have a unique set of skills I need."

"I've repeatedly asked you to call me Agent Gordon, Miss Pennington."

"I don't have time for foreplay, Gordo. Ben's been kidnapped and I need your help."

"Where and when?"

"Can you get to Seth's apartment in the next thirty?"

"Whatever you need."

"I'll be in touch."

I disconnected knowing that he'd be exactly where he promised, exactly when he promised. Seth trusted him with my life last fall and I was now trusting him with my brother's life.

"It's probably not the time but ... is everything still okay with Seth?" Adam asked.

I choked on the energy drink I was pouring down my throat and sprayed a mouthful all over the inside of the windshield.

I coughed up another of what felt like a gallon of the beverage from my lungs and felt around for a cloth to wipe the sugary liquid off the glass. If Adam thought I was ... I didn't want to think about it too hard.

"It's as fine as it can be with him at an undisclosed location and me here."

"The guy on the phone?"

I eyed him and needed to torture him just a bit. "How do you know Gordo is a guy? Might be a woman. You're the last person I'd expect stereotypical assumptions from."

He kept eye contact with me. "I'm serious."

"Agent Gordon helped out on the case last fall. He's the ATF's NoVA urban warfare command. He also sponsored Ben for an internship over the winter break."

Adam nodded, "You've built up quite the cadre of experts. Remember, we're all people too, Willa."

"No offense, Adam, because you know I love you, but right now your feelings aren't high on the list of things I give a shit about. Whatever it takes to get my brother back in one piece."

I popped the top on another energy drink and downed it. I wanted fight or flight on steroids. Steroids. That had to be what the guy wanted. The steroids had the advantage of being almost as good as cash but with the big problem of being evidence too.

I couldn't fake steroids like I could another drug. I had no idea what form they were in at the stage Damian made off with them. I wasn't faking the physical object he wanted. I was just going to have to bluff through the situation until I got Ben's location.

I stared at the phone. Where the hell was this asshole?

I stared at the phone again. Ben's location. I could track the GPS in his phone if I had my own. But I hadn't had time to replace it. I had been too busy. What else could I do? Unless ....

I redialed and the phone picked up before the first ring had barely started.

"Gordon, you've got the app Ben created for your team, right? On your phone?"

"Yeah, why? Oh."

Ben always thought I didn't listen when he talked about programming but I did. And I definitely remembered him blathering on and on about the team coordination app he'd created. And he'd have used himself as the guinea pig.

"Hold on," Gordon said.

The silence was disconcerting. I was old enough—and amped enough, thank you energy drinks—to be anxious for the sound of some clicking or *anything* to indicate Gordon was doing something, anything. I knew he was, that he was working frantically, loading the app and logging in. Ben would have made it hyper-encrypted and required passwords of suitable complexity that a normal human would fumble a bit—all things you definitely want when a team member is in trouble and the cavalry needs to fucking find him before he gets dead.

I put the can down in the cup holder. I couldn't let my emotions run away with me. Not until we got Ben free. Then I was going Kraken, *Wild Bunch*, and *The Crow* on his kidnapper's ass.

"I got him."

"Where? Can you give me a location?"

"It doesn't work like that. Not exactly. I can ping his phone but this is designed for use when we're all together. He hadn't gotten it to the point where it gives me a GPS location."

That was not news I wanted to hear.

"Okay, so we're still in wait mode?" I blew a breath out in frustration. I was fairly vibrating with the desire to inflict violence.

"Listen, I'm at Seth's place. I'll put in a call to a friend of a friend. Since I can get to Ben's phone, she should be able to get me the GPS."

"Who—"

269

He cut me off. "It's better for all of us if you don't know. She's got the access and she'll do it for me."

I nodded, forgetting Gordon couldn't see me. "The spare key is in Seth's motorcycle compartment. Code is 120789."

"What do you need?"

"The spare bulletproof vests. You'll find loaded clips in the safe next to the vests. Bring them. All of them. I'm sending you my location."

I disconnected the phone and dumped it into the spare cup holder in the console. Adam was glaring at me. "What happened to our no-guns plan?"

"No guns is my plan for you. Anybody gets shot it's going to be by me. That leaves you free and clear if the DA, who already hates me, is feeling like issuing charges. One of us in lockup is enough."

"And the bulletproof vests?"

"I'm counting on this idiot being an idiot and bringing brawn and no brains to this fight. But in case I'm wrong, I want to make sure you and Ben have some protection if things get bullety."

"Dammit, Willa. You need a vest too."

I turned to him. "Let me be clear, you are doing me a favor, which means I'm not getting you killed. Theo would never forgive me nor should he. I'm definitely not letting Ben get killed. There are a few people on this planet I would cheerfully lay my life down for and Ben is number one on that list. Besides, a vest doesn't fit over my torso holster and the holster doesn't fit over the vest. Can you get that roll of duct tape out of the glove box?"

He looked at me funny. "What do you need duct tape—" His hand stilled on the dash. "Are you actually pulling a Die Hard?"

"I'm wrapping my knuckles with it."

He shook his head and opened the glove box, pulling at the tape. "You got a knife?"

I snorted. "Any particular attributes you need besides sharp?"

"You're a scary person."

I slammed my hand on the steering wheel. "I'm never going to be in a position where I can't defend myself again, Adam. I am no one's victim."

"Willa, I met guys on the team who were not good at compart-mentalizing. Their jobs bled into their personal lives. They couldn't turn it off at the end of the day. Don't go there, please."

"My job hasn't bled into my personal life. My job *is* my personal life. My dad, our home. It's all personal. And what I said about being no one's victim goes double when it comes to my brother. I am no-joke, dead-serious, not-fucking-playing tonight. I don't care if I have to shoot someone, stab them, or rip off my own damn arm and beat them to death with it. I'll do the therapy on it later."

He sighed and started ripping down sections of tape, cutting them, and sticking the ends on the dash. "How much tape do you need?"

My phone blipped with a link.

MEET YOU THERE.

I cranked the engine. "Gordon got us a location."

My phone alerted again.

"Check that for me, would you?" I asked, yanking my seatbelt on and latching it.

"It says Seth just texted him that he's in an agency vehicle on his way home from Dulles."

Shit. This was not how I wanted to reunite with him. But there was no one I'd rather have on my team than Seth.

I pulled out of the parking lot. "Okay, have Gordon explain and divert him to the location. Seth will have all his gear with him. An-other set of hands is better for us."

I drove as calmly as possible toward the destination Gordon had sent. I made sure my speed was only ten miles over the speed limit. Cops were out on patrol and shift change was hours away. They were going to be bored and looking for speeders. Plus, the energy drinks were kicking in and flooding me with an antsy desire to move.

I cranked on the radio, my pre-workout mix began playing. It was only a few bars into a pumped-up remix of my favorite song when the music cut and the phone was ringing. Adam clicked accept.

"Sunshine, how do you keep ending up in these situations?"

Shit shit shit!

"Just lucky I guess."

"You sure you didn't break a mirror or something? Walk under a ladder? Black cat?"

"Listen, are you going to have time to back me up in between cracking jokes, Ace?"

"I got the location and I'm headed there now." His voice had lost all the humor and acquired a deadly edge.

"Excellent. ETA?"

"Ten minutes. Maybe five. I'm rocketing down the parkway, lights and sirens. I'll need to kick those off soon though. You?"

"I'm playing it safe at nine over so maybe five minutes for me too."

"Gordon's going to beat us both there. He'll do recon and set the op. It was good you called him."

"It's Ben." My voice broke a little. I shoved down my fear. My system needed an outlet before it turned on me.

"I know, Sunshine."

I saw the turn off for the neighborhood I had to crisscross before getting to the location—a self-storage business. At this time of night, it was unlikely anyone would be showing up. It backed to a wooded area and I assumed we had a final destination on the other side somewhere.

"When we get Ben free, I'm tasking Adam with his safety," I said.

"Wait a minute—"

"It's the most logical decision, man," Seth interrupted.

"But I—"

"You've had medical training, you're big enough to carry him if he's unconscious, and you can fight anyone off if you can't get to the rendezvous," Seth continued.

"Willa?"

"It's my plan, Adam. With Seth available now I've got a three-man insurgent team. You're the only one with medical training. I can't have you in the fray."

"Remember when I said you were scary?" he asked.

I nodded.

"You're very scary. You put this one to shame."

"Dude!" Seth said.

I pulled up to the self-storage and turned off my headlights as I turned right into the parking lot. I drove to the back of the lot where I knew Gordon would have set a secondary location. The brake lights of a nondescript black sedan flashed twice. I pulled in next to it.

I turned off the interior lights and got out, easing the door shut, the click of the latch the only sound I heard. I walked around the back of the truck and unlocked the tailgate, raising it. Gordon was at my side, no warning, his arms laden with the gear he'd picked up at the apartment.

"Pennington," he said quietly with a head nod.

Adam had come around to join us. "Gordon, this is Adam Carson. Adam, meet Gordo."

Gordon rolled his eyes at me under the sulfur lights in the parking lot and slung the bulletproof vests at me. I handed them off to Adam. I took the torso holster and shoved it into my hoodie pocket.

I felt the vibration of a vehicle and turned to watch a muscular black SUV, headlights off, glide up to us. It was supposed to be nondescript but anything trying that hard to go unnoticed in this area might as well have a neon sign blinking out LIVE. ARMED. COPS. Since I was expecting my own personal live armed federal cop, I was beyond happy that he'd arrived. We were one step closer to getting the show on the road. I was more than ready to let a little violence out.

Seth swung the truck around and backed into the spot next to Gordon's ATF-issued car. We all climbed in, shutting the doors to just latched.

The men all nodded at one another in that bro chin tip that they all thought was tough but really made them look like they possessed a group nervous tic. I wondered if they would do it with the bad guys too. Some kind of unspoken man alliance worldwide; good, bad, indifferent, you did the chin tip, like dogs sniffing each other's butts.

"Sunshine."

"Anderson."

I got a regular nod. It was amazing how much nuance a man could put into a simple up and down motion of his head. As a primary form of communication, it really was impressively complex. I did know him better than anyone on the planet though so maybe I was picking up what others would miss.

"Can you two make eyes at one another later? I'd like to get home sometime before dawn," Gordon said.

"Gordo, you're embarrassingly off-base. The only eyes I'm making at him right now are communicating that he'd better not turn his back to me tonight or I might cut him."

"I missed you too," Seth said.

Another eye roll from Gordon showed how much I had rubbed off on him during our interactions over the previous three months.

"Anyone have a more detailed plan than the one I've heard from Willa?" Adam asked.

"I'm sure I can recap that," Gordon said. "Make sure my brother doesn't get killed."

"Hey, I told Adam not to get killed either," I said.

"That's true," both Seth and Adam said in unison.

I cut in before Gordon could roll his eyes again. "Look, I'm not an urban warfare specialist, which is why I called you. I don't know exactly what we're dealing with here except an angry possible 'roid head who's got some kind of connection to what I'm reasonably sure is an underground fighting ring. Whether he's looking for steroids or money or his grandma's china, I don't care. He wants it, he's pissed, he's already killed one teen boy over it, and he says he's got Ben."

Gordon nodded. "I'll go recon the location the system showed for Ben's phone and we'll regroup in ten minutes."

"I'm still waiting on a text back from this guy. I don't know what he's waiting on. I'm thinking he didn't plan this out well so he's making it up as he goes."

"Are you sure he even has Ben?" Seth asked.

"There's no other way he'd have the cell number I'm using. It's a burner and only family has it. The photo was pretty convinc—"

A wave of horror washed over me, cutting through the single-minded focus I'd been indulging. I had completely forgotten my parents. Someone had kidnapped their son and I hadn't even let them enter my mind. I'd gone to a damn big box store to load up on supplies to take on the guy who was threatening the life of their little boy and calling them hadn't even occurred to me.

"Willa? Sunshine?"

"I hadn't even thought about Mom and Dad." I covered my mouth.

"Now is not the time to lose focus. Look at me," Gordon said.

What if something ended up happening to Ben and I had to tell them? Then what? They would be blindsided.

"Pennington! Look at me, right now, dammit." I'd never heard Gordon yell before, the already deep timbre of voice boomed inside the enclosed compartment of the SUV, echoing off the glass. I dragged my gaze to his face, shocked.

"I need you to dig back down inside yourself and get me the bad-ass who faced down a neo-Nazi last year. You remember her?"

"She's scary as hell," Adam said, chiming in, "and Ben's counting on her."

I nodded, slowly, letting an image of Ben's face, scared and uncertain, fill my head.

After searching my face for a second, Gordon slipped out the door of the truck and into the trees ringing the lot.

"Let's gear up, Will," Adam said.

I took the holster out of my pocket and then pulled the hoodie over my head. My compression tank was too snug to be pulled back down over the holster and allow me access to it so I tugged it off and wrapped the holster around my torso in reverse giving me access from the back. The top overlapped my sports bra just enough to be uncomfortable and I rolled my head back and forth on my neck, working out the muscles.

I slipped out of the SUV and headed back to my truck to arm up. I needed to be sure when I wrapped my hands with the tape that I left myself the freedom to pull a trigger. I realized the holster wasn't going to work backward with the hoodie unless I made some adjustments. I laid it on the tailgate, adjusting it so the sides were together, arms flopped out of the way, and stabbed down into the fabric. I dragged the knife toward me cutting two vertical slits that would be

276

hidden by my arms. I opened the door and pushed the driver's seat out of the way so I could access the gun safe.

"Will?"

I pulled my head out of the truck. "Yeah?"

"I want you in a vest," Seth said.

Adam needed to keep his mouth shut. "I can't. I can't be in a vest and fight and be armed."

"Gordon will be able to set up a perch. You don't need the gun."

I cracked my jaw, a move I'd allowed to become a habit. I'd always been a clencher but a hairline fracture intensified the tension at the worst times.

"I would say this to another agent, even Tim, if it was them. This isn't me babying you."

We both knew he was wrong. "It's dark. We don't know where they're keeping Ben. If Adam gets trapped trying to get him out then Gordon will need to focus on cover fire for them."

Seth sighed and nodded. His phone must have alerted because he flinched slightly then pulled it out of his pocket. He crouched down by the back wheel and pulled up the screen, effectively using the truck to block any light from being visible from anywhere in the tree line.

I resumed unlocking the safe. Then I loaded the magazine and chambered a round. I struggled a bit getting the gun into the holster, unused to wearing it and unfamiliar with the reverse position. I finally got the gun settled in and then leaned back in to pull a few strips of tape off the dash.

I had wrapped my left-hand knuckles with a layer of tape when Seth took over. "Flex and fist, please."

We worked quietly, him taping and me working my fist until we were both satisfied with the makeshift gloves.

"You need to get changed," I said. He was used to gearing up in odd places thanks to his years in the Army and then with the ATF. I watched him walk back to his truck and get a gear bag out. It hadn't occurred to me that I should worry about anyone wondering what the hell we were doing. Four grown adults skulking around in a self-storage parking lot in the dark on a week day, slipping into a wooded area and then changing clothes. I really hoped that if there were any security cameras, we provided some much-needed entertainment.

Seth's tactical gear was sleek and professional compared to my thrown together look. That was to my advantage. Seth and Gordon had their all black, ninja-like appearance to blend into the shadows as proper backup. I needed to look like what I was—a very pissed off, very underdressed sister.

Seth hauled out a laptop that looked like it could crush mine with its DVD drive. "Cell please?"

I handed it to him and he attached it to the laptop with a cable that had enough attachments to make a Swiss Army knife weep with jealousy. "Don't get pissy with me if my cell phone takes over your shiny new laptop and uses it to hack North Korea. You know how Ben likes to play and we've already set a precedent." I was, of course, referring to me waltzing into an ATF op last fall using my cell phone and an app my baby brother had texted me.

"I highly doubt he's trojaned a burner cell."

I cocked an eyebrow at him.

"I didn't say I doubted he was capable, just questioning his motives for giving you a cell with that kind of capability. He knows your ability to get yourself into trouble."

Offensive. Semi-true but offensive. I didn't always just stumble over volatile situations . . . I mean, sometimes I rushed headlong into them. After stumbling over them.

I shoved down another twinge of guilt for bantering while my brother was being held by some unknown quantity, but the reality was snark was how I coped. I was doing the best possible thing I could for my brother. I'd gathered a team of highly trained and extremely talented covert operatives. It was almost surreal. Had I seen something like this in a movie, I'd have called bullshit and changed channels but you fall in love with a legit James Bond–type and there are perks.

I heard my cellphone beep and looked over at Seth. He flipped the laptop so I could see the screen. It was a text from Jan, complete with the incoming number, the phone details including owner, registered address, and a blinking red dot on a map for location. A bunch of other data started scrawling down the screen and I could see all the ping locations and what looked like a device history of texts and calls. Ben was going to be so jealous when I told him about the government's latest technotoy.

"How do I respond?"

"Update her." He stood holding the laptop, scrunching down slightly so I could comfortably type. One stop shopping. Snazzy.

I replied to her that I had surveillance set up and gave her the location. While I waited for her reply even more information scrolled in including that she was law enforcement and a warning that cross-jurisdictional lines could be breached. As quickly as that warning popped up it was sucked down into the tray notifications with another popup replacing it that read WARRANT ACHIEVED.

My eyes widened. Seth gave me a curt nod. "Need to know, Sunshine."

The fact that there was "need to know" in an unofficial operation about my brother headed by me meant there was a lot more going on behind ATF scenes with my brother. Any other time I would have browbeaten Seth to tell me what the hell was going on but as long as everyone I loved, and tolerated in Gordon's case, came out of this alive I didn't care if Ben was actually secretly the head of the damn ATF.

He flipped the laptop back around and awkwardly typed with one hand. It still looked incredibly badass. He has that effect on me.

"There. Now Jan will get all the information we get when this idiot contacts you again."

"Does it work retroactively? I mean, can we just find the text from him and let it pull all that crap up like it just did."

He looked at me, squinting, obviously considering the possibilities my question raised. "I mean, maybe. That wasn't in the parameters of the program requirements. I don't even know if that kind of thing is technically possible. Or legal."

"Look, we both know Ben designed something in that system if not the whole thing despite your 'need to know' distraction. If it's possible, he did it, requirements or not. He'd code it once rather than go back and do it again. He's forever whining about how tacked-on code is so sloppy."

Movement in the tree line caught my eye and I watched with my peripheral vision as Gordon skulked out of the shadows. My senses were honing in. That was good. I didn't need anyone taken down with friendly fire. It made company picnics so tense when you had to ask the guy you shot accidentally to hand you the potato salad. And I knew if there was an incident then it was going to be me. Although if I hadn't shot him there while he was being annoying, I could probably hold off while he was saving Ben.

"I said 'need to know' because it's need to know, so keep your lips zipped, smartass." He grinned at me. It really was a shame we worked together best when someone's life was in danger.

Gordon had made it to the front of the truck when I turned and looked at him square. He froze like a cockroach and glared at me. I assumed it was a glare. It was pretty dark where he was standing and I couldn't actually see his face but it pissed him off when I overcame his Man of Stealth routine.

Another text bleeped in.

"I guess we don't need to see if the program can find those details in an old contact."

Hello, asshole.

Seth and Gordon looked over the details on the screen doing their wordless communication gig I'd seen in full force last fall and I adjusted the torso holster to make it easier to reach without having to dislocate my damn arm.

Gordon wandered back over to his car to get Adam.

"Do you want to know what the text said?" Seth asked.

"Nope. Don't need to know. I just want to know where this jackhole is so I can go stomp an extra hole or two into his face."

Seth nodded. "I know, love. Ben's going to be fine."

"He'd better be or I'm going to do more that kick the shit out of this guy."

Gordon handed out the earbuds and began laying out the strategy. He used phrases like *incursion points, fall back locations, sight lines* and then gave us the code words for when Adam got Ben to safety or if one of us got into trouble. I listened with half an ear to everything realizing the form was for the boys. All three of them knew that whatever plan I was involved in had to be fluid because I was going to spend the majority of my mental energy on honing and directing my rage.

CHAPTER

23

I SLID DOWN THE small dirt hill, scraping my exposed calf on the gravel and hard, almost frozen, clay that ringed the small industrial plot of land Ben's captor had chosen to use as the exchange point. I assumed he had thought it was a smart location with only one vehicle entrance that you'd see from all points. Of course, it was sheltered from the view of the rest of the area by a ring of trees on the other three sides.

The privacy worked much more in my favor as I looked at the assembled group of teen tough-guy wannabes. Some shadowboxed but most lounged against the work vehicles that had been left by the crew that was onsite during the day. Baby badasses tired of suburban boredom, looking to lose some of the energy and pent-up anger by becoming live action versions of action movie stars.

All totaled it looked like eight … no, Gordon had been right, there were nine. Had I been alone I wouldn't have even considered nine but with Seth and Adam, the three of us could handle it. We'd have to because in absence of a visible weapon, Gordon wasn't taking a shot.

I went back through the trees and got into my truck, a hand drawn map stuck on my steering wheel directing me how to drive around to the entrance. I cranked the engine and checked in with my crew.

"Wildcard on the move."

I might just shoot Gordon on principle for my obnoxious call sign.

"Check in again when you arrive at incursion point alpha, Wildcard. Comms open on your bud."

Yup. I was definitely shooting him, even when we got Ben out safely.

I drove out onto the parkway and exited almost immediately onto the ramp that curved around the location. Up to the first light and a right then another immediate right into the neighborhood to drive back down and curve in the opposite direction from the ramp, mirroring my trip of less than five seconds before. I passed another series of buildings that seemed attached to the work facility and found the blocked-off entrance to the equipment site. I left the headlights on as cover for when Jan and her backup arrived, the burner cell in the cup holder so she could locate me if she needed more than what Seth had already sent her.

I popped the top on another energy drink and started to drain it, hearing Adam whispering harshly. "Quit with the caffeine before your heart explodes, Wildcard."

I ignored him, finishing the can, realizing belatedly that my bladder was likely going to be close to exploding by the time we called it a night.

"Wildcard in position." I said it low in case there was another guy at the entrance that Gordon had missed in his sweep. The odds of that were infinitesimally small but I wasn't taking any chances with my brother's safety.

I ambled down the short road, my head swiveling on my neck, taking in the situation and keeping a neutral expression on my face.

"Hello?"

Hopefully, the guy running the show would identify himself and I could just break a few of his bones right away. I remember being super chatty when I was nursing a busted rib. That could have been due to the painkillers but I was willing to experiment to see what worked.

"You got my shit, bitch?"

"Braintrust located."

That was quick.

I took a few steps forward my arms loose at my sides. "What the hell is with you weak-ass boys that your go-to insult is always *bitch*, anyway?"

I scanned the group looking for my target, mentally discarding the smirkers.

"Seriously, is your vocabulary so stunted? And it's gendered bullshit, frankly."

I wandered to my right into the circle of dirt, dropping my head, forcing everyone's eyes to me and their backs to where Adam was moving to the car in the back. I didn't dare look to see Ben. Adam would take care of him.

"I mean, why are the insults always gendered? If I called you lot 'bitches' you'd be enraged because I was implying that you were weak, that you were women. Which is crap because I can kick all your asses."

That finally got his attention. A short stocky guy stepped forward, his face contorted with rage. Assistant wrestling coach, Ramsey. I wasn't even surprised. I'd never considered him as Mr. X. He just hadn't struck me as the Svengali-type. But it had to be somebody lacking morals and he fit the bill fine.

"Where the fuck is my stuff, bitch?"

"You enunciated *bitch* like it was going to hurt my feelings extra or something. Do you think I care what some sorry excuse for a man thinks of me? My boyfriend is twice your size. All over I bet."

I let the innuendo hang in the air. I needed him as full of rage and stupidity as I could get him. I needed him as distracted as I could get him. Ben's safety was all that mattered.

And the energy drinks were humming. I was feeling fairly invincible myself.

He growled and I could see him trying to control his rage. "I will beat your stupid bitch face in. Where is my stuff?"

He was five steps ahead of any of his crew, many of whom I recognized from the background of the photos Jan and I had gotten off the microSIM in Damian Murphy's car.

"Braintrust acquired and secured."

Now it was time to let the rage take over. Seth and Adam would do their part culling the players. I shrugged, planting into a back stance. "I don't know where it is. I didn't even look, honestly."

He rushed at me like I knew he would and I swung in with a roundhouse kick, kenpo-style. I put my whole body into the kick pushing up from the ground with my stance foot, just like Adam had drilled me hundreds of times. The roundhouse was a dangerous kick and, as a woman, my legs were my strongest asset.

I was off the mark though because he was moving and his thigh absorbed the force. He slid to the ground grabbing the abused limb. He'd have a hell of a bruise but it wasn't enough to stop him for long. A blow to the knee would have taken him completely out of the show.

At his howl of pain, the whole area exploded into rushing bodies. I saw the two closest to me coming in fast.

I dropped my head, tucked my arms into my sides, and brought my fists up to guard my face. They fell into a formation that was almost the exact scenario for the two-man drill. Except these two weren't going to fight fair like a drill. I steadied my breath as the first blow came at my shoulder. I dropped that shoulder away from the blow and spun, throwing my elbow up high into the face of the second guy.

The first one rushed past me and I hesitated a beat too long trying to find a way to keep facing both of them and the melee going on behind me. He managed to stop and reached his arm out to jab me in the ribs. Luckily, it wasn't the broken one from a few months ago, or a real punch, so I shrugged off the sharp, shooting pain and moved into a wide-legged stance.

These guys were all about the same height I was, so they were used to fighting someone my size. Something that was usually an advantage was now a detriment. I slid my foot back as the first one rushed again, his partner still holding his face, blood pouring out over his fingers. One man down. Correction. One boy down. They were all just kids.

When he was within range, I spun back again into a reverse kick, catching him on the back and knocking him forward. He became angrier, his inability to get engaged with me gutting his chemical confidence. He turned around and began advancing on me, swinging wildly. I deflected his wind-milling blows trying to remember a session where Adam had given me any pointers for repelling a grown man fighting like a five-year-old. The closest I could recall was the swarm drill, so I directed a side kick to his knee and when his leg slipped out from under him and he dropped his hands to cushion his fall, I front kicked him in the face. I felt his nose collapse under the thin rubber sole of my mat shoes and realized he was down too. I had just dropped my hands to my knees to suck in some much-needed oxygen when the air around me changed. The third man. Just like the drill.

I slid down to the ground on my side and spun in a move that would have made a beginner break dancer laugh at me but worked just fine for my purposes, popping back up behind the man I'd failed to cripple with my roundhouse.

He was beyond rage-filled. He was purple and spitting out curses unintelligibly. He hit out at me and I was able to dance out of the way of the first blow but the second was a haymaker and it landed squarely on my torso. The thin elastic of the holster absorbed none of the blow, leaving me with the breath knocked completely out of me. I sank down onto my knee trying to get air into my shocked lungs and enough distance to plan a return attack.

I realized someone had been shouting "Wildcard!" in my comm and that distracted me enough that he was on me, tackling me. I was pressed into the dirt, the gun digging into my spine so hard I was afraid both would break.

He outweighed me by fifty pounds, dense muscle knotted onto his small frame. My only saving grace was that his muscle pack made him inflexible. He kept jabbing his hand at my face trying to get purchase on anything he could. I used that momentum to squirm down further under him, away from fingers that could easily put out an eye.

His arms stretched over the top of me, his hips grinding me down as his feet kept slipping on the churned-up dirt. It felt like he was trying to climb me.

My hands were free and I reached around him, turning my hands into claws and jamming them into the spaces between his two lowest ribs and hooking them on his floating ribs. I yanked toward my feet as hard as I could and he bucked up away from me, screaming in agony.

I slid out farther to the side and pulled up on my hip, kneeing him in his very likely broken rib. I didn't care if I punctured his lung. I reared my hips up off the ground completely and brought a leg up, managing a laying half ax kick. It wasn't pretty but it slammed his knee into the ground and I kicked at him, connecting to his hip, getting him completely off me.

I scrambled to my feet, the urgent calls to Wildcard abandoned and my name rang into my ears.

He was up on his feet faster than I would have thought and rushing me again, his arms outstretched to grab me. I stepped to the side and planted, grabbing his arm, pulling him into my hip and flipped him. I kept hold of his arm and wrenched it back and up, stopping just past resistance.

"Jiu-jitsu, bitch."

I sucked air in and out of my lungs and keeping hold of his wrist, I put my foot on his back. I pressed down with a lot more force than necessary and it felt good to make him eat some dirt. I wasn't ever forgetting the scared look on my brother's face.

My entire body felt like a heart beat. "Wildcard finally clear."

CHAPTER

24

"**OF ALL THE STUPID,** irresponsible, idiotic, dumbass things to do, you just went off half-cocked and pulled off some movie raid. What were you thinking? Were you even thinking?"

"To be fair, Arch, she did call the police." Seth pointed at Jan, who was pressed into the couch cushions with her hands on her knees, eyes shifting from side-to-side.

She wasn't the picture of professional law enforcement calm and control; she looked like she was in the principal's office. I almost felt bad for her. Dad's rants were infrequent but legendary. But she got to leave when she wanted. I had no idea why she was sticking around except maybe loyalty. Or guilt that she hadn't at least tried to stop me.

"But she didn't let the police handle it, did she? And now look at her."

The bag of peas on my face covered a welt and nascent bruise from a well-timed elbow by the guy who tried, and failed, to beat me up. It also prevented me from seeing Seth's face. I opened my mouth to protest but my mother shook her head and adjusted the ice pack on my ribs. You'd think we'd have more of those considering how accident-prone I'd always been, but the count of ice bags handed out had been higher than normal.

"All superficial, Mr. Pennington. I checked her out at the scene and if I'd even thought for one second she needed to go to the hospital, I would have taken her myself," Adam said.

My dad paced the living room made tiny by the crowd of people. Poor Ben had to sit on the floor, Dad stepping over his legs every time he stomped from one side of the room the four steps to the other.

"Maybe you could write it up as a training exercise for the licensing paperwork," Gordon said.

"She'll be lucky if she ever gets a license pulling stunts like this." He was winding down though. There had only been three adjectives before *dumbass*. I'd heard the rants enough to know that was usually his last round. And considering the outcome, he didn't have much to complain about.

Ben had some minor abrasions, mostly from the duct tape. Sure, he was in desperate need of a shower, we all were, but he was uninjured and had a cool story to tell about the time he was kidnapped.

"Arch, dear, the kids are fine. I think we should just be grateful no one was badly hurt."

I snorted. Seven sets of eyes turned on me.

"What? I did some serious damage to that asshole's shoulder rotator. He'll be lucky if he can lift a tray in the prison cafeteria let alone weights ever again."

My mother shook her head again, trying to hide a smile.

"Willa, can you please explain to me why you didn't just let Jan handle it?"

"Arch, a word?" Seth asked, standing up and moving them toward the office.

"You bet, Seth. I've got some words for you too."

Great. Seth was going to take one for the team and I could get back to trying to find a way to work off the rest of the caffeine. My skin felt like it was crawling with bugs.

"Mom, can I shower? I mean, I know we've got company but ..."

"Oh, Ben. I think we're past formalities here."

He scampered up with a lot of energy for a kid who'd been held hostage. He'd stayed for Dad's full tirade, which I gave him credit for; he'd only ever heard them, so being on the receiving end was new.

Dad had started with Ben, giving him what for because he and Aja had been snooping. He'd moved on to Adam for not talking me out of it. Gordon had been next for a sentence or two, something about being Seth's partner and after last fall knowing what I was like. Jan had gotten a dirty look and a few mutterings.

He'd saved the majority of his ire for me. I was used to it. The times he'd utterly lost his shit had always been because of me. Bull-headed, too strong-willed, leapt before I looked. I could do both parts at this point.

I heard Dad's voice through the closed office door. He was giving Seth holy hell. Good. I owed him one for skipping town like a criminal. A crash followed.

Adam popped up.

My mother waved a hand and Adam seated himself.

"It's fine. They're not coming to blows. Arch is just blowing off steam that he's been holding onto since last fall."

I felt like my insides were trying to crawl their way out through my throat.

"Mom."

She took one look at my face and had me hauled up and hustled into the bathroom just in time for me to empty my stomach into the tub. The faintly pink liquid coating the white fiberglass was the better part of a half dozen cans of energy drinks.

"Oh, Willa. Honey, you know how bad that stuff is for you."

I responded by puking again then laid down on the floor.

"Why didn't you let the police handle it?" my mother asked, while she was cleaning me up.

The question everyone had skirted around. It hadn't been because I was reckless or stupid. I wasn't overly confident of my skills or even my intelligence.

"Last fall, after the thing with Mark Ingalls ..."

She nodded, breaking eye contact with me for just a second.

"I just ... I couldn't stop thinking 'what if Ben had been home?'"

Her eyes were back on mine, wet and shining.

"The cops would have taken too long. He was scared. I'm never going to let him be scared and alone if I can do something about it. I don't care if it's stupid or I get hurt," I said. A few tears leaked out and I was too tired to fight them.

We stayed quiet for a while. She gently rubbed my back, contorted into what had to have been an uncomfortable squat, crouched in our tiny hall bathroom.

I was curled into the fetal position; peas on my face, ice pack on my ribs, my mother pressing a cold wash cloth to the back of my neck. Throwing up was terrible, the dry heaves were the worst. I should have been able to relax. I was exhausted but Ben was safe. I'd escaped with minor bruising on my body. My ego was even intact.

Seth was home. We'd talk when we'd both come down from our unique reunion. We'd figure it out. I'd force him to talk to his parents. I'd force his parents to talk to my parents. We'd all talk and share and therapists around the world would rejoice.

I wasn't able to relax though because we still didn't know who'd killed Amanda Veitch and that pissed me off. Being sick pissed me off too. I could handle getting roughed up but being waylaid by an angry stomach was humiliating. I'd been careful to check all the labels too. All were regular sugar.

It had to have been the total fatigue that allowed my brain to finally connect the pieces. I struggled to sit up without setting off any violent reactions in my stomach, ice packs sliding to the floor.

"Willa, lie down."

"I need to talk to Jan, Mom. Can you get her?"

She handed me the wash cloth and I laid my head against the toilet lid.

Jan came in trying to avert her eyes. Obviously, everyone had heard me barf.

"Um, whatever it is can wait. You're not feeling well and—"

"I know who killed Amanda Veitch."

CHAPTER

25

WHEN SHE OPENED THE door and saw me, her whole body caved in on itself. Gone was the proud posture, pulled back shoulders. A hank of hair had worked its way loose from the clip she had twisted it up into. She stepped back to let me in and motioned me to the living room.

It was kinder to get right to it. I didn't imagine she was a sociopath, gleeful that she'd gotten away with it all these years. She had to have been terrified every time Jan visited.

"You killed Mandy."

She smothered a gasp with her hand, tears in her eyes. I gave her a minute to gather her composure. She'd been keeping this secret for a long time. From her husband and mother-in-law. From herself, at times. She'd had to have if she was able to look them in the face at holidays. There was no other way she'd have been able to sit across the table from them at Thanksgiving knowing the anniversary of the day she'd murdered Mandy was the next day. There were some cold people in the world but I didn't see her being one of them.

"Here's what I think happened. You tell me if I'm right," I said.

Courtney Veitch looked away and I saw her gaze had landed on a photo of her daughter.

"Mandy had never been happy with your interest in her brother." I paused, memories of Michael's protests about the growing bond he saw between me and Seth. I hoped he'd be happy now with the way things had turned out because he loved both of us but, like with Mandy, we'd never know.

"Your relationship was going through a natural cooling off period with her at college and you at home. Then when Kevin came home on break, he confessed to her that you two had been seeing each other behind her back for a while." I nodded to the photo she'd been staring at. "You probably had wanted to tell her about the pregnancy with him but he either didn't want to do it that way or in the heat of the fight— the fight your mother-in-law had hated to confirm to the police—he'd blurted it out."

She took a deep shuddering breath and, not meeting my eyes, nodded. I couldn't have known the details of any of the conversations, but it wasn't hard to fill in the gaps. Only three reasons for murder: revenge, money, or love.

"She waited until the family was out of the house to confront me. She called me over and said horrible things to me like that she thought I was using her brother, that I'd gotten pregnant on purpose to escape my family," Courtney said.

"She was angry. At you, at Kevin. Those kinds of conversations ... they escalate so quickly. Words got more heated. Maybe some names were called. You grabbed her arm perhaps and she pulled away or she pushed you and you pushed back."

"She tried to hit me. I put my hands out to block her and she slipped on the throw rug."

I recalled the crime scenes photos that I'd studied until I had them memorized. There was a throw rug next to the bed. The scene in my head changed from a static black-and-white image to full color with Mandy and Courtney fighting. If it hadn't happened like she said, it was easy enough to imagine it did. Her defense attorney would definitely paint that picture for a jury.

"It would have been an accident."

She nodded vigorously. She wanted to believe it was an accident.

"She slipped on the rug and fell, hitting her head on the nightstand. It probably scared both of you."

Her hands twisted in on themselves, her fingers worrying each other. "But she was fine. She didn't have a mark on her."

"And then she wasn't fine. How long did it take, Courtney? A few minutes, thirty, an hour?"

She looked stricken, her eyes darting over again to her daughter's picture. Her mother-in-law had talked about how devoted Courtney was to her own daughter. How Mandy would have loved being an aunt. Too bad she never got the chance. It was sad all around and now it was about to get immeasurably sadder.

"Maybe ten minutes. Mandy had calmed down. I think trying to hit me made her realize she'd gotten out of control. I had been trying to calm her down the whole time. It wasn't a bad thing. She had just been too stubborn to see it. I was telling her it was all going to be fine. And then she just collapsed. I tried to wake her up. I checked her pulse and … and I couldn't find one. I was in shock."

And if it had ended there, everything would have been fine.

"But then you made a terrible situation that much worse."

Courtney couldn't raise her eyes from the floor. "Kevin would have been so upset. He might not have stayed with me. I couldn't raise a baby on my own. My parents, they'd already kicked me out when I told them I was pregnant. I didn't know what to do."

For someone who hadn't known what to do, she'd certainly thought quickly enough in spite of her professed fear and shock.

"You saw the bottle of nail polish remover with its warning label that it was flammable. You just didn't know that acetone didn't burn like other flammable liquids."

"Mandy was better at chemistry. Mandy was better at everything." A bitter edge had crept into her voice. No, Courtney wasn't a cold sociopath. She was just a jealous girl who'd frozen the object of her envy into a perpetual icon of everything she wasn't. And now she was a woman who was seeing everything she'd so carefully built on a quicksand foundation of lies and playacting, slipping away from her.

I handed her Jan's card. "I'll stay with you while you wait. Detective Boyd will read you the Miranda warning and you should call an attorney before you give your statement. If you do everything by the book, if you tell her everything, it'll be better for you and your family."

At the mention of her family, Courtney broke down crying. She sobbed so hard she began to choke on her breaths and even though it took everything in me to do it, I got up and placed my hand on her back. I forced away the knowledge that she had murdered her best friend and remembered that she was a woman who was about to lose the daughter she'd done it all for. Even if they stood by her, the relationship would never be the same. Her world, as she knew it, was over.

I could understand that pain.

———

"Jiu-jitsu, bitch?" Seth smirked. Open comms could be entertaining.

I shrugged. "He'd made shitty comments about my training regimen the first time I met him. I wanted him to know what took him down."

I stared at him across the diner's table. By mutual agreement we'd decided on a neutral location for our discussion in the hopes it would force us to remain civil, and clothed, so we could actually resolve an issue for a change.

"Speaking of take-downs, nice work on the Veitch case."

"You and Jan texting behind my back?" I'd tried to sound light-hearted but the prospect horrified me. I was not up for my BF and my, and she'd die if she heard me call her this, BFF being Fs. Acquaintances worked just fine for all of us.

"Your dad mentioned it when he called for round two of kicking my ass for upsetting you and running off and not stopping you from being you. He kind of lost the bubble on that one when I pointed out that no one stopped you from doing what you were going to do. Like solving a seventeen-year-old cold case."

"I'd like to be able to say it was my crime solving super skills but it came to me while I was throwing up."

He laughed then stopped when he realized I was serious.

"I'm … are you … how, just how?"

"Mandy was allergic to artificial sweeteners too. Her mother mentioned it when I met her for the first time. So why, if she was allergic to it and they didn't even keep it in the house, would Mandy have a can of diet soda on her desk?"

He made a *go on* motion with his hand.

"It was in the crime scene photos. I saw it but I didn't see it, you know?"

"Then when you threw up ... ?"

"It just clicked. The stuff makes me violently sick because I'm allergic to it. Mandy was allergic to it. No one on the original case thought twice about a can of diet soda on the teenage girl murder victim's desk. Why would they? So it wasn't treated as part of the crime scene. The mother never saw the room. Courtney cleaned up for them. Helping. Nice of her, huh?"

I took a sip of my coffee. Sweetened with regular sugar because I wasn't throwing up for a good long while if I had anything to do about it. I'd have to find new ways to solve crimes. Getting the crap beaten out of me was getting old too.

He cleared his throat. "I need to explain to you what's been going on."

I pulled a folder out of my bag and slid it slowly across the table toward him. "I know. Here's everything my dad pulled together about the adoption and your biological parents."

Not everything though. I'd kept back the details about the murders, the prison sentence, the stuff that he didn't need to know right away.

He picked the folder up and then put it down again, sliding it back toward me.

"Hold onto this for me. For later, when I'm ready."

I nodded and put it back in my bag. It didn't feel like I was having coffee with my boyfriend. There were plenty of couples in the restaurant. Some looked happy, joking around. Some looked annoyed, hurried. I felt like we looked like we were having a business meeting.

"When did you find out?" he asked.

"The day you left. Your dad came to pick up the boxes and I got it out of him."

He laughed. It was an angry, gruff noise. It held disdain, anger, disbelief. "He had twenty-five years he could have told me. Or Michael. Michael died not knowing and he just blurts it out to you."

I touched his fisted hand. He finally met my eyes.

"I had to wheedle it out of him. I begged him to tell me what was going on with you."

"You don't beg for anything. You wouldn't beg for your own life." His mouth a hard line, his eyes cold.

I snatched my hand back and leaned forward. "I'd beg for your life, you jackass."

He opened his hands and laid them on the table, palms up, letting out a deep sigh. "I keep fucking up. I'm sorry."

I put my hand into his. "I get that it's hard. I'm not dealing well with the information and it's not even about me, but can you for one second look at it from a different perspective?"

He looked away but he still held my hand. I took that as a sign to go on.

"People do things they're not proud of because they're scared. They kept the secret because they were scared, Seth. They didn't want to lose you."

"That's stupid. It wouldn't have changed anything, not how I felt about them."

My heart cracked a little. "Oh, babe. The adoption wasn't legal. They were scared someone would come and take you away from them."

He dropped his head. I put my other hand over the top of our joined hands.

"It doesn't mean they shouldn't have told me … us."

"Do you know for a fact that they never told Michael?"

He looked up at me, accusingly, like I'd just become a party to the deception.

"I don't know that they told him or that they didn't, Seth. I'm just trying to help you work this out," I said.

He pulled his hand back slowly, a mulish set to his jaw. "That shit's not helpful, Willa."

I bit the inside of my cheek, trying to come up with the right words. I wasn't the person he should have been talking to about this. He should have been in his parents' kitchen going over all this heart-rending, family-shifting stuff with them over coffee and family photo albums. That suggestion had not even been considered.

I wasn't going to find the right words to comfort or console him. I wasn't built like that and maybe those words didn't even exist. Either he was going to get over it or he wasn't.

"You know, you've expended a lot of energy being pissed off about this. You've pushed your parents away—"

"They're not really my parents."

I leaned forward again, dropping my voice. "The fuck they aren't. Are you ten? They've nursed you through sickness, broken bones, they cheered at every stupid sports event, they paid for you to go to college, you selfish, ungrateful jackass."

He opened his mouth to protest, anger flashing in his eyes.

"Shut it, Anderson. I'm not finished." And he shut his mouth, which was a damn near miracle. "You have bossed me around since the moment we met. You've decided what was right for me and badgered, harangued, and outright ordered me to do what you wanted. Where do you think that comes from? That 'not real' father of yours. You've fussed over me and pushed me to take care of myself. You sent me to Adam, you drove me to therapy appointments and waited in the car for me at both places. Sound familiar? Maybe like that 'not real' mom of yours? You ever utter the words 'not real parents' ever again and I will personally beat the ever-living hell out of you. We clear?"

His lips were pressed in a tight line, as if to keep from telling me off. Sorry, babe, tough love time.

Then he smiled, a little. "Excellent points except I have never harangued you. I may have strongly pointed out the merits of my position but—"

"Merits, my ass. Harangued," I said.

"I'm not saying you're right but you did make a few good points to consider."

"Consider them for as long as it takes to pay the check and drive to your parents' house, Ace. I'm sick of being your emotional punching bag. I've got people who want to use me as a physical one."

I gestured to the slight shiner I was sporting. People had been staring at us as the discussion had grown heated and I was sure they thought they were watching an abusive situation unroll itself. I found, unlike in the fall, I didn't much care what other people thought of him, or me, or our relationship. It may not have been what other people thought it was supposed to look like, but it worked for us. Most of the time.

He laughed and tossed down some money to pay for the cold, untouched coffee. Then offered me his hand to help me out of my seat.

"Then you need to find a place for us to live that will take Fargo. If I'm moving in with you, she's coming with me. No arguments."

"No, ma'am. No arguments."

He hadn't needed to say the words; his smile had said it for him.

"And don't ever call me *ma'am* again, Ace. It's creepy."

The End

302

Acknowledgments

Writing the acknowledgments is the hardest part of writing a book (aside from getting it published). No book comes together without a team of people. The image of the author in an attic garret scrawling prose next to a guttering candle is picturesque but wrong. Maybe if there were a dozen people in the room … It's hard because you don't want to forget anyone and hurt them. So much of what I do is only possible because of the people in my life who stand by me, support me, brainstorm with me, and talk it out with me. Forgetting to thank one of them would break my heart.

Many thanks to the usual suspects: Matthew Clemens, Dru Ann Love, Terri Bischoff, Jessie Lourey, Heather Webber, Sherry Harris, and Lyndee Walker Stephens.

Special thanks to the Midnight Ink and Dana Kaye Publicity teams; and John Talbot.

Deep gratitude and accolades to the Fairfax County Public Library system and their staff.

My husband and daughter deserve all the credit for making it possible for me to finish this book, written during an eleven-month bout of vertigo, doctor's appointments, testing, and sinus surgery for me; vet visits for our sweet dog Karma, who was undergoing cancer treatment; and the general maintenance and upkeep of our lives. They held it together for me so I could hold it together for the book and Karma. You will find her immortalized in this book.

Finally, thanks to the readers who bought *What Doesn't Kill You*, read it, loved it, checked it out from the library, wrote reviews, and championed it. I hope you enjoyed *Dark Streets, Cold Suburbs*.

About the Author

Aimee Hix is a former defense contractor turned mystery writer. She's a member of Sisters in Crime, Mystery Writers of America, and International Thriller Writers. *Dark Streets, Cold Suburbs* is her second book. Visit her at www.AimeeHix.com.